CIVIL SECRETS

T. L. BATEY

Archway Publishing books may be ordered through booksellers or by contacting:

Archway Publishing
1663 Liberty Drive
Bloomington, IN 47403
www.archwaypublishing.com
1 (888) 242-5904

ISBN: 978-1-4808-7257-8 (sc)
ISBN: 978-1-4808-7258-5 (hc)
ISBN: 978-1-4808-7256-1 (e)

Library of Congress Control Number: 2019930250

Print information available on the last page.

Archway Publishing rev. date: 01/31/2019

To my cousin who was always up for an adventure,
My husband for supporting me,
and Owosso for inspiring the story.

1

◇

The Woods

Sam felt almost giddy as she and her cousin Nell walked along the family garden located in the far corner of her yard, hopped the barbed-wire fence separating the property from the farm field, and walked diagonally across it toward the woods. The summer sun was shining, and a gentle breeze murmured through the trees. The woods were thicker than the girls remembered, and at first, they had difficulty locating the small opening in the brush that led to the trail they had traveled in the past. At last, they spied it. Had they not used it so frequently in years past, they would never have found the entrance. In unison, the girls stepped into the trees.

Only a few feet into the woods and already it was as if they had entered another world. The trees blocked out much of the sunlight and the trees seemed to be alive with mysterious sounds. As they walked, they were surrounded by screeching, scraping and rustling sounds. Even the croaking from unseen frogs sounded surprisingly creepy. High overhead, small bursts of sunlight twinkled through the treetops.

They ventured deeper into the woods, well beyond the point where they had stopped in the past. The scene looked like something out of a movie. Vines, moss and wild mushrooms grew all around the ground and up the trees. Huge tree trunks fallen long ago littered the ground. Off in the distance, they saw an old, rusted-out red pickup truck. The brush had nearly consumed the vehicle, and only the hood and rooftop were visible.

"Who would leave a truck out in the middle of nowhere?" Sam asked aloud.

"I can't imagine," Nell answered. "But I can imagine the stuff that is living inside that truck, so don't even ask me to get inside."

"Ugh," Sam agreed. "I wouldn't think of it. Just the thought of it is making me itch."

They walked on, further into the woods, and finally spotted a small clearing in the trees where the sun shone like a spotlight creating a stage-like appearance. As they headed to the spot, it was then that Sam had the tree blind located on the perimeter of the clearing.

"Oh, look, a tree house," Nell observed.

"It's actually a hunter's blind," Sam responded. Coming from a long line of hunters, she knew a tree blind when she saw one. This one was a bit unusual in that it seemed to be completely enclosed.

"Let's climb up there," Sam suggested. "I bet the view is fantastic, and we'll be able to see how far the woods continue."

"I don't know, we're not really supposed to be in this part of the woods," Nell admonished. "We don't even know who owns it."

But Sam was already halfway up the tree. For a moment she thought that maybe she should feel funny climbing a tree as a teenager, but she didn't. "Look, Nell, whoever put up the blind nailed boards into the tree. There's a built-in ladder leading up to the blind. Come on. You don't want to miss this." Although they were the same age, Nell was usually a bit more reserved and sometimes needed some coaxing.

"Why do I have a feeling I'm going to regret this?" Nell joked as she headed over to the tree and started climbing.

Sam had reached the top and was grabbing for her backpack when she heard voices from below.

"I told you that's not part of the plan."

"I don't understand what the harm is, and I think she could help us."

"That's the problem with you—you don't think. The fewer people who know about this, the better. What did you tell her?" he snarled.

The voices were male, and they seemed to be in their twenties. They also didn't sound like they were friends. Sam suddenly felt very uncomfortable and a little concerned.

"We shouldn't be up here," Nell whispered in Sam's ear.

"Shush!" Sam mouthed to her and placed her index finger over her mouth.

"I only told her I was interested in learning more about Owosso and Dewey. I'm telling you she's trustworthy. Honestly, I don't understand why you're so riled up. Anyway, forget about it. I thought you wanted me to show you the good hunting spots."

"You're an idiot. You'd say anything to hook up with that girl."

"You're so crude. She's pretty, but that's not why I talked to her. She works for the historical society, and I think we could use her insight. Besides—"

"Shut up" the first voice commanded. "You need to talk less and listen more."

"Hey, I don't take orders from you. You came to me, remember? Wait a minute. You want it for yourself, don't you? You were never trying to help me, were you?" He sounded surprised by his own words.

"Well, I confess that you and I differ on the point of this little venture of ours."

"You were just using me, weren't you?"

The other man chuckled in response.

3

The voices continued to get louder and angrier as the two men began yelling at each other. The tension in the air was thick.

"Stay away from me."

There was a rustle, and it sounded as if one of the men was walking away.

Sam felt slightly relieved, hearing that they might be leaving. She leaned over and peered through a gap in the wooden planks of the blind. There were two men. One was standing just below the tree in which they were trapped helplessly. The second man was walking away and had reached a small clearing. Both men had their backs to the tree.

"I was afraid you'd respond this way," the man beneath them said.

"Well, get over it," the other man said flatly.

"Oh, I will," the first man replied.

Sam noticed the man directly below raise his arms and point a hunting rifle at the other.

The girls heard the unmistakable sound of the gun being cocked. They both froze, afraid to breathe.

The second man turned around, and his eyes widened as he realized the barrel of the gun was pointed directly at this chest.

Sam stared at him. His face was beet red, and his expression was mixed with shock, outrage, and fear. Sam looked over at the man holding the gun. He still had his back to them, and she couldn't see his face. From the back, Sam saw that he had dirty-blond hair and was tall and thin.

"What do you think you're doing?" the second man asked in astonishment.

"The only thing I can do," the gunman replied quietly.

"You'd really shoot me with my own gun? What kind of man are you?"

"A cautious one. I'm sorry it had to end this way, but the stakes are too high." With that, he pulled the trigger.

Sam could hear Nell breathing behind her. Then she heard the deafening and unmistakable sound of the rifle blast and watched in horror as the second man fell to the ground. He landed with a sickening thud.

"You can't leave me here like this," he pleaded. "I'll bleed out. Help me!" His words came out in a choking sound.

"You left me no choice. And I will be leaving here alone." He let out a sinister laugh, and Sam felt the hair on the back of her neck stand up. She had goosebumps on her arms.

Sam felt a pain in her arm. She looked over to see that Nell had grabbed her so tightly that her fingernails had dug into Sam's arm, drawing blood. Sam shifted uncomfortably, and the floorboards in the blind creaked. Sam looked at Nell in shock. Her heart was beating so fast it felt like a drumbeat in her ears. She held her breath and prayed their position would remain undiscovered.

After what seemed like an eternity, Sam watched, transfixed, while the gunman turned and walked away. When he was out of sight, Sam and Nell both exhaled sharply.

The sky had turned dark, and Sam heard what she thought was a clap of thunder off in the distance. "We have to get out of here," she whispered.

"What if he comes back and sees us?" Nell asked, her voice nearly hysterical.

"We can't stay up in this tree forever," Sam said, her voice shaking. "My guess is he's headed back to his car. The road is at least a quarter mile from here, so we have enough time to climb down and head back toward my house, but we have to go now."

Nell nodded in agreement. Sam slowly opened the blind door. The hinges creaked loudly, injecting Sam with additional incentive to act quickly. She descended the tree trunk as quickly as she could, her heart pounding in her throat. She jumped to the ground and felt Nell drop beside her seconds later. Both girls cast furtive glances in the direction the gunman had departed. The path appeared empty for the moment.

Sam couldn't help herself, and she looked over to where the second man had fallen. He was lying on the ground, with his body facing her. Blood had pooled around his body, and an eerie silence filled the air. His eyes were closed, and Sam wondered whether he was dead. As if being pulled by an invisible force, she edged closer to his body. When she had come within a few feet, she heard his raspy breath. He opened his eyes.

Nell hissed at Sam that they needed to leave.

"We'll go get help for you," Sam told him. "I promise." But for some reason, she couldn't move. She stared at his face. Up close, she realized he didn't look much older than she was—a few years maybe. He looked young and scared. His short brown hair had partially fallen over one eye. However, she noticed that he had dark-blue eyes and a kind face. He looked at her with such sadness. She desperately wanted to help him.

"You have to stop him," he replied. His voice was barely audible. "Find it before he does. The key is in my locker, Washington and Main, 25-18-6-5. Please, it's important."

"Find what? The key for what?" Sam gently prompted.

"Please, promise me," he begged.

"Okay, I promise," Sam promised. "But what am I looking for?"

The man gurgled, his eyes glazed over, and he was still.

Sam's stomach turned.

"Sam!" Sam heard Nell's voice at the same moment she felt her arm being violently yanked. She turned and saw Nell's eyes were wide with terror, and tears were streaming down her face. "Please, we have to get out of here before he comes back!" Nell begged through her sobs.

Sam realized they *did* need to get out of there—and fast. Without looking back, she turned toward the trail leading out of the woods, grabbed Nell's hand, and started running. With dismay, she feared her stop had cost them precious time.

Suddenly, the world was closing in on Sam. Her lungs were on fire, and she was gasping for breath, but it felt as if there was a motor inside her that was set on autopilot directing her body to get to safety. Her legs were pumping faster than she would have thought possible. She figured that adrenaline had kicked in, and she was grateful. Without it, she might still be standing back at the tree.

Now, she was flying past the trees and thick vegetation that encompassed the dark woods. Only an hour ago, the same woods had seemed so enchanted and full of possibility. But in an instant, that tranquility had been shattered, and now Sam was trying desperately to escape.

Sam kept her eyes focused forward, fervently trying to block out the gruesome scene that had just unfolded. It was hard to believe it had really happened. Her efforts were unsuccessful, as sounds and images flooded her mind. Her ears were ringing from the gunshot, her eyes were stinging, and her head felt disconnected from the rest of her body.

Sam was overwhelmed by the image of the man lying in a pool of blood. She pictured his eyes and the way he had looked at her. Then chills ran down her spine as she remembered the sinister laugh that had pierced the air. She shook her head violently to clear her thoughts and forced herself to refocus.

Sam kept running, glancing over at Nell. At fifteen, only a few months older than Sam, Nell was strong but not quite as athletic. She would keep up though; she had to. They both had to escape from the woods.

Sam reached out and grabbed Nell's hand, half squeezing it to reassure Nell and half dragging her to safety. Nell's face was ghostly pale. She had tears streaming down her cheeks, and her long, dark hair was matted to the side of her face

They ran side by side, racing up the trail, oblivious to their surroundings. They darted past fallen tree trunks, wildly over-grown brush, and the rusted-out truck that had appeared so charming before. Now, darkness enveloped them, and everything seemed menacing. Branches, leaves, and weeds sliced into their faces and limbs as they clawed their way through them to the exit and toward the glimmer of sunlight, they could now see through the thinning trees up ahead.

With a new wave of terror, Sam realized how far into the woods they had been. She turned to look over her shoulder, want-ing to confirm that they weren't being followed. With her attention diverted, she didn't notice a large tree root in the footpath. Her shoe caught under the root, and she felt herself falling, landing in a pile of dirt. The wind was knocked out of her, and her chest and throat felt like they had exploded.

For a moment, Sam was frozen. She stared down the trail be-hind them, searching for any sign of movement. To her relief, she and Nell appeared to be alone. Nell pulled Sam to her feet, and without speaking, they resumed their flight, finally reaching the opening that led to the farmer's field.

As their feet hit the plowed rows of corn, the sky opened up, and rain began pelting the girls as they exited the woods. Without caring whether the nasty farmer saw them, they crossed the field, hopped the fence, and were finally back in Sam's yard.

They didn't stop running until they reached the back door to the garage. Both girls sailed over the threshold, then slammed and locked the door behind them. Sam leaned her back against the doorframe and slid to the floor. Tucking her head between her knees, she tried to catch her breath and clear her head.

After several moments, she slowly rose and turned to peer over the window's edge. Her eyes were blurry, and she strained to pick up any movement that might indicate they had been followed. Nell's hand was resting on Sam's shoulder, and Sam could hear her struggling to catch her breath. They stood there in silence, dripping wet and shivering from raw fear.

Finally, Nell whispered, "I think it's okay."

Sam knew things were anything but okay, but also knew she couldn't say that to Nell. "Yeah, I think you're right," she replied, her eyes still fixed on the field and the woods behind it. She took one more look at the empty field before she pulled herself from the window. "Let's go inside."

As she turned to open the door leading into the house, she noticed that her parents' car was gone. She turned back and entered the laundry room with Nell close behind. They both stood motionless for a moment before finding moving to kick off their muddy shoes. Sam caught a glimpse of herself in the mirror that hung over a small, wooden bench. Leaves were stuck to her hair, and her T-shirt and shorts were soaking wet and filthy. Not that appearance was important at the moment.

She stared into the mirror for a moment. Sam was petite, with an athletic build and piercing blue eyes. Her shoulder-length hair was a dirty-blond color with a persistent wavy streak that became rather unruly in the summer humidity. Sam's face was covered with dirt, and her high cheekbones now bore scratches. The reflection mirrored her emotions—a complete disaster.

She looked over and noticed that Nell was in similar shape, except she was also sporting a long cut along her right leg, and blood was trickling down to the floor. Her khaki shorts had streaks of dirt, and her pale-yellow T-shirt now had a rip on the right arm. Somehow, though, Nell still seemed looked rather elegant, as she always did. Unlike Sam, Nell was tall and thin, with the makings of an hourglass figure. She had long pin-straight dark-chestnut hair that framed her narrow face, and dark-brown, doe-like eyes. Her hair was so dark it seemed to shine like a pool of water. She was striking in a serene sort of way.

"What are we going to do?" Nell asked quivering.

"Mom? Dad?" Sam called out.

There was no answer.

Sam needed to think. Sam opened the cabinet next to the dryer. "Here's a towel to dry off," Sam said as she handed one to Nell and closed the cabinet. "I'll go get us some dry clothes."

Sam returned shortly with two sets of shorts and T-shirts. They quickly changed, laid the soggy items on top of the washing machine, and headed into the adjacent downstairs bathroom to wash up. They had just finished when they heard the rumble of the garage door opening. Sam was relieved to hear a car pulling into the garage and her parents had barely stepped inside the laundry room through the door leading in from the garage when both girls burst into the room and started talking at once.

"Whoa, slow down!" Sam's father said. "What's all the excitement all about?"

Before Sam had a chance to respond, her mother interjected, "Well, the first thing that needs to happen is that Sam needs to explain the mess in here. I just mopped the floors."

"That's what I'm trying to do!" Sam responded. She hastily wiped up the laundry room floor while as she blurted out, "But you should know that we just saw a murder!" She threw the wet towel on top of the washing machine, and dragged Nell into the kitchen where her parents were now waiting with open mouths.

The girls told their harrowing tale, including the narrow escape from the woods. When they were finished, Sam looked from one parent to the other, expecting to see looks of horror matching how she felt. Instead, her father burst into laughter, and her mother gave her a stern look of disapproval.

"You almost had me," Sam's father said after he regained his composure. "That's quite a story. Seriously, though, you know you're not supposed to go in that part of the woods. We don't own it, and you shouldn't trespass on other people's property."

Her mother's approach was equally unnerving. "Look, I know

you have a very active imagination," she said, directing her attention to Sam. "But this is a bit much. Sue won't want Nell coming over here if you're going to start running amuck with wild stories."

"This is not a wild story!" Sam replied, barely containing her anger. Nell's mother was the least of her worries at this point.

"We're telling the truth, Aunt Lee," Nell added solemnly. "It was awful. That poor man."

For the first time, Sam's mother seemed to be paying attention. Of course, she would listen to Nell.

"We need to call the police so they can get out there like now!" Sam urged.

"You're serious," Sam's father said, looking concerned.

"Yes!" the girls nearly shouted in unison.

"Look, if we call the authorities and things are not as you say, the consequences could be severe," her father cautioned.

"What we're telling you is real. Please believe us," Sam pleaded.

Nell nodded violently in agreement.

"Well, I saw that Mike's car is parked in the driveway next door," said Sam's father. "I heard that he graduated from the police academy, so I guess we can talk to him and get his input. Stay here." With that, her father headed back through the laundry room and out to the garage.

The wait for his return was painful. The girls and Sam's mother sat on the coach in the family room in silence. What if Mike didn't believe them? The delay was killing her. What about the poor guy who was shot? Would the gunman be long gone? Worse yet, what if he was still there trying to hide what he'd done? Oh, God, what if he knew about them? Sam was so anxious her knees wouldn't stop shaking, and she could hardly sit still.

Sam was lost in thought when the back door finally opened, and in walked Sam's father and Officer Mike. Sam had known Mike her entire life. He was in his twenties, yet he still lived with his parents. He was tall—nearly six feet, as he liked to remind people. Other than that, he was exceptionally ordinary, with an average build and what seemed like, at best, an average IQ. He had dark-brown hair, which he kept cut short, and dull blue eyes. He was not particularly good-looking or interesting. In fact, Sam had the distinct impression that he had not been very popular in school and that becoming a cop was his way of finally wielding some sort of power. Sam wasn't sure he was the sharpest tool in the shed, but he had always been nice enough to her.

Mike greeted Sam's mother as he entered the room with Sam's dad. She gave him an uncomfortable smile and thanked him for coming over.

"Your dad tells me that you think you observed some unusual activity in the woods," Mike said. "Why don't you tell me about what happened?"

"First of all, we don't *think* we saw something unusual. We saw some guy shoot another guy," Sam said with disgust. "Is that normal activity for you?"

Her mother shot her a stern look, but Sam didn't care.

"Now don't get defensive with me; just tell me what happened," Mike said in what he probably thought was a calming voice but which came out as half mocking and half condescending. Sam was sure Mike was just trying to show off in front of her parents.

"Don't be rude," her mother said sternly.

At that moment, the urgency Sam felt to relay the terrifying event was replaced with a sort of uncertainty about where to begin. Things seemed to be blurred by a barrage of images flying through her brain. It was unlike Sam to be speechless—ever. However, at this moment, she was having trouble finding her voice. She looked over at Nell, who looked equally conflicted. But Nell took the cue and began to retell the events of the day.

"Well, we were walking in the woods, you know, a kind of, um, nature hunt," Nell said a bit nervously.

Sam was grateful that Nell was trying to soften the blow of the punishment heading Sam's way from her strict mother. She still didn't understand why walking through some trees was worthy of punishment, but she was certain it was coming.

Nell continued. "We saw a tree blind and ... thought it would be nice to watch some birds."

Wow! Did Nell just lie? It was a rare and kinda awesome experience. Sam was very pleased at that moment. It was a white lie and, with any luck, would hopefully draw her mother's attention away from Sam and on to the real issue here.

"So," Nell continued, "it was like a fort. It was so pretty up there that we closed the door while we ate some snacks. We were looking for hawks when we heard ..." Nell's voice faltered.

By that point, Sam's thoughts had crystallized, and she picked up where Nell left off.

"We heard a sound. We couldn't see what it was because the walls of the blind were so tall, so we had to get up on our knees and stretch up to peer out over the top. That was when we heard voices."

"We just thought we were going to get into trouble for being there, and we were ready to apologize," Nell added. "But that's when the voices got louder, and they sounded agitated."

Actually, Sam remembered shushing Nell and deciding that they should stay hidden and listen. Nell had been mortified at the time, but reluctantly held her position and remained silent. Sam was thinking that the decision just may have saved their lives.

"Anyway, that's when we heard a guy's voice say, 'I told you: that's not part of the plan,'" Sam said.

"What plan?" Mike asked.

"We don't know," Sam snapped. "Another guy said something like that he didn't understand what the harm was and that he thought he could help.

"He didn't say a name," she added before Mike could ask. "The first guy was mean. He sort of grunted: 'That's the problem with you. You don't think. The fewer people who know about this, the better.' Then he wanted to know what the second guy told her. He said that he hadn't told her anything, but the other guy shot him anyway. He fell to the ground, and ... and there was a lot of blood."

It was all sinking in. Just saying the words made Sam feel as though she was back in the woods. With him. With a killer. She wanted that poor guy to be alive, but she knew that wasn't likely. She felt nauseous. Sam looked around. All eyes were on her. No one seemed to be laughing now. Nell was sniffling.

"You really should get in there to find him before it gets too dark," Sam said abruptly. There was no way that she was going to let herself cry. She had to stay strong.

"I agree," Mike replied. "It makes sense to check it out. However, it's been raining pretty hard out there. If there was any physical evidence, it's likely been compromised now."

Sam chose to ignore Mike's use of the word *if* and instead replied, "All the more reason to get out there now. Besides, he's still out there."

"Do you need to call someone to get authorization?" Nell inquired.

Mike learned forward, giving Sam and Nell an intense look. "If you say someone was wounded, I want to get out there now. Can the girls come with me? I need them to show me exactly where this all happened. Lots of trails out there. I don't want to waste time if someone's been shot."

Sam felt rejuvenated as she shot out of her seat. "I can show you!"

Sam's mother didn't seem to react, but her father nodded in agreement. "I'm coming with you," he added.

"What if the killer's still out there?" Nell asked hesitantly.

Mike looked somber. He thought for a moment. "I think that's unlikely, but I'm armed just in case. Come on. We've gotta go!"

"Yeah let's get out there!" Sam said.

"Lee, I'll head over there with Mike and the girls," Sam's dad said to her mother.

"Okay, I'll call Sue," she responded, looking very unhappy and more than a little put out.

The girls grabbed raincoats and headed outside. With a mixture of trepidation and excitement, they walked into the back yard, hopped the fence, and crossed the field. The rain was coming down in sheets, so hard and cold that Sam felt as if she were being punched by a hundred fists. That was Michigan weather for you. One minute it was sunny and eighty degrees, and the next, it was rainy and cold. They reached the small opening to the woods, and the girls paused.

"Since your flashlight is bigger, maybe you should lead the way," Nell suggested to Mike.

Sam knew what Nell really meant— "Since you are the one with the gun, you should go first"—and she was happy for the suggestion.

Mike also seemed pleased with the thought. He drew himself up taller and donned an official-looking expression as he proceeded. Apparently, the direction of the trail was not as obvious to Mike as it was to the girls, and he regularly asked for guidance on which way to proceed. After several minutes, Mike asked how much farther down the trail the blind was located. Sam and Nell looked at each other, searching for an answer.

"We're not really sure," Nell answered. "I mean, we were just exploring the area on our way in, and our exit was a blur. Sorry."

They continued to walk for a while, this time in silence. Luckily, the lush trees shielded them from much of the rain. The mixture of trees, including oak, maple, and pine trees blended together to create dense coverage from the outside world. Sheltered from the elements, an eerie calm lingered overhead. However, the chill lingered, and the girls felt cold, soggy, and very tired. Sam was starting to think they would never find the blind when, finally, she saw the large tree with the boards nailed into the trunk. She looked up and saw, with mixed relief and anxiety, the tree blind in which they had been captive earlier that afternoon.

"There it is," she said, pointing at the tree. Her voice cracked as she forced out the words.

"Okay, now where were these gentlemen standing?" Mike asked.

"They weren't gentlemen," Sam said. "Well, at least one of them wasn't."

"All right, where were the men standing?"

The girls forced themselves to remember the events of the day and to recall where on the ground the men would have been standing.

Sam walked about fifteen feet from the tree. "I think they were standing somewhere in this area," she said, pointing in a circle around where she now stood.

Nell looked at the area, up to the tree, and said, "Yes, that looks about right to me."

The area was soaked from the rain, and it was filling up like a swimming pool. After inspecting the ground for a few moments, Mike said, "Well, I don't see any sign of a struggle or any blood. Are you sure we're in the right spot?"

"Yes, we're sure," Sam answered for both girls. "Besides, we already told you: there wasn't a struggle. The first guy started to walk away. The second guy cocked the shotgun and shot him. I think he shot him in the stomach."

"Okay," Mike said in an uncertain tone. "I'm sure the rain hasn't helped our search, but where's the body?"

Sam looked up at the blind, then turned to stare at the empty place when the man had been lying. "He's ... he's gone!" she said, barely able to control her emotions. She knew now that the man had likely died right in front of her, and his empty eyes haunted her. They probably would for the rest of her life.

"Maybe he was able to crawl back toward the road," Nell offered.

"Or maybe the killer moved the body," Sam speculated.

Mike made a sweep of the general area and then returned to the group. "Look, it's not that I don't believe you, but without a body or any blood, I'm not sure what I can do."

"Well, how about calling in a search party to look for the body," Nell offered helpfully.

"Uh, or maybe look for the killer." Sam almost sneered.

"Give me a complete physical description of the, uh, both men," Mike requested.

"The guy, the one that was shot, was, like, average height, kind of stocky, and he had brown hair," Sam began.

"And he was wearing jeans and a brown shirt," Nell added.

"What color were his eyes?" Mike asked.

"I'm not sure," Nell responded.

"Blue, Sam said quietly.

"Okay, how about the other guy? What did he look like?" Mike prompted.

Sam stared at Nell, realizing that they could not give Mike a description of the second man. After several long moments, she looked up at Mike and said, "We don't know. We never saw his face."

"Did you see any distinguishing features?" Mike suggested.

"He was sort of tall and wearing jeans and a black T-shirt," Nell replied.

Sam could hear the man's voice in her head. She recalled her promise to get help. His strange request. Could she really find it? She pulled herself away from her thoughts to answer Mike's question.

"He was wearing a blue baseball cap and had blond hair," Sam added.

"How tall was he? Was he taller or shorter than me?" Mike asked.

"He was about your height, I guess," Sam responded.

"I just don't know," Nell replied.

"Anything else?" Mike asked. "Something that might distinguish him from a crowd, like a tattoo or piercing?"

Again, the girls looked at each other wishing, suddenly, that they'd seen more.

"We're sorry, but he never turned to face the tree. That's all we have for you," Sam answered.

"That's okay, girls," said Sam's dad. "You might remember more later." He'd been so quiet on the walk over, Sam had forgotten her father was with them.

"Well, it's getting late," Mike said. "Let's head back now." Mike saw the looks on the girls' faces. "I have to call this into the station, and I'll check to find out whether anyone fitting the description showed up at the hospital. If he suffered a gunshot wound to the abdomen, he wouldn't have had much time to get medical attention before he'd die from the blood loss. I'll try to get some guys out here tomorrow to conduct a search, though. There's nothing more we can do here tonight."

"Come on, girls. You heard Mike. Let's head on home now. Your mother will be worried," said Sam's father.

Sam was beside herself. It had never occurred to her on the way into the woods that the dead man wouldn't be there. She had wanted him to be there alive. In fact, though she had steeled herself for the grisly scene and even for finding the killer still lurking in the area, she had not been prepared for this, finding nothing and being silently mocked by Officer Mike.

Worse yet, she hated the fact that her parents had thought for a moment that she would make up such a story. Her parents were both so strict, and so against excitement of any kind, they always seemed to disapprove of whatever she was doing. Yes, she had an imagination at times, but she would never, never lie, and she never got into any real trouble. You'd think they'd realize that by now.

She felt they were leaving the woods empty-handed and that, as a result, Nell's and her reputations were somehow tarnished. This was too important for anyone to ignore.

Worst of all, she felt that she had failed in her promise to get help. Sam stomped her way along the trail leading back to her house. By the time she had reached the field, she was in a very bad mood.

They parted company with Mike at the back door to the garage. While the girls headed inside, Sam's dad hung back to talk with Mike. Sam didn't care what they were saying; she just wanted to put this day behind her.

The rest of the night passed uneventfully. Nell had secured permission to stay another night, provided that they stay in the yard. Sam, Nell, and her parents ate dinner in near silence, no one really knowing what to say. It was clear that Sam's father had filled in her mother while the girls had changed for dinner because her mother didn't broach the topic of the day's events. Despite the lack of a lecture, Sam somehow still felt that her parents were looking at her with some measure of disapproval.

After dinner, the girls headed upstairs, mumbling that they were exhausted and heading to bed for the night. Once they were in Sam's room with the door closed, they changed into their pajamas and dropped, exhausted, onto Sam's bed.

"What the hell happened today?" Sam asked out loud.

"Shh," Nell cautioned. "Let's not add getting grounded for swearing to the list today."

"Well, I'm sorry, but I can't wrap my head around what happened today."

"Me either," Nell agreed. "It almost seems like we imagined it all."

"Don't you start too," Sam snarled. She had been laying on her bed. Now she returned to a full upright position and glared at Nell.

"Whoa, that's not what I meant; I know what happened, and

nothing anyone says is going to change what I know," Nell said reassuringly.

"Sorry, this whole thing with my parents really pisses me off, and I'm upset that we didn't find - him."

"What made you stop to talk to that man? I mean, it was very brave and kind of you, but what made you do it?" Nell asked.

"I don't know, when I saw him lying there, something just drew me to him."

"Hey, how come you didn't tell Mike about what that poor guy said to you?" Nell asked gently.

"I didn't hear you offer it up either," Sam retorted defensively. However, when she saw the look in Nell's eyes, her tone softened, and she continued. "Well, at first my mind was focused on getting Mike out to look for the guy in the woods and I totally forgot what he'd said to me. Then, once we were there and there was no body, I figured I'd sound completely unstable if I described a conversation with a ghost.

"I can't believe we didn't find his body or any evidence of his death. I mean, I think we watched him die. Based on what Mike said, it doesn't sound likely that he survived. Plus, he was so still when we left. I think I was the last person to talk to him.

"Something was awfully important to him, Nell. So important that he begged me to find it, whatever it is, as he was dying. He didn't say, 'Tell the police.' And I'm not sure the police would even follow through on his request. Plus, I promised him I'd find it. I can't go back on a promise.

"It's weird, but I feel a connection with him somehow. I know that sounds crazy, since I never met him before."

Nell studied Sam's face for several minutes. "Well, then let's find the *it*," she said in a matter-of-fact voice.

"Really, you'd be up for that?" Sam asked, shocked and excited at the same time.

"Well, you did say that this was going to be the best summer ever. You promised me adventure, and I intend to make you live up to that commitment," Nell said with a twinkle in her eyes. And then she became more solemn. "Plus, a promise is a promise."

"Then it's settled," said Sam. "We're going to fulfill that man's dying wish. We can find what he wanted us to find and then give it to the police."

"Okay, but let's start our quest tomorrow," Nell said mid-yawn. "I feel like I haven't slept in a week."

"Right, good night," Sam said as she rubbed her eyes. "And Nell?"

"Yeah?"

"I'm so lucky to have you."

"I feel the same way about you."

That night Sam's dreams were flooded with images of the man lying on the ground begging for help and of a shadowy figure lurking in a dark forest. She was running after someone whose face was never quite visible, but his chilling laugh was unmistakable, and it echoed into the darkness as he made his escape.

2

◇

The Plan

Sam woke before Nell the next morning, with her brain still buzz-
ing from yesterday's events and the excitement of their upcoming
adventure. She looked over and saw that Nell was still asleep on
the roll-away bed next to her. Through her bedroom blinds, Sam
could see that the sun was out and shining. The storm had passed,
and it was a new day. As she laid in her own bed, Sam's thoughts
turned to Nell's arrival just forty-eight hours ago.

After four long years, Nell and her family were finally moving
back to Owosso, Michigan. Sam's mother and Nell's mother were
sisters, and the two families had always been extremely close. Born
less than a year apart, the two had been inseparable since birth.

As young kids, they had spent an inordinate amount of time together, often venturing out of Sam's yard and into the neighboring
fields. Sam smiled when she recalled the many days spent in the
forest fighting off the wicked witch and rallying the forest crea-
tures to engage in battle. Sam still sported a scar on her knee from
one adventure which ended when she fell out of a tree. Tomboy
though she was, Sam considered herself to be somewhat athletic,
but she recognized that she would never be graceful like Nell.
Luckily, the thought didn't cause her much concern.

After their "battles" in the forest, the girls would often retreat to the pool in Sam's yard where they would swim for hours. Then suddenly, when Sam had been nine years old, Nell's father, Hank, had accepted a job in Grand Rapids. Sam and Nell had been devastated. At the time, it had seemed as if life could not go on. Despite the distance between them, and the differences in their personalities, the bond between the two had never been broken.

She sat back and thought about how amazing it was that they were so close given their different personalities. As alike as they were in their thoughts, they were quite different in a number of respects. In addition to the obvious differences in their height and physical builds, the girls' personalities were also distinct.

Nell, for example, enjoyed attending church and participating in church youth groups. Truth be told, Nell's mother was the one who required the family to attend church every Sunday, but Nell didn't seem to mind. She actually just enjoyed meeting people and attended services simply because she had a nice time.

Unlike Sam, Nell was a bit girlie; she loved wearing frilly dresses covered with lace and having ribbons in her long, dark hair. Nell was also often shy, quiet, soft spoken, and easily intimidated by authority figures. She tended to keep her thoughts to herself, except when it came to Sam with whom she shared everything. Sam was always envious of Nell's incredible patience and concentration. Nell usually took her time in evaluating things and in coming to a conclusion. As a result, her actions tended to be slow and carefully thought out.

Nell was also honest, intelligent, kind, hard to offend, and quick to forgive. All in all, she was a faithful and loyal friend. Her one fault, if she had one, was that she was a bit naive when it came to trusting other people and judging their characters. She took people at their word. Consequently, she was often shocked when her trust was misplaced.

Sam, on the other hand, usually only attended services with

Nell and mostly just to spend more time with her. Left to her own devises, Sam would have completely avoided the loud, creaky benches and the usually off-key singing. Also, although Sam enjoyed a structured environment at school, watching the mass of people file into the church always struck her as being oddly similar to cattle being herded into a barn. She also harbored an irrational fear that lightning would strike as she entered the church, as a not so subtle sign that she didn't quite fit in there. She routinely breathed a sigh of relief that Nell never pressed the religion issue.

Also, unlike Nell, Sam detested wearing dresses or anything with frills of any kind. She had found that such attire was usually itchy and drafty and not well suited for much of anything. Plus, wearing those kinds of clothes made her feel like a fraud somehow. She felt most comfortable wearing jeans and a T-shirt or sweater.

As for temperament, Sam could not be described as shy. Although she was more reserved in group settings and around new people, Sam generally spoke her mind, something that got her into trouble on more than one occasion. She believed that you should respect your elders and persons in positions of authority, but that respect could be lost based on the behavior—regardless of age. She was thoughtful, well-spoken, and polite, when not provoked. She was daring but not reckless, smart, strong and opinionated, but she was also loyal and honest to a fault.

Even for her age, Sam had a sharp analytical mind. She had the ability to quickly assess a situation and act on her assessment. She performed especially well under pressure and rarely second-guessed herself once she had decided. She had high expectations for herself and others. Unfortunately, she had already learned that her expectations of others were rarely met, which left her a bit less open-minded than Nell. As a result, she was slow to warm to new people and did not give out her trust easily. Once her trust had been broken, it was nearly impossible to regain.

They were, however, *exactly* alike in that they both craved adventure, culture, and learning in general. They loved reading and particularly liked a good mystery and learning about history, both things they had not often found in their little town. In past summers, they had blown through the library's collection of books at record pace. With their respective character traits, Sam and Nell were actually the perfect complement to each other.

The time spent while the families lived apart had been difficult on the girls, despite their regular contact. They had so much catching up to do. This feeling had prompted Sam to promise Nell that they would have the best summer ever.

Thinking about her promise, Sam slowly rolled out of bed and walked over to her dresser. Pulling out her swimsuit, a clean T-shirt, and a pair blue shorts, she dressed without realizing she was doing it. Sam let out a half laugh as she compared her prior plans to what they had experienced in the woods. The list of activities she had prepared seemed so childish now.

Even the planning for Nell's arrival all seemed ridiculous now. The hours of waiting for her aunt to call, the polite period of time to wait before driving over to greet the family. Her mother forcing her to clean up her room. Like Nell would care, and her aunt and uncle had never set foot upstairs to Sam's knowledge. She grinned when she recalled that she had merely shoved most of her stuff under her bed. She would deal with it later.

Her thoughts now drifted to her hometown. Owosso was a small town. There were no malls, and entertainment was largely limited to seeing a movie at the cinema. The movies were rarely current and frequently had some sort of glitch in the middle of a show. Then there was bowling at the bowling alley or shopping at the JC Penney, the only retail store in town (conveniently located next to the bowling alley). Given the limited options, Sam and Nell were generally forced to create their own entertainment.

Making matters slightly more difficult was the fact that Sam's family lived in a subdivision outside of town. The two-story colonial home was nestled on two acres and tucked in the back of the subdivision. Quaint, yes, but not usually chocked full of excitement. The development itself was flanked by a dirt road which led back to town, and M-52, a two-lane highway. The local radio station, WOMP, sat directly opposite the entrance to the subdivision. Known for its "soft rock," the red glow from the WOMP sign had always been a bit of an embarrassment to Sam. Even before she knew what kind of music she liked, she knew she didn't enjoy WOMP music. She was thankful that her house was located far away from the ridiculous blinking light.

For some reason, the most attractive part of Sam's home seemed to be the farm field just beyond her yard. The area closest to Sam's house was used to grow soybeans and other crops; however, the smell of livestock and manure could not be avoided on windy days. The farm itself was surrounded by an old barbed-wire fence which had been neglected over the years. There were several downtrodden spots that made crossing it easy to cross and thus providing passage to the woods beyond—the same woods that had for so many years had seemed like such a magical and mysterious place. Everything had changed now.

Her brain began filling with thoughts and images from the prior day. The events replayed in her head, despite her desire that they stop.

"Why are you staring at me?" Nell asked, her voice puncturing Sam's daydream.

"What?"

"Why are you staring at me?" Nell asked again.

"What? I, um, didn't realize I was staring. I've just been thinking. I didn't realize you were awake," Sam replied.

"You're dressing already. Are you okay?" Nell asked.

"Yeah, I guess. You?"

"Honestly, I'm not sure. I suppose so," Nell answered. "I'd like to forget that yesterday ever happened.

"I know, but we can't," Sam responded softly. "We have to re-member for him. We must help him."

"I know," Nell said. Her large brown eyes filling up with tears.

"And in order to help him, we need a plan," Sam said.

"I agree." Nell drew a deep breath.

"But before we come up with a plan, we need to eat. Let's grab some breakfast and head outside to talk."

"That sounds wonderful. I'm famished," Nell responded.

After Nell tossed on a swimsuit and a cover-up, the girls made their way downstairs to the kitchen. The house was quiet, leading Sam to guess that her mother was outside. Sam opened the pantry and was thrilled to see a box of Fruit Loops instead of the typical bland stuff her mom usually bought. She held the box up and saw that Nell was equally excited. They were just finishing up when Sam's mother entered the house from the patio.

"Oh, you two are finally up, I see. Nell, did you sleep okay, dear?"

"Yes, Aunt Lee, thanks for asking," Nell replied politely.

"What's the plan for today?" Sam's mother asked, looking at Sam.

"Um, I think we're just going to hang around and relax," Sam said vaguely.

"Okay, I think you should stick around the house today," her mother responded. It was more of an instruction that a suggestion.

Sam grabbed the cereal bowls, walked to the sink to rinse them off, and placed them in the dishwasher.

"Come on, Nell. Let's go float around in the pool for a while."

"That sounds nice," Nell said quietly. "See you later, Aunt Lee."

"Don't forget sunscreen, girls."

Sam hastily grabbed a can of sunscreen from the counter, waved it at her mother to acknowledge the instruction, then gently pulled Nell outside the patio door, closing it behind her.

Once they had applied the sunscreen and were in the safety of the pool, they started talking.

"Okay, what exactly did he say to you again?" Nell asked, clearly referring to the man in the woods.

Sam thought for a moment. "He said, 'You have to stop him. Find it before he does. The key is in my locker, Washington and Main, 25-18-6-5. Please, it's important.'"

With vivid clarity, Sam remembered how the man's eyes had glazed over, and then he was still. So very still. She stared at Nell for several moments.

Finally, Nell broke the silence. "Hmm. That's not a lot to go on. What's at Washington and Main?" Nell asked.

"No clue," Sam responded. "No, wait. I do know. It's the bowling alley."

"The bowling alley? That's strange," Nell said.

"Yeah, it is," Sam responded. "And we need to go there."

Nell just looked at her with a mixture of dread and determination.

3

◇

Vindication

After floating on rafts in the pool for so long that Sam's fingers felt like prunes, she rolled over and looked at Nell. "So, Nell, let's go over and make nice with Mike. We should make sure he gets some people over to check out the woods. Plus, I was thinking, based on the direction the second guy headed, I'm guessing that his car was parked somewhere closer to M-52. We could ride our bikes over that way and—"

"You know we aren't supposed to ride out on the highway," Nell interjected. "Plus, you told your mother we were going to hang here today."

"I know. I know," Sam said, waving her off. "Apparently, this summer, we're breaking all the rules. You know, in the interest of justice."

"Well, if that's the case, then ride we must," Nell said, putting her hand in the air as if she were taking an oath. "My mom said I can't overstay my welcome here and that I have to come home for a few days, so we'd better head out soon."

"Okay, let's go," Sam said as she slid over her raft and headed for the pool ladder. "I'll tell my mom we're going for a bike ride and then we can take you home."

29

After they had both dried off, they headed to Sam's room to change clothes. On the way back downstairs, they passed Sam's mother, who was carrying a laundry basket.

"Say, Mom, Nell and I are heading out for a bike ride."

"Well, I guess that's okay, but Nell's mother asked me to bring her home this afternoon, so don't be gone long."

"We won't be," Sam responded and motioned for Nell to follow.

"Nell, let's grab the bikes and walk next door to Mike's. We can head off from there."

"What if your mom sees us?"

"Oh, good grief, let's deal with that if it happens. Come on."

Sam led the way, walking her bike down the driveway and then up Mike's. Nell followed. Leaving the bikes on the side of his driveway, they made their way up to the front door and rang the bell. Sam was pleased when Mike answered the door, notwithstanding his obvious surprise to see them.

"Um, hi, Mike," Sam started. Now that she was standing here, she wasn't sure of a tactful way to ask whether he would be doing what she thought he should. "I, well, we, were wondering whether someone's been out to check the woods for, you know ..." Her voice trailed off, but she was doing her best to look as polite as possible.

"Hmm, I should have figured you'd follow up," Mike responded with just the slightest bit if annoyance mixed with surprise. "I called in a report last night and put the word out at the hospital to alert the police station if any gunshot victim was admitted. My partner and I will be checking out the area later in the day."

"I bet the, well, killer parked his car along M-52 and walked into the woods. You should probably check along the road," Sam added.

Mike smiled and said, a little too condescendingly for Sam's liking, "Yes, we planned on checking out that area."

Realizing that, for the moment, they couldn't do anything more, they thanked him and left. After they were on their bikes and were riding safely out of earshot, Sam turned to look at Nell. "Hey, so what do you think those guys were talking about?"

"The guys in the woods?" Nell repeated. "I have no idea. It could have been anything. The whole thing still gives me the chills."

"The first guy mentioned Dewey," Sam reminded her. "He had to have been talking about Thomas E. Dewey."

"Oh, yeah! That, makes sense," Nell said. "How many Deweys can there be? Especially in this town, he's like our claim to fame.

"Remember: he also mentioned something about a girl. I wonder who she is," Sam said.

"Me too," Nell agreed. "It might help if we were able to talk with her. Although it didn't sound like he said that much to her. Do you remember what else he said?" Nell asked.

"Yeah, he said he wanted to learn more about Owosso."

"Okay, so if that's the case, wouldn't he have done some research on a computer or gone to the library?" Nell suggested.

"You would think so," Sam replied. "But what's there to know about Owosso? This is the most boring town on the planet."

"Well, it was until last night," Nell corrected her.

Sam nodded in grim agreement.

They had reached the exit of the subdivision. Sam took one look at the red, glowing WOMP sign, jammed down on the pedals of her bike and beckoned Nell to keep up. Riding took all of their concentration now. M-52 was a busy road, for Owosso, and the girls kept riding off the road and onto the gravel shoulder to avoid approaching cars. After what was probably a little more than a mile, they girls spotted what looked like a gravel car path leading off the highway and toward the woods. Sam knew at once that this was what they were looking for.

"Come on," Sam said, pedaling hard off the road and onto the path. "Let's see if we can find anything before the cops do!" Sam steered their bikes off road and onto the gravel drive.

The hard rain had left the shoulder of the road waterlogged, and the gravel was still swimming in pools of muddy water. They carefully left their bikes on the grass and walked over to the path to check out the area.

"Look at those rows of water," Sam said. "Don't they look like tire tracks?"

"Yes, they do," Nell agreed. "Come over here. There are a ton of cigarettes here on the ground. Ew."

"There's a load of beer cans too," Sam observed.

After several moments of surveying the area, Sam suggested they follow the gravel path into the trees to see whether there was anything unusual. Noting that Nell seemed worried, Sam turned to her, "Relax. There's nothing to worry about."

"Yeah, right, that's what I thought yesterday." But she fell in step with Sam as she headed toward the trees.

They had only ventured a short way down the path when the sound of tires rolling over gravel caught their attention. Sam suddenly tensed at the sound of crunching rock behind them. Realizing the sound was coming from behind them, they froze, not knowing whether they should make a beeline for the road or hightail it into the woods. They stared at each other, having a silent discussion with their eyes.

They heard a car door open, and a familiar voice called out: "You can come out now, I saw your bikes on the side of the road." To their relief, they recognized Mike's voice.

"Crap," Sam muttered. He would pick now to start taking an interest in this.

Locked in step, the girls headed back toward the road.

"Hey Mike," Sam said as casually as she could. "We weren't hiding. We were just out riding and thought we would stop here and check out the area."

"Girls, I promised you I'd look into the matter, so don't go playing amateur detectives," Mike admonished gently. "By the way, this is my partner, Tom," he said, motioning to the tall, blond, good-looking man standing next to him, who smiled and waved. Both girls gave a half wave in acknowledgment.

"We weren't playing anything, but what's the harm in us looking around a little?" Sam asked.

"Look, I'm not exactly sure what transpired here last night, but I think you should be safe and stay as far away from the woods as possible. Plus, I can't have you jeopardizing any potential evidence."

"Oh, now you believe us," Sam said sourly.

"I never said I didn't believe you. I just said I didn't have any hard evidence to go on," Mike responded.

In a clear effort to change the direction of the conversation, Nell said, "What brings you out here now? We thought you weren't going to have time until later this afternoon?"

"Actually, we were headed just up the road to interview a victim of one of those break-ins," Mike answered.

"Break-ins?" the girls asked in unison.

"Yeah, there have been a number of unsolved break-ins over the last several weeks. A few fires that look to be arson. Mostly commercial establishments have been affected, with a few residential. No one has been hurt, and nothing of any substantial value has been taken, but it's got residents on edge. The police chief has placed an emphasis on catching whoever is behind the crimes."

"Now that you mention it, I do remember my folks talking about a bunch of break-ins," Nell said. "Do you think they're all related?"

"It's hard to be sure at this point," Mike replied. "Although this amount of criminal activity is unusual for the town. It could just be some kids having a lark, but we can't let it continue."

"What have the thieves taken?" Sam asked.

"Mostly low-value stuff, books, photographs, and miscellaneous things," Tom answered. "Still, it's got the town pretty upset. This kind of thing just doesn't happen here. Well"—he looked around— "as long as we're here, we might as well take a look around. You guys should head on home."

"Would it be okay if we stayed here and waited while you searched? I mean, we would stay right here by the car," Sam promised.

"I don't think there would be any harm in them staying by the car," Officer Tom remarked, making him instantly likable in Sam's book.

"Fine," Mike said with a half frown. "But don't leave the car."

"Got it," the girls promptly replied.

As Mike and Tom headed into the woods, Sam perched herself on the hood of the cruiser to wait. She knew she probably should have asked permission but figured it would be more palatable to Mike than her sitting inside the cruiser. After a bit of coaxing, Nell hopped up next to Sam.

The sun was now out in earnest, and the girls leaned back on the hood, soaking in the rays. The sun was warm and relaxing. Nell was just remarking how she could feel herself drifting off to sleep when they heard a shout from Tom, then rustling of leaves and branches making its way closer. Soon, Mike emerged from the trees looking visibly shaken. Both girls quickly slid off the hood and landed in a near salute position next to the car.

"You guys were gone for a while," Nell said. "Did you find any clues?"

"I'm not sure about a clue," Mike said with obvious concern, "but we found a deceased male, apparent victim of a gunshot. A shotgun was located next to the body."

At first, Sam thought Mike might just be trying to yank her chain, but a closer read of his face revealed he was serious. His face looked grim, and he was clearly shaken. She was simultaneously stunned, scared, and relieved. She would have preferred that no one had been shot, and the thought of a dead body out here was scary, but at least she hadn't imagined it all. But that also meant there was a killer on the loose. What if he had seen Nell and her running out of the woods? She shuddered at the thought.

"Where did you find the body?" Sam asked. "Was it near where we told you?"

"No, it was nowhere near the area we inspected last night. We found the body about a quarter mile from where we were last night, leaning up against a tree."

Nell looked like she was going to pass out or throw up. "Oh my word, I ... I can hardly believe it." Her voice rose to a high pitch, and then faltered. "Is ... is it the guy we described last night?" Nell asked with a quivering voice.

"It could be. The clothing generally matches your description. After we speak with your parents, we would like to have you come to the mor— ... well, come and see if you can identify the body."

"How many guys do you think were murdered in these woods last night?" Sam asked in an irritated tone.

"The body showed evidence of suffering a gunshot wound to the abdomen. That's not necessarily evidence of a murder."

"So what, you think he shot himself in the stomach—with a shotgun?" Sam asked incredulously. "My dad has told me about this kind of thing and said it's nearly impossible to shoot yourself there."

"Well, it is difficult, but not impossible," Mike replied. "Just last year, we had a fella who was out hunting alone at night. He grabbed his shotgun off from the bed of his pickup. When he pulled on the barrel, the trigger must have caught on something, and the gun fired. It happens. In any event, I need to call for backup and then I need to get you two home."

Mike reached into the car, spoke into the car radio for a few moments, and returned to where the girls were standing. Then they waited. Nearly, ten minutes later, several other official-looking vehicles showed up, including an ambulance.

"Well, they're not going to be needing that," Sam said, eyeing the EMS.

"That's harsh," Nell admonished.

"Sorry."

"Okay, time to go," Mike said. "Let's load up your bikes on the back of the cruiser, and I'll take you home."

"We can ride back on our own," Nell offered.

"I'm sure you can, but I want to make sure that you get back safe, and I want to speak with Sam's parents."

"Fine, but we're riding in the front," Sam piped up. "My mother will have a stroke if she sees us sitting in back like a couple of criminals."

"I wouldn't have it any other way," Mike said with a smile.

The ride home passed much more quickly than the ride out. Sam was apprehensive of her parents' reaction. The look on Nell's face confirmed that she was having the same thoughts. Within moments, they were pulling into Sam's driveway. As Mike got out and started to unload the bikes, Sam turned to Nell and said, "I'll probably catch it for riding on the highway. Don't worry. I'll tell them it was my suggestion. I'm going to try and keep it simple. We were out riding, we noticed the gravel path, and we stopped."

"Got it," Nell replied.

They exited the car, helped Mike pull the bikes into the garage, and headed for the back door. Sam took a deep breath and pulled on the handle. The three of them entered the laundry room single file. To Sam's disappointment, she noted that her mother was in the kitchen. Despite the presence of the car in the garage, Sam had hoped maybe she was out running errands. Her mother turned to look at the group as they entered the house.

"You guys were gone for quite a while. We were just about to send out a search party." She pointed outside where Sam saw her father mowing the lawn. "Oh, hi, Mike. How are you today?"

"Fine, thanks for asking. But I'm afraid I have a bit of bad news," Mike continued.

"Have the girls gotten into some trouble?" Lee asked.

Nice, Sam thought. *I get good grades, I've never been in trouble with anyone outside this house, and she goes straight to "have the girls gotten into trouble?"*

"No, no, on the contrary, I need their help."

At this moment, Sam's father entered the house. He had apparently seen Mike's cruiser in the drive and had come in to see what was going on. The two men exchanged a brief greeting before Mike continued.

"Unfortunately, we found a body in the woods off M-52, apparent gunshot victim."

Both girls looked at Mike, silently praying that they could skip the part where they were riding their bikes on the highway and that Mike had found them conducting their own search.

"Based on the girls' physical description, I think we may have found the man they saw last night." Mike looked at the girls and continued talking. "I saw the girls and picked them up so I could talk with you—and Nell's parents, of course. I'd like to arrange a time for the girls to come in to town and see if they can identify the body."

Sam had braced herself for her parents' wrath once they'd heard the story. Instead, she realized that Mike had just totally saved them. With that one act of unsolicited kindness, he instantly transitioned from slightly weird and dorky next-door neighbor to potential ally.

"Well, I ..." Sam's mother began, and then her words apparently failed her. She turned to her husband. "Jim?"

"I just can't believe that something like this could have happened in our neck of the woods," Sam's father said. "But as long as the girls are up for it, I say they should help the police in any way possible. Mike, we can get Nell's folks on the phone now. I'm sure they'll agree with us that the girls should help if they can. Once they give their permission, you just tell us when you'd like the girls to head downtown."

The grown-ups situated themselves at the kitchen table, and Sam's father picked up the phone to call Nell's parents. Sam nudged Nell, motioned toward the family room, and walked out of the kitchen. She signed as she sat down on the sofa. She could hear her dad's side of the conversation on the phone. There was a brief discussion of the recent events, and it was clear that Sam's dad had already informed Nell's parents of the previous day's ordeal. The conversation soon turned to Mike's discovery and his request for the girls' assistance in identifying the body. The girls were only half listening to the conversation taking place in the other room.

"What do you think it's going to be like, seeing a dead body?" Nell asked.

"Well, we've kinda already seen one." Sam said.

Nell just looked at Sam with her big doe-like eyes.

"I know," Sam responded softly. She knew how upset Nell was. Honestly, I'm not sure what to expect. But seeing the body lying there can't possibly be as bad as watching him get killed. Let's just concentrate on doing our part to catch that sicko who shot him."

"Nell just nodded.

Sam heard the phone being hung up, and her father walked in to the family room. "Okay, girls, I've spoken with Nell's father, and we all agree that you both should do whatever you can to help the police. If you are up for it, Hank and I will take you downtown at three o'clock this afternoon. Mike is arranging for us to go today, even though it's a Sunday, so Hank and I won't have to take time off work. We both would prefer to take you girls. Your mothers are pretty shaken up by this. Plus, Mike suggested that you might feel more comfortable without so many people milling around like they would be during the weekday. Is that okay with you?"

Sam's "Yeah" was quick and unqualified.

Nell's response was a quiet, but firm "Yes."

"Okay, we'll stay with you while you check to see whether you recognize the, um, body. In the meantime, why don't you guys go relax at the pool? You've had a lot of excitement in the last twenty-four hours."

Suddenly filled with exhaustion, the girls agreed with the suggestion. They had changed into their swimsuits and were lounging on pool rafts just a few moments later. As they floated in the pool, they kept their conversation focused on stress-free topics like cloud formations, the shade encroaching on the yard from the nearby trees, and the pool temperature. When they ran out of safe topics, they drifted in silent thought.

A while later, Sam's mother called out that they should get dried off and be ready to leave in about twenty minutes. Startled out of their daydreams, the girls wobbled off their rafts, quickly dried off and headed inside to change. Although it was a warm day outside, the thought of walking into a morgue raised goose bumps on their arms, so both girls elected to wear jeans and a T-shirt. Still feeling a chill, Sam threw on a sweatshirt.

"Oh hey, I keep forgetting, here's the baseball hat I borrowed from you during our last visit," Sam said, handing her the cap.

Nell tossed her hair into a messy bun and pulled the cap over it. They headed downstairs, nodded to Sam's dad, and the three of them piled in the car. As they pulled up to the county building, Sam felt cold all over. She pulled up her hoodie before getting out of the car. Nell's father met them on the front steps, and they all walked in the building together.

"How are you doing, honey?" Hank asked his daughter with obvious concern. He was always so sweet. Much softer and emotional than the rest of their parents.

"Oh, I'm doing okay, Dad," Nell answered. Her voice was a little shaky, but Sam noted that her performance was believable. She knew Nell was freaking out but that she would never let on to her parents. She was particularly close to her father, and Sam knew that Nell wouldn't want to worry him.

As they stepped inside the building, they saw Mike waiting for them with a reassuring smile on his face. Sam felt relieved when she saw him. Inside it was a little muggy thanks to the air-conditioning being turned off for the weekend. Mike had only turned on a few lights in the hallways, so the building had an empty and slightly eerie feeling.

He led the group down a long hallway to an elevator. Their shoes were loud on the marble floor, leaving an echo behind them, further adding to the creepy experience. When the elevator doors opened, everyone stepped in, and Mike pressed the button for the basement. The elevator lurched downward, and with it, so did Sam's stomach. After only a few short moments, the doors opened to a nondescript hallway. Mike turned right and led them down a narrow passage. He stopped at the end of the hall in front of a set of large metal doors.

"Okay, this is it, the morgue," Mike said unnecessarily. "Once we're inside, the coroner will roll out the body for us. When the coroner lifts the sheet, just focus on the face. Take your time and let me know if you think you recognize him. Don't rush yourself, and there's no pressure. If you don't recall seeing the face, that's okay. Let me know when you are ready to head in."

Sam felt Nell grab her hand. She looked straight ahead and said, "Ready."

"Okay, here we go." Mike swung open one side of the doors and led the procession into the room. Sam saw that they were standing in a room the size of a small classroom. An entire wall was lined with small metal doors that reminded her of the antique refrigerator her grandfather had once owed. There were several metal tables in the center of the room and she started to think about her last science class. Beginning to realize what the tables were used for, she looked away. Then she noticed the odor. The room smelled like a combination of a funeral home and bleach.

Mike cleared his throat and then introduced everyone to the coroner. Without waiting for a request, the coroner opened one of the small metal doors and reached in. Sam heard squeaking, like the sound of tiny metal wheels rolling and slowly out rolled a metal table. With a loud clank, it came to a stop about a foot from where the girls were standing. On it lay a motionless body covered by a sheet.

"Are you guys ready for the face to be uncovered?" Mike asked with concern.

"Do it," Sam replied without looking at him.

Mike nodded to the coroner, who removed the material covering the head. A strong smell of chemicals pierced Sam's nose. Unconsciously, she took a step backward and covered her mouth and nose. She saw Nell cover her face.

Sam forced herself to focus. There he was, the brown-haired, red-faced man from the woods. However, all the color was gone from his face, and his skin had a sickly white hue to it. It was hard to believe this was the same guy from, the same man Sam had spoken with.

Sam turned away from the body and looked at Nell. Nell's face was red, and her eyes had welled up with tears. Sam's stomach felt like someone had punched her, and she felt light-headed. The whole experience was surreal. She was overcome with sadness, seeing him lying on the table. Looking at a dead body wasn't nearly as awful as watching what had happened in the woods. She was more sad than scared at the moment. She couldn't help but think about how young he looked and how much life he should have had left to live. He looked peaceful now. At least death had removed the terror from his eyes.

"That's him," Sam announced. The sound of her own voice was deafening.

"Are you sure?" Mike asked quietly.

"Positive," both girls answered in tandem.

"What was he wearing when you found him?" Sam asked.

"Jeans and a brown shirt," Mike replied.

"Well that's it then, isn't it?" Sam said to no one in particular. She spoke, but her head felt foggy, like she was in a haze. She had desperately wanted to know what had happened to her, but this was the confirmation that she didn't really want.

"It seems that it does," Mike responded softly.

"Do you need the girls for anything else, or can they go now?" Hank inquired.

"You guys can head on home. I'll prepare statements for the girls to sign, including their ID of the body, and drop copies off at your homes later today or tomorrow. Thank you for coming here today and for your help. I'm sure this wasn't easy on any of you," Mike said.

Everyone except Mike and the coroner headed for the exit. As they reached the door, Sam stopped, and addressed to Mike. "You found the murder weapon, right?"

Mike looked surprised. "Well, we won't know until we get the coroner's report and conclude our investigation whether it was murder or not, but yes, we found a rifle next to the body."

"Were there any fingerprints on the gun?" Sam continued.

"We have not concluded our investigation yet, but so far, the only prints on the gun belong to the victim."

"Huh," Sam murmured. "Hey, do you know what his name was? It just feels like we should know his name." She felt horrible that she hadn't asked his name right away. She was a little overwhelmed by it all, but there was a real person who had died. Well, who was killed.

Mike eyed her for a moment before answering. "We believe that he's Fred Gray. Remember that there's an ongoing police investigation. Please don't share anything you know with anyone outside of your family—and the police department of course," Mike added.

Sam heard Nell promise that they would, and she nodded in agreement.

"One more thing, I thought that, given the girls' ages and the nature of the event, it might be a good idea to keep their names under seal for the time being. I've requested and been granted an order to seal the records, including witness names."

Sam saw that both dads seemed to be relieved by the approach. She was grateful too. It hopefully meant the whole town wouldn't be talking about them. She certainly didn't need more people asking her questions. This was a small town, and people certainly talked.

With that, the group made their way back to the elevator and out into the warm sun and fresh air. After being in the basement morgue, heading outside perked up everyone's spirits. The late afternoon sun was warm and relaxing, and Sam was grateful for it.

"Well, I guess we should be getting home," Hank finally said.

"Yeah, it's getting to be dinnertime," Jim agreed. "Thanks for meeting us up here, Hank."

"No problem. Have a good evening," he replied.

The girls said their goodbyes and then headed to their respective cars.

As Sam sank down into the front seat next to her father, she wanted nothing more than to go to bed and sleep for a week. But she felt bonded to Fred somehow, and she knew this journey wasn't over. However, she vowed to put it out of her head for the remainder of the night. She leaned her head against the window and stared outside. She smiled as she saw a man walking his dog down the sidewalk. Everything seemed so quiet and normal out here.

As they pulled out of the parking lot, Sam vaguely noticed a black SUV and heard a faint hum as it idled in place. She turned her head back toward the dog who was now having a grand time rolling in the grass. That was what she needed to see.

The trip home was quiet with only the radio intermittently interrupting Sam's thoughts. When they entered the house, they saw that Sam's mother had dinner waiting. Sam ate the meal quickly and, after assuring her parents that she was going to be fine, went upstairs for the night. Her head was swimming with thoughts and images for some time. Then, blissfully, she fell into a deep slumber.

4

◇

A History Lesson

True to his word, Mike dropped off statements for each of the girls at their homes the next day. Nell called Sam to talk as soon as Mike had left.

"What did you think about your statement?" Nell asked.

"It seemed pretty straightforward," Sam answered.

"Yeah, I thought so too," Nell agreed. "But reading it was strange; it was like I was reading about someone else. I still can't believe we were there."

"Listen, Nell. We really need to get that locker," Sam stated. "I haven't done what I promised Fred I would do." Sam decided to start using his name. She felt that it was a way of showing her respect. "We need to get that key—or whatever it is that we're supposed to find—before the killer does. I hope it's not too late."

"I know," said Nell. "But it's not like we've had much choice. Our parents have kept us cooped up since it happened."

"I've been thinking about it, and I can't imagine why he'd send us to a bowling alley."

"It does seem weird. But I'll figure out how to get us there," Nell promised. "I also think we should probably do some research. How about I ask my mom if you can come over later this week 'to go to the library,' and we launch our investigation?"

"Perfect," Sam agreed. "It would be a lot easier if my parents would get a computer like the rest of the world instead of forcing me to go to the Library every time I need to use one. Hey, I thought you had one?"

"Yeah, I do. It's packed with my dad's stuff. It's not much good right now since the internet hasn't been hooked up yet. We'll have to do it old school til then." Nell answered.

After some amount of finagling, the girls secured the necessary permissions for Sam to go to Nell's house that Friday and stay over for a few days. It was surprising that nearly a had passed since Nell's arrival and the gruesome scene in the woods. It was a welcome relief for Sam to get out of her house and away from her surroundings. Just looking out her backyard made her feel tense, sad, and guilty. Sam arrived at Nell's Friday afternoon with her duffel bag, pillow and library card.

As her mother pulled the car into the driveway, Sam thought how happy she was that Nell's family had been able to buy back their old house on Crust Drive. She had a lot of good memories in the house. Plus, it was located just outside the main part of town, which provided better access to activities. The house was a sprawling ranch-style located within walking distance of the high school and Emerson Elementary School. Main Street and the center of the town were only a few blocks away.

Sam couldn't contain herself when they pulled into the driveway. She had flung open the car door before the vehicle had come to a stop, raced across the driveway, bounded up the steps and was through the front door before her mother had gotten out of the car. The front door opened to a small foyer, which led directly to the family room. Beyond the family room was the spacious kitchen.

Sam heard Nell's voice before she actually saw her. Her voice emanated from behind a mountain of boxes. Apparently, they were still unpacking.

"Hey!" Sam called out. Nell's face peered out from a large box. She smiled and both girls immediately began talking at once.

"Hi, Aunt Sue, Uncle Hank," she called over, remembering her manners.

"Hello there; nice to see we're not completely invisible," Nell's dad said and laughed.

"Nice to see you too," Sam heard Aunt Sue call out a greeting, but she knew that the moms were busy getting caught up as well.

"Well, we should probably make sure you're completely un-packed," Sam said with a wink. She was dying to be alone to talk freely with Nell.

"Sounds like a plan," Nell agreed.

Nell led Sam through the kitchen and down the hallway, past the main bathroom, and to the bedrooms. She stopped at the en-trance to what had always been the room used by her brothers, Bill and Mark. Gone were the bunk beds used by Nell's brothers, and in their place was her trundle bed, a small dresser and a desk. "Since my brothers are both in college now, Mom and Dad said I can have their old room. It's a lot bigger than my old room. Plus, it's at the opposite end of the house from my parent's room—so there's less of a chance that they break up our late-night chats."

"Brilliant!" Sam agreed.

After unpacking most of Nell's stuff, the girls were enlisted to help with a few boxes scattered throughout the house. By five, the house was sufficiently in order, and everyone dropped, exhausted, into the nearest chairs in the family room.

Sam sat back and observed the adults. She noted for the first time, how different their parents were physically. Her mother was short, barely five feet in height, her hair was ash blond and her eyes were bright blue. Sam had recently learned that her mother had been homecoming queen when she'd been in high school. The thought seemed bizarre to Sam. In contrast, Nell's mother was several inches taller than her sister, her hair was dark-brown, nearly black, and her eyes were light brown. They didn't look like sisters.

Sam then looked over at Uncle Hank and compared him to her father. Sam's dad had brown hair and dark-blue eyes, while Nell's dad had blond hair and brown eyes. Both fathers were tall, but while Sam's father was athletically built, Nell's father's frame was just plain skinny. Sam's dad worked at a local automotive supplier, while Nell's dad was an accountant. It seemed to Sam that their appearances matched their jobs, or vice versa.

The interests were also markedly different. Sam's dad spent much of his free time working on the family cars, grooming the lawn, or starting some project around the house. When he wasn't occupied around the house, he enjoyed hunting and fishing, so he usually sported a tan.

Uncle Hank, on the other hand, was an avid reader and could usually be found in his chair reading a book. When he wasn't reading, he enjoyed going to museums or experiencing other cultural events. Sam had never seen Uncle Hank with a tan, or without his black socks on, come to think of it. In short, the dads were polar opposites. Luckily, it had never prevented the family from being close with one another and enjoying time together.

The girls tried to make polite conversation for what they thought was a reasonable time before excusing themselves. They were anxious to discuss their plan in earnest. The door had hardly latched closed before Nell started firing out thoughts. Sam was impressed to hear that Nell had figured out how to get them to the bowling alley. Since Nell's mother was generally a bit against those types of places, they had figured that a trip there was going to require one or both of the dads. Actually, Nell had somehow managed to convince her mother that she needed a new pair of sneakers, and Aunt Sue had agreed to take the girls to JCPenney the following morning. It was the only department store in town and conveniently located right next to the bowling alley, which made it perfectly situated to launch their search. The girls went to bed that night anxious to find out what they would learn.

In the morning, Sam awoke to the smell of bacon. She looked over and saw Nell sit up and yawn. "Man! I love it here; your mom always makes the best breakfasts!" Sam exclaimed, hopping out of bed and pushing the trundle into storage.

"It does smell good," Nell admitted. "Thank goodness my mom's a good cook. It almost makes up for her eternally sour disposition."

Sam had to admit, her aunt didn't seem very happy, though she was always nice to Sam. Their mothers were so similar, very serious, and mostly suspicious of their daughters. If Sam thought about it, she supposed it was probably the way they'd been raised, and maybe they were just trying to be protective. Whatever the reason, it was kind of a drag most of the time.

"Hey, did you tell your mom that we wanted to go to the library this weekend?" Sam asked.

"As a matter of fact, I did," Nell said smiling. "I talked to both of my parents. I told them that we'd finished all our own books and that we wanted to do some reading—both which are true. My mom was thrilled. Well, as thrilled as my mom can get. She even offered to drive us there and pick us up either today or tomorrow. Her complaining was actually pretty minimal."

"Nicely done, Nell," Sam said with admiration.

"And, you know, she's not entirely comfortable with us riding our bikes across M-52," Nell added.

"What is it about that road?" Sam asked rhetorically. "It's only two lanes. It's not exactly the Autobahn."

Nell gave a little groan of embarrassment. "I don't get it either, especially since we just moved away from a big city. But for now, we have to work with our parents' issues."

"I know," Sam mumbled. "I can't wait until we can drive."

"Plus," Nell continued, "I told my dad that I was so excited to be back home and that I wanted to learn more about Owosso. Also a true statement. He thinks it's a great idea—so much so that he suggested we visit some of the local landmarks. He suggested we take a tour of the castle on Sunday. I was thinking it couldn't hurt to check it out."

"You've been hard at work," Sam admired. "Is your mom going to be okay with that?"

"She'll have to be since it was my dad's idea," Nell said, smiling. "So I was thinking, we'll hit the library this afternoon, see what we learn. Tomorrow, we check out Curwood Castle and then map out the rest of our sightseeing excursions/investigations afterward."

"Perfectly planned," Sam said.

Nell accepted the compliment with a small curtsy.

With the plan in place, Sam followed Nell into the kitchen for breakfast.

"Okay girls, I want to get going in a few minutes. The store opens at nine thirty, so we can be in, out, and have the rest of the day," she said.

"Okay Mom", Nell said, getting up from her chair.

Sam followed Nell into the bedroom.

"Nell, the bowling alley doesn't open until 11:00. I know because I went to a party there not too long ago. We need to stall."

"Crap, Okay." Nell answered.

Sam hopped in the shower before her aunt could stop her, and made a production out of drying her hair afterwards. Nell took her time trying to decide what to wear. It was ironic that that they were now working so hard to use up time when it seemed that they spent the majority of their time trying to make their parents move faster.

Finally, at around ten forty, they were out of excuses, and Aunt Sue ushered them into the car. Luckily, they spotted a neighbor walking her dog, who motioned them to stop and chat. That used up almost five minutes. Thanks to Aunt's Sue's driving, the trip to the store took another ten minutes.

"Okay, I'll stall my mom in the shoe department. You head next door to the bowling alley and see if you can find the key. If she asks where you are, I'll tell her you're shopping. I just won't tell her you're shopping for a key," Nell said.

"Got it," Sam responded.

Nell's mom parked the car, and they all headed inside. As they walked, Sam noticed a side door to the bowling alley. It was only a few yards from the store. The entered the store, and Nell and her mother headed straight for the shoe department, which was located in the back of the store.

Mumbling something about checking out a swimsuit, Sam stayed near the front door. Looking over what appeared to be a list of some kind, Aunt Sue nodded her understanding without looking up. Sam was out the door and inside the bowling alley seconds later.

Once inside, she had to stop for a moment to let her eyes adjust to the darkness. After a moment, she saw that the place was nearly empty. She noticed a bored-looking teenager manning the shoe rental counter, and was surprised to see a couple putting on bowling shoes midway down the alley.

Beyond the shoe counter, Sam spotted a row of lockers. It now made sense that the numbers he listed must indicate a locker number and the combination. She made her way over to the lockers as nonchalantly as possible. She kept reminding herself of the numbers Fred had given her, 25-18-6-5.

Sam scanned the locker numbers until she found locker 25. She looked over her shoulder to make sure no one was watching. She tried to act casual as she reached out and tried the combination 18-6-05. She held her breath and pulled down on the lock.

For a second, nothing happened, but at last the lock fell open. She opened the door and peered inside. She saw a pair of bowling shoes, a towel, and a score card. No key. Befuddled, she continued to stare at the contents as if hoping a key would appear.

When that failed, she picked up the items one by one to look at them more closely. After she had fully inspected the items and had come up with nothing, she started to return them to the locker. In her frustration, she dropped one of the shoes.

As she bent over to retrieve it, she accidentally stepped on the shoe and noticed a slight tear in the sole. Carefully, she prodded the sole away from the shoe. Buried deep in the sole, she saw a small, fragile-looking piece of paper. The paper was yellowed with age, and the edges were tattered. Carefully, she opened the fold. Written in long hand, in the most proper writing Sam had ever seen, was a note that read:

> What once was lost for preservation
> Rediscover for our great nation
> The Founders' faith was set in stone
> There the journey's path will be shown.

Her heart was racing, and she could barely breathe. She stared at the message, rereading it several times before she realized she needed to get back to Nell. As she placed the shoes back into the locker, a small black book slid out from inside the shoe. Her exhilaration at finding the clue left little incentive to read a book.

Flipping through it quickly, it seemed to be an ordinary journal of some sort. It had a few motivational notes and then some comments about a family fight. It reminded her of the journal she knew her uncle Hank kept. She shoved it into her back pocket. Then she carefully returned the rest of the contents, minus the handwritten note, back to the locker, closed the combination lock and exited the building.

In her haste, she nearly collided with a man walking up the

sidewalk toward the bowling alley. He gave her a funny look, but she barely noticed. Lost in thought, she mumbled an apology, and continued on.

She reentered the department store, keeping her eyes peeled for Nell. She stopped near a rack of clothes for a moment to regain her composure, then headed to the shoe department.

"There you are," Nell's mother announced from several aisles over in the shoe department.

"Um, I'm sorry if I kept you waiting." She hoped that Aunt Sue wouldn't ask her where she had been.

"Hey, Mom, these really feel good," Nell said loudly in an effort to redirect her mother's attention. "But if you don't like them, we can wait. I think I could get a few more months out of my current shoes."

"No, no, these are fine, and they're on sale. We might as well get them now. I'll go pay for them. You girls stay close. We need to head home for lunch."

"Okay, we'll just be over here looking at the jeans," Nell informed her mother.

Once they were safely out of range, Nell started in on Sam. "What took so long? I had to try on every shoe in the store and pretend that there was something wrong with each one. I don't even need new shoes," she grumbled. "Thank heavens, she saw an old friend of hers from high school. Otherwise, we would have been busted."

"Well, your sacrifice was worth it. Look what I found," Sam exclaimed, her heart still racing with excitement. She reached in her pocket, carefully extracted the note and handed it to Nell. "Be careful; I think it's really old." She gave Nell a list of the locker contents and confirmed that she had not found an actual key.

Nell delicately opened the note and gasped with surprise as she read its contents. "Wow! What do you think it means?" she asked.

"I can't even manage a guess at this point," Sam responded,

mesmerized by the note and its unknown meaning. "But I think it must be what Fred meant by the key. It seems odd that he would keep something so valuable at a bowling alley. We definitely need to make that trip to the library," she added.

"Okay, girls, let's head home now." Nell's mother's voice felt like a cup of cold water had been poured on Sam's head. She was so lost in thought that she jumped at the sound of her aunt's voice. Sam carefully refolded the note and placed it back in her pocket, and the girls joined Nell's mother.

Hey Mom, since we're out, would you mind dropping us off at the Library now? I mean, I was just thinking that it might be more convenient for you, and I'd love to pick up some books.

Aunt Sue eyed Nell for a moment, her furrowed brow almost twitching. Sam knew that she liked things to be very planned out, and wasn't used to making decisions on the fly. Sam held her breath.

Well, I suppose that would be okay. What about lunch?

I'm not hungry, Nell said.

Oh, I'm so stuffed from that amazing breakfast, that I couldn't possibly either anything until dinner, Sam quickly added.

After another moment of hesitation, Aunt Sue miraculous agreed.

5

◇

Research

Sam was bursting with excitement as they headed to the Library. It felt like firecrackers were exploding inside her, but she had to pretend like everything was normal. It felt like an impossible task.

Finally, the ivy-covered walls of the building were in front of them.

Nell's mother parked the car and turned to look at them in the back seat. Okay, what time shall I pick you up?

Sam gently kicked her, willing her to buy them enough time.

"Oh, well, it's hard to say. I haven't been here in forever, and I can't wait to check out what they have. Remember that, dad suggested I, well, we take his cell phone and call when we're ready to come home? Ya know, if that's still okay.

Sam inwardly groaned that neither she nor Nell yet had cell phones, despite the fact that most of the other girls their ages did. Apparently, their parents thought that it was an unnecessary luxury in their quiet little town.

With a sigh, Aunt Sue begrudgingly handed Nell the phone. Sam knew that this bit of freedom would never have come without her uncle. He was so nice.

"Thanks Aunt Sue, we really appreciate this." Sam said.

Nell followed Sam out of the car and they approached the building. It sat on the corner of M-52 and M-21, or Main Street as it was called in town. The exterior was a deep red brick with a similarly colored roof. The front steps rose ceremoniously to the main entrance, which was topped with a rounded concrete arch. Ivy enveloped much of the building. It truly was a striking.

The children's library was located on the first level, so the girls made their way up the narrow flight of stairs to the main collection. They located a free table in the far corner of the room and sat down to review their plan.

"Okay, do you want to research Dewey or Owosso?" Sam asked.

"Hmm, I'll take Dewey."

"Okay, I'll tackle Owosso," Sam replied.

Unfortunately, there were only two computers in the library, and much to their disappointment, they were already taken. As they scoured the card catalogs, they each made a list of reference materials. After a while, they split up and began pulling books from the shelves.

Sometime later, they met back at the table. Each of the girls bore arms laden with a tall stack of books. The books slid from their arms and landed on the table with a loud thud prompting looks of disgust from several other occupants. Sam ignored the stares and set straight to work searching through the materials for information.

After reading for nearly an hour, Nell lifted her head up and started talking in a hushed voice. "Hey, did you know that Thomas Edmund Dewey was a US prosecuting attorney who busted a number of racketeers, served three terms and governor of New York, and was the Republican presidential nominee in 1944 and 1948?"

"I knew about his run in the one presidential election, but not the other stuff," Sam replied.

"It says here that he was offered the position of chief justice of the US Supreme Court by President Nixon in 1968, but he turned it down," Nell said, reading on.

"What an idiot," Sam said, a little too loudly. "What else does it say about him?"

"Not much," Nell replied. "Most of the books say the same thing. The microfiche station is open now, so I'll see if I can find any interesting articles about him."

"Okay, good luck," Sam said. She dove deeper into her books, so deep that she barely noticed when Nell returned some time later.

"Nothing," Nell grumbled.

"Really?" Sam said. "I'm actually finding out a lot of interesting stuff about this town. For instance, did you know that Owosso was named for an Indian chief named Wasso? Or that Owosso Woodward Furniture was used in the White House for decades? Also, the first Beatles record was stamped here in Owosso. Then, of course, there's a lot of stuff on James Oliver Curwood. Your dad was right: he wrote like thirty books. I always thought that he lived in Curwood Castle, but apparently, he only wrote in the castle. He lived over on Weston Street. Must be nice to have an entire castle just to write in."

"This town is more interesting than I thought," Nell admitted. "When I struck out on Dewey, I read a few articles about Owosso. Did you know that Owosso was supposedly part of the Underground Railroad? Apparently, there were even tunnels underneath some of the homes. It sounds like they may also have been used for storing alcohol back when it was illegal"

"All of this is interesting, but how does it help us?" Sam posed.

"Good question," Nell agreed. "I'm not sure."

"I don't mean to interrupt, but I couldn't help overhearing a part of your conversation," said a voice from behind Nell.

The intrusion made both girls jump out of their chairs as if caught in the middle of some wrongdoing.

"I'm really sorry, I didn't mean to startle you," said the voice. Sam regained her composure and focused her attention on the source of the voice. It came from a boy who looked to be about the same age as the girls. He was tall, athletically built, with sandy brown hair and deep blue eyes. His hair was cut short. It was slightly tousled on the top, leading Sam to wonder whether he had curly hair. He looked like a jock.

"Hi, my name's Dean," he continued.

"Uh, hi, I'm Sam, and this is Nell," she offered. She had introduced them more out of habit than politeness.

"So, um, like I was saying, I couldn't help overhearing part of your conversation. It sounds like you guys are researching Owosso. What did you do, take on a summer paper project for extra credit at school?" he joked.

"No," Sam answered, her guard up. "Nell just moved back to Owosso, and we were just doing some research for fun."

"Well, it didn't sound like you were able to find what you were looking for," Dean observed.

"Not exactly," Nell agreed.

"Yeah, sometimes you just can't find what you need in this library, small town," he said with a shrug. He looked over at the one still-occupied computer. "They need to spring for more computers."

"Do you spend a lot of time here?" Nell inquired.

"Sort of." Dean answered. "My mom's the director of the library here, so I work here a few days a week. She says that I can learn while I stay out of trouble. I like to read, so it works out okay."

"Anyway," he continued, "a lot of Owosso's history apparently didn't make it into the books. At least that's what my mother is always telling me. We had a guy in here a few weeks back doing some research on Owosso. He seemed to be disappointed in his search too. I gave him the same advice. Of course, he didn't seem real bright to start with, and he didn't want any help. Anyway, if you want to learn more, I'd be happy to help out if I can. Also, you might want to talk with some of the locals or members of the chamber of commerce. The aged love to talk about the old days."

"We were thinking about taking a tour of Curwood Castle and some of the other landmarks," Nell mentioned.

Sam shot her a warning look, but Nell seemed unfazed.

"That's cool," Dean replied. "If you want, I can hook you guys up with some special tours of the castle, Curwood's house, and the historic homes. My mother has forced me to attend one too many dinner parties with the historical society folks."

He paused for a moment. "Honestly, I'm not a total dork. I just sound like it right now," he added with obvious embarrassment. Anyway, let me know if I can help. You guys are the first two people under the age of fifty to come in the last few weeks, so I guess I'm a little relieved to be around my own kind."

Sam assessed his features and behavior. He was maybe sixteen or seventeen. "Uh, thanks. We'll let you know," Sam said, a little dismissively. She found herself oddly attracted to him, and the feeling made her sweat a little.

Dean smiled and headed back to the other side of the library.

"He was nice," Nell said.

"Kinda pushy," Sam retorted. "I mean really, what kind of a loser spends so much time here?"

"Well, we're here," Nell challenged.

"Oh, yeah," Sam acknowledged. Suddenly she realized that she was being a jerk. "Okay, he was nice."

"Cute too," Nell added. "Plus, I think he was scoping you out."

"No way, shut up!" Sam ordered. "Now you're just trying to annoy me." She closed the book she had been reading. "I can't concentrate now. I say today was a bust. Are you ready to call your mom and have her pick us up?"

"Sure. I think you're right; we're done for the day. But you're wrong about Dean," she said with a giggle.

Sam scowled at her and stood up to start re-shelving her books.

Nell walked off to a corner to call her mother. Several minutes later, she joined Nell at the table, and they headed back to the steps leading to the exit. On the way out, Nell spotted Dean, and he waved to them as they descended the stairs.

When they returned to Nell's home, they grabbed two sodas out of the fridge and headed to Nell's room. As Nell closed the door, she frowned and said, "You know, I just really thought that this was going to be easier. I thought we were going to be able to find a clue today that would help us understand the note you found."

"Me too," said Sam glumly. "Hey, you have a new computer," she exclaimed, pointing at the shiny silver laptop on the desk in Nell's room.

"Oh yeah, my dad got me a new one. He figured that I would be needing it for school. Dad must have unpacked it for me. We're going to have high-speed internet. Dad uses it for work, and he said it will help me save time with school research projects."

"Hopefully the internet will be up and running in a few days. We have to be careful though. I got a long lecture from my mother on what the computer can be used for. She won't come out and say it, but apparently, she's afraid I'm going to meet some serial killer online or use it to look at *inappropriate materials.*" Nell rolled her eyes in obvious irritation at the lack of her mother's trust. "My dad knows me so much better. He knows I'd never do that kind of stuff."

Sam nodded in agreement. "Your dad is the best. Hey, let's go over what we know," she suggested. "Maybe all our research will shed some light on what we found."

They retrieved the note and reread its message. After several moments, Sam said, "I know this is going to sound silly, but I think the message is talking about something valuable, like a treasure of some kind." She looked at Nell as if waiting for her to laugh.

Nell cocked her head to the side for a moment. Then, slowly, she said, "You know, I think you might be right."

"You do?"

"Yeah, *what once was lost for preservation, rediscover for this great nation,*" Nell regurgitated. "It makes sense. Something was hidden to preserve it. The note says that it should be found. It clearly was important to Fred that we find the note. He must have been trying to figure it out too."

"That's what I thought," Sam replied. "But what was hidden, and what were they preserving it from?"

"No idea," Nell answered.

"Okay, let's go over the second part," Sam said. "*The Founders' faith was set in stone, there the journey's path will be shown.* Who are the Founders? Do you think this means we're looking for a rock with a message on it?"

"Founders, Founders ... set in stone," Nell muttered. "It could be referring to the Founding Fathers, you know, like in history class, the Founders of the United States. But I never read anything about the Founding Fathers being from Michigan. As for the stone part, I don't know of any stone monuments in Owosso, do you?"

"Nope," Sam replied. "I haven't a clue what this note is trying to tell us. Did your dad happen to mention anything about a lost treasure?" Sam added half-jokingly.

"No," Nell responded with interest, "But I think that's a great idea."

"Girls, dinner's almost ready," Nell's mother called.

"Follow my lead," Nell whispered as they both started toward the kitchen.

After they had set the table, and everyone had settled down to a dinner of hamburgers and fries, Nell began her subtle inquisition.

"Hey, Dad, we learned some really interesting things about Owosso today. We never knew this town was so fascinating."

Nell and Sam took turns regurgitating a few of the more interesting details of the town's history to show that they'd done their research and to establish their enthusiasm.

"We're really looking forward to Curwood Castle tomorrow,"

Nell added. "I know it's small, but having a castle in our own town is really cool."

Nell's dad chuckled. "I'm glad you're enjoying learning about this town. It has an impressive history."

"Uncle Hank, were any of the Founding Fathers from Michigan? I mean, it seems like we had a lot of interesting people come out of this town."

"Hmm," he responded. "I don't recall ever reading anything like that. Although you are correct that Owosso has produced a number of well-known and successful people."

"I read that it was originally settled by an Indian tribe," Nell mentioned.

"Yes, yes, you are correct," Nell's father said. Then he launched into an extended explanation of the original Indian settlers who decided to farm the area. "Yes, the original settlers purportedly established a farm right about where Central Elementary School is now."

He continued talking about crops and treaties until Sam thought her head would fall off. However, she forced herself to maintain a look of absolute fascination on her face. When Nell's dad paused to take a drink of water, Sam seized her chance.

"So you're sure you don't remember anything about the Founding Fathers being from Michigan?" she prompted, gently trying to redirect him to the question.

"Pretty sure, the Founding Fathers lived in the original colonies. Michigan was not a state back then. As for Owosso, it was formed around 1838, I think." He paused for a moment. "Gosh, I'm not sure if I even know the names of the original settlers of the town," he said to himself before addressing the girls again. "There are several families, like the Grays, who have lived here for quite a long time, but I'm not sure who is formally credited with establishing the town."

"Dad, have you ever heard any stories about buried treasure in Owosso?" Nell almost blurted out.

Nell's dad gave a hearty laugh. "No, can't say as I have, sorry. I don't think this town is *that* exciting. Why do you ask anyway?"

"Oh, I don't know," Nell responded, her cheeks growing red. It's just that we found out so many interesting things today, I uh, half expected to hear about legends of lost treasure."

"Well, I suppose anything is possible, but I wouldn't hold out a lot of hope."

"Now, girls," Nell's mother chided, "I hope you're not cooking up some mystery."

"Don't worry, Mom," Nell cut her off. "We're just having fun learning about the town. We're not cooking up anything."

"Sue, there's certainly no harm in the girls doing a bit of research on their hometown. In fact, I think it's a wonderful idea."

Sam saw her aunt shoot her uncle a disgusted look, and she suppressed a smile. Uncle Hank had their back.

"Girls, how about if I drop you off at Curwood Castle after church tomorrow?" Nell's dad said, in obvious effort to move the conversation along. "You guys can take your time enjoying the castle and grounds, and I'll pick you up around two thirty."

"Sounds good, Dad, thanks," Nell said with appreciation.

Sam had forgotten about church. Nell's family attended church every Sunday. Before Nell had moved away, Sam had sometimes accompanied the family to the Methodist church they attended. Having only experienced the regimented structure of a Catholic mass, Sam found the Methodist church a bit less stuffy. Actually, she would still have preferred to skip the experience altogether, particularly this week. But she didn't want to make Nell feel bad, so she kept her feelings to herself.

After dinner, the girls helped clear the table. As they were headed for Nell's room, her mother called out, "It's such a nice night.

Why don't you guys go out for a walk instead of being cooped up in your room?"

Reluctantly, the girls agreed. They grabbed their shoes and were out the door before Aunt Sue could suggest that she join them.

Nell's house was located on a quiet street nestled in a subdivision bordered by Emerson Elementary School and the only high school in town. The girls decided to walk toward Emerson since the road curved and they'd be out of sight more quickly.

Anxious to gain some insight on the note, as they walked, the girls rehashed what they had learned during the day. After going over and over their research, including their conversation with Nell's dad, they agreed that they still didn't have much to go on. Before they realized it, they were on the school playground. They made themselves comfortable on swings and tried to make sense of the clue. For a while, they swung without talking, each one trying to come up with an idea or suggest a lead.

"Holy crap!" Sam exclaimed so suddenly that Nell nearly fell off her swing. "*The Founder's faith was set in stone.* Isn't the castle made of stone?"

"Yes, I read that the castle was built using fieldstones from a farm nearby," Nell answered. "You don't think there's a treasure buried under the castle, do you?"

"I don't know," Sam answered with enthusiasm. "But it makes sense. I can't believe we didn't think of this before. The castle is pretty old."

Sam considered it for a moment. "I wonder if James Curwood had some connection to the Founders," she asked rhetorically. "And what does Thomas Dewey have to do with any of this? Nell, I think we're going to need a little more time at the castle than we expected."

"I suppose anything is possible. I'll arrange it with my dad," Nell agreed.

Relieved that they finally had something to go on, they headed back to the house. Although they walked in silence, Sam knew they both had the same thought: What would they find at Curwood Castle?

Alone in Nell's room, Sam plopped on the bed and felt something hard. Reaching into her back pocket, she pulled out the book she had found in the locker.

"Oh, yeah, I forgot that this was in the locker too," she said tossing it onto the bed. "It seems to be just a daily journal of some kind. I only scanned it, but I think it just talks about family stuff."

She pulled out the note and read it out loud. Nell used a dictionary to look up the meaning of each of the words, hoping that it would help them decipher the code. Two hours later, they weren't any farther ahead and the words on the aged paper were still just as mysterious as before. Panic filled Sam as Aunt Sue called them to dinner. Another day had passed, and she still didn't understand what Fred wanted her to do. *I mean, I went where he told me and found the note. But what did it mean?*

At dinner, conversation turned to the annual Curwood Festival starting in a few days. The event took place over the course of four days starting on the first Thursday in June. The festivities celebrated one of Owosso's favorite citizens, and author James Oliver Curwood. During Curwood Days, the streets in the center of town were closed off, and the area was filled with rides, games, music, arts and crafts, and food. The entire event culminated in a parade down Main Street. It was easily the most excitement the town saw all year.

Sam never missed Curwood Days. Suffering from motion sickness for most of her life, Sam was not partial to many rides, but every year she and Nell would tackle at least one ride and stay on until Sam had overcome her urge to be sick. She was confident that the look on her face, and the shade of green that she was certain she became, was more than a little off-putting to others on the ride. However, Sam was proud to say that she had not yet actually gotten sick.

After they had conquered Sam's fears, they would reward themselves with sodas and some carnival food while they walked around and played a few games. Sam particularly enjoyed the tents in which you could dress up in period clothing and have your picture taken. She looked absolutely ridiculous, but it was so much fun.

After dinner, the girls helped clear the table and load the dishwasher, then retreated to Nell's room. They closed the door and pulled out the note to again read its message. They read and reread the paper countless times. In the end, they were still as mystified as they'd been after the first reading. They didn't know who wrote the message or what it meant.

Realizing they weren't making any headway, they agreed to put it away for the evening. After considering every inch of Nell's room for a proper hiding spot, they elected to store the note in a pencil case under the trundle bed. Sam absentmindedly tossed the black book into her backpack.

"Let's play some video games," Sam suggested. "I need a diversion."

Nell's brothers had graciously left her their old television and equally old video games. Although a bit dated, they were still fun. The distraction worked, and they played until Nell's mother poked her head into the room to tell them it was time for lights out. They dutifully turned off the games and crawled into bed. Nell in her bed, and Sam in the trundle beneath her.

"What a day," Nell sighed.

"Yeah," Sam agreed. "I wonder who wrote the note and what it means."

"I know, me too," Nell agreed. "This whole thing seems like something out of a book. Do you think we should tell Mike what we found?"

"Not yet," Sam responded. "I know we talked about finding the key and then turning it over to the police, but that just doesn't feel right to me for some reason. I think we need to know more before we bring in Mike. Can we keep this to ourselves for a little while longer?"

"Okay, sure," Nell replied. "It's fun to have a secret like this."

"My mother's right. I'm a bad influence on you," Sam said jokingly.

"Oh, trust me: my mother would insist that it's the other way around," Nell said.

Clearly their mothers shared some similarities.

Exhausted from the day's excitement, Sam quickly fell fast asleep. Once again, Fred's face swarmed her brain. His eyes kept urging her to help him, to figure it out and find it, whatever *it* was.

6

◇

Curwood Castle

Sunday morning dawned, finding the girls awake, showered, and dressed bright and early, an unusual occurrence for what was typically a lazy day if Sam had her way. They hastily ate a breakfast of cereal and juice, waving off Nell's mother's suggestion for a heartier start to the day.

Shortly after nine, Nell's mother summoned everyone to the car. They all dutifully piled in, and soon they were pulling out of the subdivision. The girls sat in silence while Aunt Sue speculated about who they would see at church.

Sam tried to take her mind off the castle so the wait wouldn't drive her mad. She looked out the window, lazily watching the trees go by. Slowly she realized that they'd passed the church where Nell's family used to attend services.

"Hey, did you guys, um, change churches?" Sam asked. She hoped that they had not decided to convert to Catholicism. She still didn't have a firm grasp on all the proper etiquette. All the standing, sitting, kneeling. She always seemed to be in the wrong position; she never found the right reading in time; and the pull-out kneeler routinely seemed to slip out of her hands landing with a loud crash. The harder she tried to be quiet, the louder she seemed to become. She shook her head to erase the embarrassing images from her head.

"Well, not really," Nell's father answered. "The church we used to attend is undergoing some renovations right now. We have friends who attend the First Congregational Church over on Weston Street, so we thought we'd attend a service."

"We'll be returning to *our* church just as soon as possible," Nell's mother chimed in.

Nell rolled her eyes at her mother's Stalin-like dedication to her chosen church.

Sam had to admit that Nell's mother was a bit rigid. Nell speculated that her mother only attended church out of some sense of obligation and for public perception. Sam was starting to agree with Nell's assessment. Aunt Sue was a good person, but she was so negative all the time, even in the face of happy occasions.

The remainder of the ride was silent. A few minutes later, the car pulled into a parking lot and Sam saw the church towering over them. From the outside, you could see large stained-glass windows on several sides of the structure. Everyone climbed out of the car and began walking toward the entrance.

Up close, Sam could see that the church was made of large field-stones, and it looked very old. The building looked different than most churches Sam had seen, and she wasn't sure what to make of it. Suddenly she became anxious. Old things tended to creak, and Sam always seemed to be the one generating those sounds. Already she envisioned a mass of people turning to scowl at her after she committed some church faux pas. Unfortunately, the more nervous she got, the clumsier she seemed to be. Thankfully, Nell would be there for support.

"It looks old," Nell said.

"It is old," her father responded. "It is one of the oldest churches in town. It was originally founded back in the 1830s."

They climbed the stone steps and entered the lobby. As they

walked further, the ornate details of the church came into view. Inside, the church was very pretty. The east entrance boasted a beautiful balustrade, and two balconies were observable on one side. At the front of the church, a black altar sat atop while marble. Behind the altar was a massive organ covered by an ornate gold screen. In all, Sam found the structure rather interesting.

As the church started to fill up with people, Sam and company found themselves seats. The church bells sounded overhead in a low, serene call. Soon, everyone was seated, and services commenced shortly after.

Sam was thankfully able to avoid any major incidents. She never felt comfortable singing out loud, but there was no need to worry. Her voice was easily drowned out by Aunt Sue. Nell's mother had a horrible singing voice, and Nell suspected that she was tone deaf. Nevertheless, Aunt Sue belted out every song at the top of her lungs. The experience was always part torture and part amusement.

The service itself was tolerable. Thankfully, the minister was on the younger side. He was interesting, and best of all, the process was relatively quick. Before long, church was over, and people started to file outside.

Nell's parents struck up a conversation with another couple on the way out. They had hardly moved a few feet from the pews and were standing in the aisle. Much to Sam's dismay, the minister came over to greet everyone. Upon learning that Nell's family had just returned to the area and were visiting the church for the first time, he insisted upon giving them a tour. It was clearly a thinly veiled attempt to secure new members for the church, but he did seem friendly enough.

Sam started to panic. Her uncle *loved* learning about everything and anything. They could be here for hours.

Uncle Hank must have seen the look of concern on her face, because he subtly leaned over and said, "Relax, girls, the castle doesn't open until one." With a quiet chuckle, he coaxed them in line to join the tour.

Although Sam knew that it was too early to get in to see the castle, she was nonetheless anxious and jittery. She would much rather have been sitting outside the castle, ensuring that they were the first to get in, than be dragged around an old church.

Pastor Dan, as he introduced himself, was a short, stocky little man. His skin was pale white, as if he hadn't seen sunlight in ages, and his dark-brown hair was thinning on top, but his small dark-brown eyes were filled with kindness, and he had a hearty laugh.

He led them to the front of the church and started the tour up on the altar. He began talking about how the church was one of the first in town, established by the very first settlers, and he discussed some of the church's history.

Then he described the origins of the black-stained oak altar and the organ with its lovely gold screen. He spent an inordinate amount of time discussing the organ, and Sam had to force herself to pay attention.

Next, he turned to the stained-glass windows adorning the north and east window. At least Sam could appreciate those, they were vibrant and beautiful.

"Ah, the windows honor the town's original pioneers, the Weston and Gray families," Pastor Dan informed them. "The families gave so much to the town—and to this very church, by the way. In fact, both families are still quite active in the community to this day, or to be more accurate, their descendants are. Since this town's birth, they have been staunch supporters of its prosperity. They were and still are truly inspirational in their thoughtfulness, giving, and dedication to the preservation of this town's history.

"Edward and Adam Gray, the ones who helped to found this town and this church, were also highly intelligent and innovative thinkers of their time. Edward Gray fought in the Civil War. He returned a hero and lived the rest of his life serving the community both by providing his exceptional legal skills and in his many community activities. Over the years, the church has undergone a number of renovations and remodels, and in 1892 the windows were dedicated to the Gray family along with the Weston family for all of their community service."

Sam was only half listening. She wanted to get to the castle. But the sound of the name Gray gave her a jolt. She thought of Fred Gray and what she knew she needed to do for him. Overhead, she could hear the last rings of the church bell.

Pastor Dan was still rambling on. "Oh, and Adam Gray gave the church the magnificent bell you heard ringing. Such a wonderful family. You know, when the bell was donated, it was the only bell in town. They used to use it as a fire alarm and to signal curfew."

In response to the girls' bewildered looks, Pastor Dan explained that many years ago, the town had an established curfew, a time by which everyone should be inside their homes.

"Those were different times he said, with a wink."

The girls tried to look interested, but it was getting increasingly more difficult with each passing minute.

The tour continued as Pastor Dan showed them the rooms used for youth groups and the church offices. At this point, both girls were wondering what else he could possibly show them. They were careful not to ask any questions or show too much interest for fear that he would launch into another story. Besides, Uncle Hank was asking enough questions for all of them.

To Sam's immense relief, the group resurfaced near the exit. Pastor Dan was still talking as he walked them outside. Apparently, he wanted to get in one last lecture on the windows, as he led them outside on the grass. The sun was already hot, and Sam stayed close to the building for the shade. In her effort to keep up with the others, she tripped on something and landed spread eagle on the ground. It was to Nell's great credit that she didn't laugh.

"Ever the graceful one, aren't I?" Sam said with a grin. Rubbing her toe, she looked over to see what had prompted the fall. A small cement slab jutted out of the corner of the building. On it was a metal plague which read: "1854 original church site."

"As you can see, we are rather proud of our little stone church," Pastor Dan said admitted. "I thank you for indulging me today. I do enjoy an opportunity to introduce our church to new folks like you."

"It was our pleasure," Nell's father immediately replied. "Thank you very much for taking the time to introduce us to an amazing architectural and historical monument."

Finally, it was clear that the tour was officially over. Everyone else thanked Pastor Dan for the informative tour. Sam tried her best not to sprint toward the car. However, she was first to get in the vehicle, followed closely behind by Nell. She was relieved when her aunt and uncle entered the car and closed the doors. She was anxious to leave.

"Well, that was quite an interesting tour, don't you think girls?" asked Uncle Hank. He'd clearly enjoyed himself.

"It was a fine tour," Nell's mother said reluctantly.

"Yeah, Dad," Nell said unconvincingly. "But it was kind of long."

"I agree, it was a little long, but it is in keeping with your desire to learn more about Owosso," he joked. "Plus, think of it as a nice distraction. Now, we have just enough time to run home and change before heading off to the castle."

With that, he headed back to their home.

"Well, they need to eat some lunch before they leave," Nell's mother said.

They were back at Nell's house a few moments later. Although they had no appetite, the girls knew better than to try and skip a meal under Sue's watch. They forced themselves to eat the sandwiches she had made for them.

When Nell's father entered the kitchen a little later, the girls nearly pounced on him. He tried to hold them off by reminding them that the castle was still not open yet. However, Nell promptly responded that arriving a bit early would give them an opportunity to appreciate the grounds without a horde of people and they could be one of the first people inside once it opened.

"You know, Dad, I read that the castle doesn't have air-conditioning, so I bet it gets really hot with a bunch of people in there," Nell informed him with all due sincerity.

"All right, you've convinced me," her father said surrendering to their will. "Let me grab my keys, and we'll be off."

The girls dashed to the car and were in a near state of fits by the time he approached the car. Trying to sound matter of fact, Nell suggested to her father that maybe they should take the cell phone, more as a convenience to her father. She explained that they really wanted to enjoy the tour of the castle and grounds as well as the view of the river. Her father thought it was a good idea, and with phone in hand, they were on their way.

As the car turned down Curwood Castle Drive, Sam was struck by what they saw. The castle was small, by castle standards, but impressive in its execution. It was perched on a slight hill in the crook of the Shiawassee River. The castle, modeled after a seventeenth-century French chateau, was built of slate, stucco, and fieldstones and was trimmed in copper. It was picturesque.

The lawn was perfectly manicured and brightly colored flowers and well-groomed shrubbery enveloped the grounds. In the background, the river sparkled like flowing crystals in the bright sun. The entire sight looked like it came out of a fairy tale. As they pulled up to the driveway, the turrets loomed overhead coming to dramatic points at the peaks. Sam was imagining what it would have been like to be a young girl using the castle as a playground.

"Okay, girls, give me a call when you're ready to come home," said Nell's dad.

Their daydreams interrupted, Sam and Nell mumbled their agreement and scrambled out of the car. They gave an obligatory wave to Uncle Hank, and started up the driveway. It still wasn't quite one, and it looked as if they were the only ones there.

Wanting to seize the opportunity, Sam linked her arm around Nell's and led her up the path.

"Okay, now we need to check out the grounds first, while no one is here to ask any questions. I'll go this way," she said, pointing to the left, "and you circle around the castle to the right."

"Got it, but what are we looking for?" Nell asked.

"I'm not sure. Anything and everything, I guess," Sam replied. "Keep an eye out for anything that looks like it has an inscription on it, and anything that seems out of place."

"Okay, but what if someone sees us?" Nell asked.

"The truth—your dad dropped us off early, and we're admiring the grounds until the castle opens. They are pretty, right?"

"Gorgeous, yes, okay."

Sam slowly made her way around the castle. She passed a plaque set in a large rock that noted that the castle was designated a Michigan historical landmark. She stopped and inspected it for a moment. The rock wasn't moveable, and she was unable to find anything out of the ordinary. It wasn't like she was expecting a flashing arrow or an "X marks the spot," but she had expected to find some indication that the land on which she stood had a secret to tell.

Sam thoroughly inspected every stone, step and bush, convinced that the answer was there waiting to be found. She had nearly made her way halfway around the building when a voice behind her inquired "May I help you?"

Sam was sure that she jumped, but as she turned, she forced herself to paste a look of enthusiasm on her face. Standing before her was an attractive, tall, blond woman who looked to be in her forties. Her hair was piled high on her head in a bun, and she was dressed like a librarian. The look on her face clearly told Sam that she was not happy.

"Hello, I was just admiring the beautiful grounds until the castle is open. Do you work here?" Sam asked.

"I do. My name is Barbara Johnson. I am in charge of the castle tours. I must tell you that the tours are *inside* the castle, and we generally ask that guests refrain from walking on the grass or disturbing the vegetation."

At that moment, Nell appeared from around the corner. Her face registered surprise at finding Sam conversing with an adult in the bushes. Sam could also tell by looking that Nell had come up empty-handed as well.

"Oh, there you are," Sam said with feigned surprise to Nell. "Nell, this is Barbara. She's in charge of the tours here. I was just about to tell her that you recently moved back to Owosso and that we're spending our summer learning about the history of this town."

With that, Sam turned back to Barbara. "I do apologize if we gave you any concern. We weren't aware we weren't allowed on the lawn. The architecture of this building is just so awe-inspiring; I couldn't help viewing the stone and copper work up close."

Succumbing to Sam's charms, the woman's attitude changed. "Oh, I wouldn't say that you're not allowed," she said, now with kindness. "We just try to minimize traffic on the grounds to preserve its beauty. I must say that I'm impressed that young ladies such as yourselves are taking an interest in your town's history, very commendable. Well, since you're here, why don't we start a tour?"

The girls had not planned for such an occurrence. In fact, they'd rather hoped that they could blend in with a group and conduct their investigation while the tour guide was preoccupied with others. Seeing that this was not going to be the case, the girls decided to make the most of the situation.

"That would be lovely," Sam responded.

On the way back to the castle door, the girls asked a number of questions about the landscape, in part to keep up appearances and in part hoping that the guide would reveal something they'd both missed. However, if Barbara had inside information regarding some hidden treasure located on or under the grounds, she didn't let on to the girls.

As the party stepped inside the castle, Sam felt transported back in time. She stopped in the great room of the castle to take in the detail. Its arched ceiling accented by dark wooden beams drew her attention to the simple but large fireplace over which was mounted what looked to be a moose head. On either side of the fireplace were built-in bookcases packed with books behind glass doors. In the front of the room sat a modest writing desk and chair.

As Barbara pointed out various aspects of the room and explained their significance, Sam scoured the room. She walked closer to the fireplace to inspect for any inscription, mark, or other clue; peered into the dusty book cases; and finally scrutinized the desk. The latter was a difficult task to accomplish without appearing too obvious. Since the desk had no drawers or other openings, Sam could only spend a few minutes admiring it before it was clear that Barbara was moving on to the next room. Sam dropped her sunglasses under the desk, so she could inspect its underside, but the effort was wasted. There was nothing unusual about the desk, and clearly there was no hidden compartment.

At this point, a few new faces appeared in the doorway. A middle-aged couple with what appeared to be their ten-year-old daughter, another couple in their twenties, and a tall, blond, lanky man who looked to be in his thirties. They were obviously there for the tour.

Barbara explained that she'd just started a tour with the girls, who politely introduced themselves, and she invited the newcomers to join the tour in progress. She gave them a short summary of the significant aspects of the room and then the expanded group continued through the building.

Thanks to the additional people, Sam and Nell were now able to wander off a bit, taking more of a hands-on approach, although being careful not to let Barbara notice the extra-close inspection. So far, the castle was not revealing any secrets. However, the girls both felt that the castle turrets held the clue.

The group slowly climbed the narrow staircase leading up to the tower where James Oliver Curwood had purportedly done so much of his writing. From the top, the view was beautiful. Windows adorned every angle of the turrets providing perfect frames for the lush grounds below, the cascading river, and Curwood Park, which lay just down the way. It was easy to see how Curwood had found inspiration here.

As Barbara launched into a lengthy discussion of the various books written by Curwood, Nell and Sam again did their best to analyze the structure and its contents. Between the two of them, the girls stared at, poked, and prodded every inch of the tower.

Sam made it a point to test each and every floorboard in the room, lightly bouncing up and down and side-to-side on each section in effort to uncover any loose boards that might conceal a hiding spot or a clue. She felt silly and a little self-conscious bobbing up and down like child who had consumed too much sugar. However, she maintained an expression of what she hoped looked like unbridled enthusiasm on her face and prayed that no one would ask her what she was doing.

From across the room, Sam could tell Nell was conducting a similar type of inspection on the walls of the room. Sam wasn't sure which would upset Barbara more, Sam's inane bouncing or Nell's fingerprints on the aged wallpaper. It came as no small shock to both girls that they were able to conclude their respective examinations without a reprimand from Barbara. The girls conducted similar inspections of the remaining rooms and turrets, all of which left them empty-handed.

After searching every inch of the last turret, the girls met back near the stairs with small sighs escaping from their throats. They knew just by looking at each other that the search had been a failure. Although interesting from a historical perspective, the castle seemed to be devoid of any secrets. Sam closed her eyes, hoping that she could divine some hint or clue.

"Nothing," she muttered.

"I'm sorry?" Barbara answered. Apparently, Sam had said that aloud.

"Oh, sorry, I was just thinking that, um, nothing could get me to leave this place if I lived here. It's just so fascinating."

"That's nice, dear. As I was saying, this castle stands as a wonderful architectural treasure, a legacy to a remarkable individual's life and a time capsule of days gone by."

"She had to use the word *treasure*," Sam said under her breath. "What a cruel joke. Is there a basement?" she asked Barbara.

Barbara looked at her as if she had just spoken a foreign language.

"No, why?"

Sam had no idea how to respond. Luckily, Nell saved her.

"Oh, we read that lots of the homes from this period had large cellars where they stored preserves and that kind of thing. Our mothers love to can."

"Oh, yes, well, as you know the castle was never used as a residence. So, unfortunately no basement and no preserves."

"Of course. How silly of us," Nell said, trying to minimize the awkwardness.

Sam gave Nell a look of appreciation for her efforts.

"All right then, if there are no more questions, please follow me downstairs, and you can exit out the front door."

The tour was officially over. Nell and Sam thanked Barbara and headed outside. The warm sun did little to lift their spirits. For a moment, they stood motionless and silent, each trying to figure out what they were missing.

"Let's go sit by the river for a while before we call your dad. I'm just not ready to go home yet," Sam said.

Nell merely nodded in agreement, and they walked down the path that led to the river. They sat down on the grass near the water's edge. Nell stared at the flowing current while Sam's gaze was locked back on the castle.

Part of Sam felt as if the castle were gloating back at her as if to say, "Ha! You didn't find it." In her mind, she retraced her steps in and around the castle. She was convinced the search had been thorough. Her gut told her there was no treasure here. "Nell, do you think the treasure—or some clue—is really here? I mean, short of reading every book in that castle or ripping out the floors or walls, I don't think it's here."

After a thoughtful pause, Nell responded. "No, I don't think it's here. I even stuck my head in the fireplace to see if anything was hidden in the chimney. I don't think we missed anything."

"Well, this just sucks!" Sam suddenly exclaimed with exasperation. "I can't believe we're no farther ahead than we were two days ago." She picked up a pebble and skipped it across the river.

"I know. I know," Nell responded, completely in agreement. It was clear she wanted to comfort Sam, yet being equally disappointed, could not find the words. After several long minutes, Nell glumly suggested they call her father and have him pick them up.

"Fine," Sam agreed. But as Nell reached into her pocket for the phone, Sam sudden shot upright and sat rigid as a statute. "We're idiots! Absolute idiots! How could we be so stupid?" Now she was on her feet, pacing.

Nell jammed the phone back in to her pocket and was now on her feet as well. "What do you mean?" she said, utter confusion forcing her face into a contorted expression.

"Don't you see?" Sam said, wheeling around to face Nell. "We were so close to the next clue and we didn't even realize it!"

"What are you talking about?" Nell asked, now in earnest.

"'The Founders' faith was set in stone, there the journey's path will be shown.' It's the church."

"What church?" Nell asked, still completely bewildered.

"The church we just spent the last two hours at! Don't you remember? Pastor Dan referred to it as the *stone church*."

"Okay, so it's a stone church," Nell said.

"So it's a stone church with windows honoring the town's original settlers, you know, the *Founders!*"

"The clue was never about the Founding Fathers!" Nell nearly shouted. "Remember in the woods Fred mentioned wanting to learn more about Dewey? He must have thought that Thomas E. Dewey was part of the clue."

"Or he was just trying to throw the other guy off," Sam responded. "Clearly, Thomas Dewey wasn't one of the founders of Owosso, we know that based on our research." Sam silently kicked herself for not thinking to research the town's founding families when they had been at the library.

"We need to get back to that church," they said at the same time.

After taking a moment to try and compose herself, Nell pulled out the cell phone and dialed her father. Not sure of how they were going to be able to convince her father to take them back to the church, Nell merely informed him that the tour had concluded and they were ready to be picked up.

Knowing that they had, at most, twenty minutes before her dad arrived, they sat back down on the grass and discussed how best to approach him. They racked their brains, but each idea seemed worse than the last. Since neither of the girls wanted to lie, it made matters more difficult. Finally, when they knew they only had moments before Nell's father pulled up, they settled on a plan.

"Okay," Nell said, "I actually thought the church was quite charming. I mean, I was anxious for the tour to end because I wanted to get here, but otherwise, I found it quite interesting. I will tell him that I liked what I heard about the youth group program, and I would like more information about how I could attend. It's not perfect, but I think it's the best we've got," Nell concluded.

"I'm surprised you don't want to come clean with your dad," Sam said.

"Even my dad wouldn't go along with this," Nell replied. "Besides, I actually am interested in getting involved with a youth group."

They heard a car horn, looked up, and saw Uncle Hank parked in the driveway. They both smiled and waved. As they stood up and headed toward the car, Sam whispered, "You're up."

In their flustered state, they nearly collided with the lanky guy who had taken the tour with them.

"Beg your pardon," Nell said to the man.

"Sorry," Sam called out hastily as they continued to the waiting car.

Nell reached the car door first. "Hey, Dad! Thanks for taking us here. We had a great time!" she exclaimed. Her voice was full of enthusiasm. "What an amazing place," she continued as the girls climbed in the car. "Oh, Dad, you should have stayed. You should have seen all of the old books by the fireplace, the cool, old writing desk, and the turrets; well, it's every girl's dream!"

"Yeah, Uncle Hank, thank you so much for suggesting this tour. It was so interesting. It is so peaceful here. It's no wonder Mr. Curwood loved to write here. I could hang out by the river for hours."

Uncle Hank laughed warmly. "Well I'm glad you girls liked it. It also sounds like you learned a lot."

"We did!" they both responded in unison.

Uncle Hank put the car in gear and started down the driveway. Sam glanced at Nell.

"Say, Dad," Nell began, "while we were sitting by the river, we were talking about church today. We both feel really bad that we weren't more attentive to Pastor Dan. It's just that we were so excited to come to the castle, and the tour was so unexpected, we didn't have the proper focus."

"That's okay, girls," Uncle Hank replied.

"Well we were wondering," Nell said, the pause revealing her uncertainty. "Could we stop back by the church on the way home? I, uh, would like to tell Pastor Dan in person that I appreciated the tour and that I actually had a few questions about the history of the church."

"You do?" her father said with obvious surprise.

Taking a clue from Sam, Nell began to discuss the architecture of the church. "Yeah, Pastor Dan referred to it as the 'stone church,' and we realized that kind of look is not very common. Plus," she continued, now with more confidence, "I liked what I heard about the youth group program. I was wondering if I could get more information about it."

"Well, your mother won't like you joining a youth group outside her church, but the truth is that the renovations could take another month or more. Your mother is next door visiting an old friend, so I suppose we have a little time. How about if I drop you off, run a couple of errands and come back for you? I would like to pick up a new book downtown. Unless, of course, if you wanted me to come with you."

"Oh no, Dad, we're fine," Nell replied. "You've been chauffeuring us around today. Please, run your errands. I'm sure we'll be with Pastor Dan for hours," she said with lighthearted mocking. "Take your time. If we finish up first, we'll just wait for you on the church steps."

"Okay, sounds good," her father said. "But let's keep this between us three for now. No sense in getting your mother upset."

"Our lips are sealed," the girls replied.

1

◇

The Second Clue

Although the trip from the castle back to the church was probably less than ten minutes, it felt as if they were never going to get there. Sam had to hand it to Nell; she had worked her father like a pro. She had bet herself that getting back to the church was going to be much more difficult. Figuring that they could use all the help they could get, she was particularly grateful that Uncle Hank was so easygoing.

Finally, they arrived back at the stone church. It took every ounce of self-control Sam possessed not to hurl herself out of the car the minute the steeple came into view. She thanked Uncle Hank, exited the car calmly, and ascended the stairs to the church. Nell was right by her side.

When they reached the top, Nell grabbed Sam's arm and whispered, "Okay, now what? Where do we start?"

"I have no idea," Sam answered with dismay. "You're the church expert. How about we head back into the church and check out the windows a little more closely?"

"Okay, I'll take the ones on the north wall," Nell offered.

"I'll check out the east windows," Sam responded.

They pulled open the main doors and stepped inside. Ten feet ahead were the interior doors leading to the pews, altar, and the marble platform. Sam tested the doors and found that they were unlocked. She carefully pushed on one of the doors, obviously afraid that they would be announcing their presence. To both of their relief, all was quiet. They made their way down the aisle and to the ornate windows. It seemed so strange to be the only ones inside.

"Keep an eye out for anything on the floor or anywhere else that seems noteworthy," Sam quietly suggested.

Nell nodded her head in agreement, and they went their separate ways.

So far, nothing seemed out of the ordinary to Sam. The pews seemed unremarkable, and everything was as it should be. Sam now stood staring at the stained glass dissecting every detail. The colors were breathtaking, particularly with the afternoon sun streaming in. It was clear that the north and east windows paid respect to the Gray and Weston families. However, they revealed little else. The remaining stained-glass windows were, in Sam's opinion, typical for a church.

"Anything?" Sam called over as quietly as possible.

"Nothing," Nell answered.

"What are you looking for?" a familiar voice asked.

Both girls jumped, and Nell let out a shriek that sounded like a strangled bird. As they turned to locate the source of the voice, they saw Dean, standing near the altar with a broad grin on his face.

"You!" Sam exclaimed.

"You scared us half to death," Nell complained, holding her hand over her heart.

"Gosh, I'm sorry. I didn't mean to scare you guys," he replied with obvious remorse. "It's just that you both looked so intense." His head hung a bit lower as he walked closer to them.

"What are you doing here?" Sam demanded.

He could have demanded the same of the girls but instead he answered, "Another one of my glamorous jobs. I'm filling in for one of the maintenance guys who's on vacation. Not too exciting, but I can use the extra money during the summer. Plus, my mom volunteered my services," he said with a shrug of his shoulders. "Heaven forbid that I have too much free time."

"What have you guys been up to?" he asked. Despite the choice of words, Sam had to admit that he seemed genuinely interested in being friendly.

Sam's mind raced as it searched for a response. Finally, an idea came to her. "Well, it's a bit embarrassing," Sam said, "but we're on a scavenger hunt of sorts."

"Really?" he replied with interest.

Sam was surprised that Dean didn't make fun of them. "Yeah, we thought we'd make learning this town's history a bit of a game. We attended services here earlier today. Pastor Dan gave us a little tour, but we thought we'd come back to learn more, right, Nell?" she prompted.

"Yeah, yeah, and I thought I might check out the youth group," Nell replied.

Oh no, thought Sam, *now he's going to take us to Pastor Dan. We'll never get to do a proper inspection.*

Dean leaned in a little closer to the girls. "Pastor Dan can be a bit long winded; I can get you that information if you want," Dean offered.

"That would be great, thanks," Nell said.

Sam breathed a sigh of relief.

"So earlier, you guys seemed to really be enjoying the windows. Are you guys into stained glass, or is it part of your hunt?"

"A little of both," Nell responded.

"Hey, Dean, how much do you know about this church?" Sam asked with a sudden sparkle in her eye.

"Well, a little bit, thanks again to my mother and all of those luncheons and dinner parties. It's one of the oldest churches in town. It may even be the oldest church in town, but of course, there are one or two other churches in town that also claim the title. The original founders of Owosso formed the church shortly after settling here. I think it dates back to like 1838. This is not the original building, but the current church is built on the foundation of the 1854 or 1855 church. I don't remember the details, but I think the church moved and then was rebuilt.

"The windows you guys were admiring were added in 1892, I think. They honor the town's founding families, the Grays and Weston's. They were big supporters of this church and general do-gooders of the town. What else can I tell you about the church?"

Sam latched on to the word *founders*. She was thinking about it when she heard Nell ask about hidden passages.

"I, uh, watched a show with my dad, one time and it indicated that some churches built in hidden areas to their structures. I just thought that this church being so old and all ..." Nell's voice trailed off. Sam knew that she instantly regretted having asked the question.

Before he could answer, a door near the front of the church opened, and Pastor Dan appeared.

Sam thought that her heart was going to explode out of her chest.

"Well, hello there; I remember you girls from earlier today," he said. "Did you enjoy the services?"

"Oh yes, we did," Nell answered. "And thank you so much for the tour. We really enjoyed hearing about the history of this church."

"I'm delighted you enjoyed it. As I say, this church really does have an amazing history. Did you come back to speak with me?"

Before either of the girls could answer, Dean responded. "Actually, they're friends of mine. I had promised them a tour of the church, but I guess you beat me to it."

"Oh, so sorry about that, Dean," Pastor Dan said apologetically. "You know me: I love my church. However, let's see." He rubbed his chin as if in thought. "I believe that I neglected to show them the organ and the bell tower. You might also be able to tell them a bit more about the youth group program.

"If there's any interest, please feel free to show them around, just lock up when you are finished. With all the recent break-ins, we can't be too careful. So sad that we have to think that way." His voice trailed off for a moment before he continued. "Well, I have to head out to visit a member who is home ill. I'd best be on my way. So nice to see you again, girls." With a smile and a wave, he was gone.

"You're welcome," Dean said, as soon as the coast was clear.

"For what?" Sam asked.

"I figure you didn't really want to involve Pastor Dan in your search."

"He is very nice," Nell said, "But no, we weren't planning on spending more time with him today."

"Would you like my ten-cent tour?" Dean offered.

A silent but intense internal struggle was playing out inside Sam's head. She did *not* want to involve anyone else in their search, but she was dying to find the second clue. They didn't know this Dean guy, and she was loath to bestow her trust in someone on a moment's notice. He was, however, rather handsome—in a way that made her uncomfortable.

Sam was becoming more convinced that Fred had given her the clue to finding a treasure. She could *feel* that they were on the right track and close to finding the treasure or at least the next clue. She knew that they needed Dean's help. She looked over at Nell, who nodded.

"Sure, but we would like to keep our scavenger hunt our little secret," Sam reminded Dean. "We don't want people to think that we are total dorks." She was trying to play off Dean's comments about himself. "What with Nell moving back and all, her image is critical." She said the last with mock drama.

"Absolutely," he replied. "Would you like me to pinkie swear?" He held his right pinkie up in the air.

Both girls had to laugh. They looked at each other and came to a silent agreement.

"I don't think that will be necessary," Sam answered.

"Okay, let's test out your tour guide skills," Nell said, gently teasing him.

"All right then, off we go. And we're walking," he said in effort to imitate a professional tour guide. "Oh, and in answer to your question, there aren't really any hidden areas, but the doors to the organ and the bell tower are sort of, well, discreet. The organ was apparently really expensive, and they try to limit access. The same sort of goes for the bell. It's old, delicate, and they don't want people playing with it. But I can show you if you want."

"Lead the way, tour guide," said Sam. She suddenly felt the need to fix her hair and was annoyed with herself for feeling that way.

As they made their way to the front of the altar, Dean pointed out areas of interest and recited facts he knew. Most of the information had already been relayed by Pastor Dan, but somehow coming from Dean, it was less boring.

Dean led them through a door near the front of the church, down a hallway and through another door. The organ was just up these stairs and to the left. The three of them climbed the narrow steps almost entirely in the dark. At the top of the stairs, the girls could see something shining brightly. Once they reached the top, they saw the source of the glow, the organ. It was massive, and its golden pipes reflected light in all directions.

"You can see the entire congregation from here!" Nell exclaimed.

"This is really amazing," Sam remarked.

"Yeah, it's pretty cool, but let me say that you don't want to be up here when they are playing that thing," Dean told them. "It's super loud!"

After admiring the organ for a few minutes, Nell and Sam tried to subtly inspect the area.

"Can I help look for anything?" He asked.

"No, er, have you seen anything that seems unusual up here?" Sam asked.

"No," he replied, "but I have to admit that I haven't looked that close."

"Oh, Pastor Dan mentioned that this organ was special."

"It is, to him," Dean responded. "Like I said, it's expensive, but I don't know if there is anything unusual about it. We can look around though."

The three of them looked over every inch but found nothing. No loose floorboard, no hidden compartment, no clue, no nothing.

Finally, it was Nell who said, "I don't think we're going to find a clue for our, um, scavenger hunt here."

"I don't see anything of particular interest," Dean said in agreement.

"I agree. Let's move on," Sam chimed in.

"Your wish is my command," Dean said, with a half bow. He led them back down the stairway and along the hallway leading to front of the church near the offices. He stopped at a nondescript door, pulled out a set of keys and unlocked it.

"Ladies first, but watch out—it's really dark until you reach the top."

Sam headed up first. The stairs were narrow, wooden, and smelled faintly of mold. The darkness only intensified her desire to reach the top, and in her haste, she tripped up the stairs. Nell caught her arm and helped her regain her balance. Both girls giggled, knowing that Sam had a special knack for falling up, not down, stairs. Dean seemed genuinely concerned when he asked how Sam was. He didn't laugh. He got points for that. Sam called down that she was fine, and they continued to climb until they reached the other door.

Sam tried the handle. "It's locked," she announced.

"Sorry. I forgot there was a second lock. Here's the key." He handed her a key on a heavy ring. Sam inserted the key in the lock and turned, but nothing happened.

"It's an old lock. You need to turn it hard," Dean suggested.

Sam used both hands and turned the key with all her strength. Slowly, the key turned in the lock, and they heard a loud click. Sam pushed the door open, inhaled a deep breath of fresh air and stepped out onto the bell tower.

Sam found herself standing on a small wooden platform encircled by half walls that enclosed the area and anchored by four stone pillars that led up to the pointed roof overhead. In the center of the platform sat a huge bell. It looked as if it had been there for ages. It was a deep brown color with streaks of light green clearly due to aging.

On one side of the bell was a long crack. Sam immediately thought of the Liberty Bell and wondered to herself whether all bells cracked over time. Looking closer, Sam saw that the bell was actually supported by, and rested on, a large wooden frame of sorts. She also saw the words "Cast in 1856, West Troy, NY" on the side of the bell.

"It's really beautiful," Sam heard Nell observe. The voice was a surprise to Sam. She had become so focused on the bell that she had forgotten she wasn't alone.

"Yeah, this bell is pretty cool," Dean said in agreement. "You want to ring it?"

"Can we?" Nell asked without trying to hide her excitement.

"Sure, Pastor Dan won't mind." He walked over, picked up a think rope and handed it to Nell. She beckoned Sam over, and the girls pulled down together. The bell began to ring. Its tone was deep and rich. After several pulls, they released the rope so they could watch the bell swing gracefully back and forth. The sound was entrancing. It was somehow solemn and sad to Sam, although she couldn't explain why she felt that way.

"What a joyful sound," Nell commented.

"You think?" Sam said. "I think it sounds kind of sad."

"Why do you think it sounds sad?" Nell said with a note of surprise in her voice.

"I don't know. It just does," she responded.

"I have to agree with Sam," Dean offered. "Church bells always sound sad to me. Maybe it's because they have been used a lot to signal tragic-type things, you know, fires, funerals, the infamous Owosso curfew." He added this last, imitating an eerie voice.

"But they are also used for things like weddings and church services," Nell replied,

"My point exactly," Sam retorted, now with a grin.

"Shame on you!" Nell said, giving her a mock disapproving look.

"Oh no! You guys cracked it!" The girls looked horrified, then turned to see Dean laughing. They glared at him, and he threw his hands up in the air as if to surrender. "I'm sorry. I'm sorry. Bad joke, I know, but I couldn't resist."

"Mean," was all that Sam could muster.

"Enough of this goofing around," Sam stated. "We've got a job to do here. Nell, do you mind taking that half of the area, and I'll take this half?" she said, motioning to one side.

"No problem."

"What can I do?" Dean asked.

"Nothing," Sam replied as kindly as she could.

"Oh, come on. You guys can trust me," he nearly begged.

"I think we should put him to work," Nell suggested.

"Fine," Sam said, capitulating. "First, what do you know about this bell?"

"To be honest, not much more than you probably already know. I know that the Gray family, Adam or Edward Gray, I can't remember which one, purchased this bell and donated it to the church back in 1856. The families were loaded with money. That probably explains the windows too," he joked with a chuckle. "Although they probably ended up paying for those as well. The church has a way of coaxing contributions out of its families. The bell was used as the first fire alarm and cracked somewhere along the way. Despite the huge crack, it was never replaced. I think, because it was the first bell in town, it holds a special honor. People just can't bear to get a new one."

"Anything else?" Sam prodded.

"Sorry, that's it," Dean answered.

"Okay, Dean, check out the bell itself. Since you're taller than us, you should be able to see the top of the bell as well as underneath. Let us know what you find."

"Got it."

For several minutes, the three worked silently. Much as they had with Curwood Castle, the girls gently pressed, poked, and prodded their way around the tower. Every stone, screw, and board was tested. The area was relatively small, only just leaving enough room for each of them to move around, so the search proceeded at a steady pace.

Suddenly, Nell squeaked with excitement, "Hey, I think I found a loose board over here. Check it out!"

Sam was at her side in an instant. She saw the board and it did indeed appear to be loose. It gave way just enough to almost see beneath it; however, the nail holding it in place prevented further inspection.

"Here, try this," Sam said as she handed Nell a small mirror she had retrieved from her purse.

Nell took the mirror and held it down by the board. She adjusted the angle several times until the light pierced the darkness. To their great disappointment, they saw only solid wood below. "What now? Do we pull up the boards?"

"Uh, I said that Pastor Dan wouldn't mind if you rang the

bell. But I'm pretty sure he would mind me letting you rip up the floorboards. Plus," he said, coming over to stand with them, "that floorboard looks the same as any wooden plank exposed to the elements."

"He's right," Sam said. "We were just so excited to find something that we let our minds race. Did you find anything, Dean?"

"There's nothing on the exterior of the bell. It's dark on the inside, so I couldn't see very well. If I can borrow that mirror, I take a second crack at it, no pun intended."

Sam groaned and rolled her eyes.

"Here you go," Nell said, handing the mirror to him.

Sam's original search conducted on her portion of the tower had turned up nothing. Her fingers were sore from tugging and pushing on the stone and wood. Despite her efforts, she had not observed so much as a scratch.

Disgusted with herself, she turned her back on the wall she had been inspecting, put her hands behind her back and thought, If I wanted to hide something up here, where would I put it?

When she came to the realization that all her ideas were too obvious, she then starting thinking about the longevity of structures and people's propensity to renovate, rebuild, and repair.

Without realizing what she was looking for, she started to walk close to the bell housing. She walked around the wooden frame several times without stopping, analyzing the frame and trying to understand how it all came together. Sam had several engineers in her family and had come to appreciate, if not always understand, how things worked.

Next, she started carefully touching the wooden support. It was heavy and sturdy despite its years, so her bare hands were unable to so much as budge the structure.

"Anything?" Sam called to Dean.

"Other than the date the bell was cast, which you saw, there's nothing on top of or inside the bell, except for the ringer, of course," Dean announced. "I'm sorry."

Sam resumed her circling. Midway around she tripped and landed face-first on the floor. Embarrassed by her lack of coordination and her hands and knees still hurting from the fall, she didn't move for a moment.

"Are you okay?" Nell asked.

"I'm fine, but this church keeps tripping me up, huh?" Sam said, now managing a slight smile.

"I tripped out on the lawn earlier today," Sam offered up to Dean.

"Hey, at least you keep going," Dean said with encouragement. "If it makes you feel any better, I'm always falling over or into stuff."

"It does actually, thanks," Sam replied. "Ouch, I think I got a sliver in my hand." Carefully, she used her nails to extract the sliver. "Okay, now that the drama has passed, we can ..." Her sentence stopped abruptly, and Sam was motionless as she stared straight ahead.

"Sam?" Nell said. "What's the matter?"

"I think I might ..." She began crawling on her stomach toward the bell. "Nell hold my feet and make sure that I don't fall down the cavity under the bell. I don't want to go three for three today."

"Okay, but what are you doing?" Nell asked.

"Not sure, give me a minute," Sam replied. She inched herself forward until more than half of her body was wedged in the wooden frame surrounding the bell. Just above her head was a large wooden beam.

What caught her attention were four gold-colored bolts. When she looked closer, she saw tiny numbers imprinted around the heads. Having assisted her father with countless home-improvement projects, she was used to seeing nuts and bolts. However, these bolts had the numbers 0 through 10. The numbers were so small, she had to look twice, but she was certain of her finding. All four bolts were the same. It also struck her as odd that there were four bolts placed so close together and that they were gold rather than silver. She tested the first bolt with her hand, but it didn't move.

"Hey, do either of you guys have a quarter?" Sam called out.

"I might," Nell said, rooting around in her pockets. "What do you need it for?"

"It might be nothing, but there are some unusual-looking bolts under here. They sort of look like screws. I'm just curious to see if they move."

"I found one," Nell said.

"Great, pass it to me," Sam replied as she reached out her hand.

"I can't reach you. You're too far away," Nell said apologetically.

"Here, hand it to me. I have longer arms," Dean instructed.

Then Sam felt Dean's hand in hers. As he pressed the metal into her hand, it felt almost like a shock from static electricity. God, he made her feel strange.

She grabbed the coin, inserted it into the top of the bolt, and tried to turn it. It didn't budge. Undeterred, and thinking about Dean's advice on opening the door to the tower, she used both hands and turned with all her strength. Slowly, it moved.

She tried the same thing with each of the bolts, and after much effort, all were able to be rotated. Unfortunately, nothing else happened. She continued to stare at the bolts and eventually an idea began to form. She tried moving the bolts to 1-8-5-6. She could hear what sounded like gears turning, but nothing happened.

"Hey, I think I found a lock of some sort. I just turned the bolts to 1856, the year the bell was donated by nothing happened." Next, she tried 1838, the year the town was supposedly formed. Again, she heard gears turning, but again nothing else happened. "Give me some dates to try," she called out.

"Are you serious?" Nell called back with surprise and disbelief in her voice.

"Yes, I know it sounds silly, but I have to try it."

"How about 1892, the year the windows were dedicated?" Nell called.

Sam tried the number, but there was no movement.

Nell and Dean took turns suggesting dates, each of which Sam dutifully tried.

Then Dean suggested that they consider other significant events in the town's history. They exhausted their collective knowledge of significant dates in Owosso's history, but still no luck opening what Sam was convinced was a lock.

"You know, Sam, maybe it doesn't work anymore, or maybe it was never a lock at all," Dean proposed gently. "Maybe it's just decorative."

Sam wasn't listening now, she had a thought. "Hey, Nell, you did that big paper on the Civil War, what year did it end?"

"Eighteen sixty-five, why?"

Feeling a little foolish, Sam didn't explain what she was thinking. Instead, she turned the coin back to the first bolt. She moved it until the number 1 was at the top.

This is ridiculous. This only works in the movies, she said to herself. Still, she turned the next three bolts so that the numbers 8, 6, and 5, respectively were directly on the top. As the final bolt stopped in place, there was a load click and the beam made popping sound. At first, Sam thought she had broken something.

"What happened?" Dean asked anxiously.

"Please tell me nothing is broken," Nell added.

Instinctively, she had closed her eyes. As she opened them, she noticed what looked like a tiny drawer protruding from the opposite side of the beam she had been working on.

"No, everything's fine, chicken little," Sam teased. "I think I found a drawer of some sort. Hang on. I need to crawl in a little more."

This area left little room for navigation. Sam felt like she was playing the game Twister as she forced her body over another piece of wood and up toward the newly discovered drawer. She was just able to get her head up high enough to look into the compartment. It was, most definitely, a hiding place. The opening was small and nestled inside was small metal star.

With trembling hands, she gently lifted it out of its container and held it up to look more closely. It was rather heavy for its size, and its edges were sharp as if it had just been cut out of the metal from which it was made. It seemed sturdy and delicate at the same time.

After turning it over in her hands several times to inspect it from every angle, she turned her attention back on the drawer. It was devoid of any additional contents or markings of any kind.

"Well? Are you trying to kill us with suspense?" Nell demanded.

"Sorry, I'm coming out, and I'll show you." Slowly she closed the compartment. Extracting herself proved trickier than her entrance. She was entangled with the beams that seemed to be everywhere. Her excitement was mounting, and her heart was beating faster and faster. Nell and Dean seemed to be excited too, since they started tugging at her feet to help her get out faster.

At last, her head finally cleared the last support, and she was out. She looked up to see Nell and Dean staring at her. They looked funny, as if they were ready to attack her at any moment. Sam was covered in dirt, grease, and cobwebs, but she was beaming as she turned to show off her discovery.

"It was so cool," she said. "I remembered Pastor Dan saying that Edward Gray fought in the Civil War. I figured that the end of the war was a significant date, so I turned the bolts like a combination lock to 1865. When I finished, a drawer popped out. I reached inside, and I found this." She opened her hand to reveal the star. "I checked the drawer, but there was nothing else." She added the last before they could ask.

They each took turns holding and inspecting their discovery.

"What do you think it is?" Nell asked aloud. "I mean, I know it's a star, but what do you think it's for?"

"I don't have the foggiest," said Sam. Then she turned to Dean. "What do you think?"

"It could be anything or nothing. For all we know, it could just be a metal star. By the way, you have a little dirt on your nose," he said quietly.

"It was totally worth it," Sam said, only mildly embarrassed. She pivoted toward Nell, who swiftly removed the offending mark and motioned that Sam was good to go.

In the distance, they heard a car horn beeped several times. At first it didn't register, then after several more beeps, Nell exclaimed, "My dad! I totally forgot!"

"Oh no, me too, and I look like I've been playing in dirt."

"He's a guy. He probably won't even notice," Dean offered.

"Yeah, but her mother will," Sam answered, as Nell nodded her agreement. "Luckily I fall a lot. Hopefully, it'll explain my appearance this time as well."

After making sure that Sam was somewhat presentable, they all scrambled back the way they had come, locking the doors behind them. When they reached the steps outside the church, Nell waved to her father to signal they were on their way.

Sam turned to Dean. "Look, thanks for helping us today, we really appreciate you saving us from Pastor Dan. But seriously, you ..."

"Relax, it's our secret. I promise not to tell anyone anything. You have my word. You can trust me. Besides, this is the most excitement I've had in weeks. I owe you guys."

"Okay, um, thanks again. We'd better go before Nell's dad gets upset." As she started to walk away, Dean called her back.

"Hey, give me a call if you want any more help. I'd give you my home number, but I don't have a pen. Wait a minute."

He dashed just inside the doors and returned with what must have been the pen used for the sign-in book.

"Hold out your hand," he said to Sam. Once again, he was holding her hand, and she was at a loss about what she was feeling. "Here's my number." He wrote on her palm. "And you can feel free to call me at home or at the library."

"Okay, uh, thanks," said Sam, pulling back her hand, feeling awkward and self-conscious.

"Yeah, Dean," Nell added. "Thanks for all of your help today, and thanks for not telling anyone."

"No problem."

Not wanting to keep Nell's dad waiting any longer, they sprinted down the steps to the waiting car.

In the parking lot, Sam noticed another car idling. It was a black SUV, and it seemed familiar somehow. However, her mind quickly returned to the events of the day, and lost in thought, she waved goodbye to Dean as he headed back into the church to lock up.

8

◇

Mr. Miller's Information

In Uncle Hank's car, Sam was counting her considerable luck. First, her uncle was, as ever, in good spirits when they reached the car in the church parking lot. He had teased them a bit about keeping him waiting, but it turned out that he had run into an old friend and was himself a bit behind schedule in arriving to get them. He hadn't failed to notice that they were with a young boy, but after a question or two, he let it drop.

Second, she couldn't believe that they had actually found a hidden compartment today and that it had yielded the metal star that was now safely tucked in her pocket. She kept her hand on her pocket, just to make sure that it was secure. She could tell Nell and Dean thought perhaps the star was just that, a star placed in a piece of wood, maybe for purely sentimental reasons.

Despite their obvious skepticism, Sam was certain the star was the second clue to finding whatever it was Fred had wanted her to find. Although she was young, she had good instincts, and they were telling her that the find was important. She just didn't yet know how or why. She very much wished that Fred had been able to tell her what she was looking for. It would have made things easier.

100

Back at Nell's house, the girls found out that Sam's father would be arriving soon to take her home. And, true to the girls' concerns, Nell's mother immediately noticed Sam's appearance.

"My word, what happened?" she said, motioning at Sam. "Your clothes are filthy, and you look like you've been playing in a pile of dirt. What will your mother think I've done?"

"Mother, this is no reflection on you," Nell informed her. "We were outside at the castle and ..." Clearly wanting to avoid mentioning the second stop at the church, Nell paused.

Not wanting Nell to have to lie or to get grief from her mother on her account, Sam interjected, "I tripped and fell. Kind of like I did at the church earlier today. I need to be more careful looking where I'm going. I'll go get cleaned up before my dad gets here."

"That's a good idea. Nell, go ahead and gather up her things for her while she gets ready."

"Sure thing, Mom," Nell said.

Once they were out of sight, Sam showed the phone number on her palm to Nell, who agreed to write it down so Sam could wash her hands. In the bathroom, Sam quickly washed her hands and face, fixed her hair, and brushed off her clothes into the wastebasket. Then she joined Nell in her bedroom.

Sam closed the door behind her and sat down on the bed next to Nell. "So, what do you really think about the star? I mean, I can tell you think that it might be nothing."

"Well, I have to admit it's not much of a clue," Nell said, obviously trying to be sensitive in light of Sam's excitement. "It's just that it's not much to go on. It would be nice if it said, 'Go here and you will find a big ole treasure chest.' Also, it could just be that when the bell was donated someone left the star inside for any number of reasons—good luck, sentiment—we just don't know."

Sam felt a rush of disappointment. She got up from the bed and went to the window, sighing and shaking her head. She felt crestfallen.

"*However*," Nell continued, "if it was just a star, why would it be hidden in a secret compartment? Why wouldn't they just affix it to the bell or wooden frame? Plus, you said the combination was 1865, the date the US Civil War ended. Hey, you know, I think President Lincoln was assassinated that year as well. You're right that it is a significant date."

As she kept talking, Sam could tell that Nell's enthusiasm was growing.

"You know, it could be nothing, but I do think it's something," Nell finally concluded.

"Eloquently put," Sam teased. "Seriously, thanks for sticking with me on this. I think it's something too. But the real question is, what's the clue? The star has no writing or any other markings. So far, we haven't found anything that tells us where we should be looking next. If there is a treasure, I don't think it's at the church. You heard the pastor: the church was renovated several times and moved. If the treasure was there, someone would have found it. The first clue clearly indicated a starting point: *The Founders' faith was set in stone, there the journey's path will be shown. Journey* must mean that we have to follow the trail somewhere else. But where? The star we found today must be the second clue. There has to be another clue."

They proceeded to discuss the wording of the first clue for several moments. Then they each offered their thoughts on their tours of the stone church and the possible significance of the star. Sam pulled it out of her pocket again, and they scrutinized the small metal object.

"On the ride here, I thought maybe a clue was inside, but looking now, it's clear that it's solid," Sam noted. "Ouch," she said as she scrapped her finger on the point of the star. "And the injuries continue."

"Yeah, it's really pretty, but what does it tell us?" Nell posed.

"Your dad's here," Nell's mother announced from the family room.

Sam grabbed her bag, which Nell had packed. "Hey, is your internet access still being hooked up tomorrow?" she asked.

"I think so, why?"

"Can you do some research on the church?"

"Absolutely. I'll dig up everything I can. I'll also see if I can find out anything about that star. Who knows? Maybe I'll hit the jackpot."

"Okay, I was thinking about what Dean said about the older folks in town knowing more about the history of this place. What you think about me talking with my neighbor Mr. Miller? Remember the retired high school principal? He's in his seventies, and I think he is, or was, involved in the historical society at one point. I could ask him some general questions."

"I think it's a great idea," Nell answered.

By now, they could hear grown-ups talking in the other room. "Okay, I'd better go."

"Good luck!" they said to each other, together. They gave each other a hug, and Sam headed out the door.

On the way home, Sam's mind kept replaying the day's events and going over and over the clues they had so far. Part of her wanted to show the star to someone, but somehow, she knew it wouldn't help. The other part of her kept thinking about how it felt when Dean held her hand.

As they pulled into her driveway, Sam saw Mike's cruiser in the driveway next door. "Thanks for picking me up, Dad," she said climbing out of the car. "Is it okay if I head next door to say hello to Mike?"

"I guess that's fine. But don't be too long. I'll take your stuff inside so your mom can wash them."

"Okay, I will." She crossed the side yard separating her yard from Mike's parent's house, hopped up the front steps, and knocked on the door. A minute later, Mike answered the door.

"Hey there, how have you been? Come on in. I haven't seen you in days, I figured you weren't talking to me," he said jokingly.

"Been over at Nell's. How's the investigation coming?"

"Oh, I see how it is, just pumping me for information." He pretended to act insulted.

"Oh, please, you're not offended," she retorted. "Besides, I saw a guy murdered; don't I have some interest in the killer being caught? I can't stop thinking about what we saw; it was horrible. I still see his face in my dreams."

Sam was an emotionally strong person and wasn't about to burst into tears. On the other hand, Mike should understand why she needed to know what was going on.

"Okay, I'm not offended. I'm happy to keep you in the loop as much as I can. Since it's an ongoing investigation, I can't share everything with you, but I promise to do my best."

"Thanks. Do you have any suspects?" she inquired.

"Unfortunately, we don't really have any viable suspects. The deceased seemed to be a nice guy, quiet and kind of kept to himself, but people seemed to have liked him. So far, it doesn't look like he had any enemies, and there doesn't seem to be a motive to kill him."

"Did he have any family?"

"Yes, he has family in town," Mike answered. "He was single, but his parents and his siblings all live here. The Gray family is pretty upset. Do you know the Grays?"

"No, no," Sam responded, trying to suppress her shock. "I attended church with Nell this morning and the church had these big stained-glass windows dedicated to the Gray family. Small world, huh?"

I must be an idiot, Sam thought. *Why didn't I make the connection before? There's only one Gray family in town.*

"You must be talking about the stone church. Those windows are pretty amazing. Yeah, well, the Gray family has been very involved in the town for many years, since the beginning, I believe. Sad to have to deliver such news to them. They are good people."

Mike paused for a moment before continuing.

"So what else have you been up to, other than following my investigation?" Mike asked.

"Not much, just hanging out with Nell. It's so nice to finally have her back here. We went to see Curwood Castle today. Other than that, nothing exciting."

"You've probably had enough excitement for the summer," Mike said. "You sure you're doing okay after seeing what you did? You know, if you want to talk about it, you should. That's some scary stuff you had to see."

"Thanks, Mike, that's really nice of you. Actually, I'm fine. I mean, I don't think I'll be heading into the woods anytime soon, but I'm okay. Really. I'm still just trying to process all of it."

In truth, she didn't feel fine at all. It seemed that since the incident, her emotions were constantly swirling and changing. She was certainly traumatized by Fred's murder, but she was also sad and curious. She felt like she'd been stuck in a swirling vortex since she saw the murder. She couldn't quite clear her head. Just thinking the word *murder* seemed surreal. Tring to figure out Fred's message helped to focus her mind on something productive and off the terrifying event in the woods.

"Okay," Mike said. "I just wanted to let you know that if you have any lingering feelings of fear or concern, that's normal. Make sure that you talk to someone about them."

"I promise. Well, I'd better get back home. My parents will wonder where I am. Thanks for keeping me in the loop. I really appreciate it." Sam was a little confused by the comment. She wasn't sure why she should be fearful.

"Anytime. See you later," Mike said as he walked her out the door. "Tell your folks I said hello and thanks for the tomatoes."

"Sure thing."

With a wave, she was out the door heading down the sidewalk. She entered the house. The smell of pot roast simmering in the kitchen filled the air. She said a quick hello to her mother and retreated to her room to collect her thoughts before dinner.

With a sigh, she sank down into her bed. Suddenly, she was exhausted. It felt like it had been weeks since she last slept. Talking with Mike had sent her mind racing again. Being on a treasure hunt, real or imagined, was fun.

But she remembered the look in Fred's eyes shortly before he'd died. He'd wanted them to find it, whatever "it" was. It was obviously important to him that they find it before the killer did. What the hell was it? It had to be a treasure of some sort. At least it was a treasure to Fred.

She desperately wanted to fulfill her promise, but she didn't have much to go on. She mulled over all of the clues in her head countless times. Still, she was no closer to finding out what the next step was. Again she questioned herself as to whether they should fill Mike or someone else in on what she and Nell had discovered to date. She was, after all, only fifteen. What made her think she had the expertise to hunt down a treasure of any kind, with a killer on the loose no less?

They'd found the star by using the date the Civil War ended to open the secret compartment. The Civil War, clearly, she was no expert on either.

She knew her parents would throw an absolute fit if they knew what she was doing. She had to admit she couldn't really blame them. It did seem a little ridiculous, two teenage girls looking for a treasure that may or may not exist. In the end, she decided to put off any decisions until tomorrow. She was simply too tired and confused to determine the appropriate next step. She would enjoy dinner and then make it an early night. She doubted her parents would object.

Sam awoke the next morning well refreshed. The nightmares continued but felt like, in a way, they were keeping her on task. She had decided that she would relax around the pool for a while. It helped her to think. After lunch, she would go for a walk. Mr. Miller was usually out puttering with his lawn or out in his garden in the afternoon, so the chances were good that she would run into him.

Her plans were slightly altered as her mother appeared in her doorway and insisted that she clean her room.

"I've hardly seen you since Nell got back in town, and your room looks like it was hit by a tornado," her mother complained.

"Right, Mom, I'll clean it up right after breakfast." To be fair, her room was a little trashed. Clothes were strewn around at least half of the room. Some of them landed there in the daily quest to determine what to wear, a task that seemed to become more important to her the older she became. In any event, she would tackle the problem after she had some food in her stomach.

A search of the kitchen cupboard revealed a box of Pop-Tarts. She grabbed two without toasting them and headed back to her room. She hastily fished out clothes scattered about the room and under the bed and deposited them into the clothes hamper in her closet. She scanned the room and decided that it was clean enough.

She then decided to go directly to Mr. Miller's. After changing into a clean shirt, shorts, and flip-flops, she called out to her mother that she was headed to the Millers and was out the front door in near record time.

As she walked toward the Miller house, she thought about how to approach him. It wouldn't be too hard to get him telling stories. The only problem would be in focusing him on what she needed to know.

As she approached the Miller's driveway, she saw Sunny, his golden retriever, in the backyard. The Millers had no family in town and were always grateful for company. They were a little too long-winded sometimes, but they were good people and had always been nice to Sam.

As she rounded the corner of the house, Sunny saw her and came bounding over. Sam dropped to her knees, and Sunny nearly knocked her over. Large paws landed on Sam's shoulders, and Sunny gave her a wet kiss on the face.

"Hey, Sunny, how are you?" Sam said, scratching the dog's ear. "You are such a good girl."

"Hello, stranger! Good to see you," called Mr. Miller.

Sam looked around and saw him standing in the middle of his garden.

"Hi, Mr. Miller. How are you?" she said walking toward him. His garden was small, but it was chock-full of beans, corn, tomatoes, and other vegetables. Plants climbed up to his waist and higher in some sections of the garden, which explained why she hadn't seen him at first. Wearing green overalls and a fishing hat, he was nearly invisible.

"Oh, can't complain, thanks for asking," Mr. Miller responded with a wide smile. "My garden is doing well this year. I can hardly keep up with it. Say, do you mind holding my bucket while I pick the peppers and cucumbers? I'll give you a cut of the findings," he said with a chuckle.

"Oh, sure, I'd be happy to," she answered. "And you don't have to share the fruits of your labor. Playing with Sunny is reward enough."

"That dog sure does enjoy seeing you," he responded. "You can come as often as you like. I got a new box of dog bones for her in the garage cabinet next to the fridge. Always feel free to help yourself. Your folks have a key."

"Will do, thanks."

Sam exchanged some small talk with Mr. Miller as he picked vegetables out of his garden and tossed them into the bucket she was holding.

"I heard about that death in the woods behind your house. Heard it might have been a murder. I've been thinking about you and your cousin. Are you okay? That's pretty heavy stuff. The whole town is talking about it. You girls were very brave."

"Oh, yeah, well, thanks. We were all pretty shaken up about it at first, but we're okay. I'm focusing on the good stuff and just enjoying being back together with Nell."

"You sure?" he said, giving her a solemn look. "There's no shame in being scared after something like that happens near your home. Make sure that you girls discuss your feelings with someone and get it out. Don't bottle up your feelings. You know, I used to be a counselor at the school, not just the principal. If ever you want to talk, just let me know."

"Thanks, Mr. Miller, that is very nice of you, but I'm doing okay, honest. Nell too. We have talked to each other and our parents. But I appreciate your offer. I really do."

She quickly changed the subject.

"So, Mr. Miller, Nell and I decided to take on a little summer project, so to speak. With Nell moving back to Owosso and all, we thought it would be nice to learn a little of the town's history. We've seen all the movies at the theater and read nearly all the books in the library, so we thought it would be fun to learn our town's legacy."

"Really?" Mr. Miller said with a laugh. "You girls are pretty special. Not many kids your age would undertake such summer activity. I have to commend you for your interest."

"Thanks." Suddenly feeling a little nervous, she tried to explain their interest. "It all sort of started with the upcoming Curwood Festival. We go every year, of course, but we really didn't know much about who the festival was named for. We realized that our town has some interesting history. The trouble is, the library couldn't really give us much detail about when Owosso was first formed. We learned that the name came from the Indian Chief

Wasso, but the early history of this area is still a bit fuzzy. We decided that we need to take a hands-on approach in educating ourselves.

"Yesterday, I attended services with Nell's family at the stone church, and afterward we took a tour of Curwood Castle. It was pretty cool. I understand that the windows honor the founding families of Owosso. After seeing them, we were hoping to find out more."

"I say, you girls have really put your hearts into this project. How fantastic! You know, I used to be quite active in the historical society, and I still volunteer from time to time. I might be able to help."

"Seriously?" Sam said with genuine excitement and relief. "That would be great. Can you tell me what you know about when the town was formed, who its founding families were, and stuff like that?"

"Well, I might not have all of the details, but I certainly think I can fill in some gaps," Mr. Miller said. "Here, grab these tomatoes and let's head up to the porch. I'll get us some lemonades, and I'll tell you what I know."

Bubbling with anticipation, Sam settled herself into the porch swing and anxiously awaited his return. Thankfully, he reappeared a few moments later, bearing the drinks as promised.

"Okay, where shall I start?" he inquired. He removed his hat and ran his hand over his thick gray hair.

"Start with the first people who came here to live," she suggested.

Sam listened intently as Mr. Miller told her how the Weston brothers, John and Louis, were first to settle in the area, and encouraged others, including the Comstock family, to buy land here as well. The Westons had apparently set up a log-cabin trading post near what became the corner of Main and Water Streets.

"Elias Comstock, as you probably know, built Comstock Cabin, the one-room log cabin. It was built in 1836 and was the first permanent residence in Owosso. The first church services were also held at the cabin. The cabin was reportedly moved several times before it came to rest over by Curwood Castle. Of course, as you know from your tour, the castle was not constructed until 1922.

"In 1837, Michigan officially became a state, and Owosso was in the running for the state capital. We lost by one vote, and it was cast by our own legislator. Imagine how different our lives might have become! We'd be big-city dwellers.

"Anyway, the next settlers to the area were several of the members of the Adam Gray family and the Edward Gray family. More homes popped up, and the Weston boys set aside the area now known as Fayette Square for a public park in 1838.

"In the 1840s and '50s, the population continued to grow, and by 1852, there were five hundred people living here. More churches established a presence in town. As you know, one of the oldest churches, the First Congregational Church, also known as the Stone Church, was established. It is now located at Washington and Mason, but I believe it was originally built elsewhere shortly after the town's formation. Another one of the old churches is St. John's Church, which was built at Washington and Oliver Streets.

"The first formal schooling took place in a log cabin. The first official school building was erected in 1840 near Washington and Mason Streets. It was later relocated East of Mason Street to make room for Salem Lutheran Church. In 1846, a bell was purchased for the school by children bringing in their pennies. Pennies, can you imagine that? Sam could tell that he enjoyed talking about this stuff. A look of delight and amusement lit up his face.

"Anyway," he continued "the Union school, as it was then called, was constructed in 1858, and it sat on the same site as Central School is today.

"A few years later, a third building was erected for the school, just south of the prior building. The old structure was torn down. Shortly before construction started on the new building, the original bell purchased with the kids' pennies was destroyed in a fire. That same year, Edward Gray purchased and donated a bell for the school, and he paid for construction of the platform on which the bell stands.

"Despite the fires, the school and the bell, have remained there ever since. Although I think they expanded the building a couple of times. Later, the middle school and the high school were built where they stand today."

"Central School had fires?" Sam asked with surprise. She had attended that school, but she didn't remember talk of any fires.

"Oh yes," Mr. Miller said with a look of sadness. "There were a few. I'm not sure of all the dates, but I know that on April 1, 1900, a fire broke out, and two firefighters died. It was tragic. Luckily, no students were there at the time. The school was later rebuilt on its foundation. The school was nearly completely destroyed again in 1945. Most of the building was leveled. They rebuilt. Just a few years later, they began constructing a new building, in 1949 I think, to replace the out-of-date structure. In 1950, the cornerstone of the present Central School was set."

"What about some of the original homes in the area?" Sam gently prodded.

"Ah yes, well, Adam Gray built a home at Washington and Oliver. His brother Edward, built his home over at M-52 and Weston. Hang on a minute. I'll be right back," Mr. Miller said suddenly.

He got up and entered the house. He returned several minutes later with a small pamphlet.

"Here you go," he said, handing it to her. "This is a copy of the map that the historical society uses for walking tours. It shows most of the historic homes and businesses in town. You can keep it if you like."

"Thank you," Sam said. "This is really helpful."

"You're welcome. You and your cousin might enjoy taking the

tour. The homes are beautiful, and being inside them really gives you a feel for the periods in which they were built. The Adam Gray house is probably the most impressive residential structure in town. The architecture is stunning, and the attention to detail both inside and out is quite remarkable. Plus, the tour really lets you get up close and personal with our history."

"You said that Adam Gray was one of the first settlers here, right?" Sam coached.

"Yes, ma'am. He was indeed. Adam also became very involved in the town. He was once of the first lawyers, and he later became a judge and then a US Senator. I'm not sure when the home was officially donated, but it is now maintained by the historical society and is open for tours.

"Rumor has it," he said, leaning toward Sam and lowering his voice for dramatic effect, "though it's never been officially confirmed, that Adam used the house as part of the Underground Railroad to assist former slaves flee to Canada.

"There were also rumors that there were tunnels under the property connected to one or more other houses that were part of the railroad, and for some bootlegging. Folks do like to imbibe in some alcohol from time to time." Mr. Miller winked at her when delivering this bit of information.

"According to the rumors, there are secret hiding places all over town. The family never admitted to the tunnels. If there are tunnels, my guess is that they were used for storage of family items, perhaps some of value, which would explain why they wouldn't want to talk about them. It's kind of like having a modern-day safe room."

Mr. Miller continued talking. "Anyway, Adam's brother was equally impressive. Edward was one of the town's first entrepreneurs. He established several successful businesses at a young age before he followed his older brother into the study of law. He, too, became a successful attorney. He is also quite famous in these parts for being part of Michigan's Fighting Fifth during the Civil War."

"Did he die in the war?" Sam asked with a touch of sadness.

"No, no, he survived and returned to live out his days here in the town he loved. He didn't die until 1870 or 1880, I believe. After the war, he returned to a very active life here in town. Among a great number of things, he donated his legal services to benefit the town and he was instrumental in seeing to it that Central School was rebuilt. He was a good man, very kind, thoughtful and generous to family, friend and town alike."

"What became of Edward's house?" Sam questioned.

"Oh, it still stands where he built it over on what is now M-52, though back then I think it was called Mulberry Street. It's not too far from Central School actually. It has been turned into a bed-and-breakfast.

"What was I saying? Oh, Adam and Edward were both fine gentleman and upstanding citizens, generous to a fault. They loved their family and their town. In fact, they built a home for their sister, Elizabeth Gray Adams, that still stands on Oliver Street near Central School.

"Of course, over the years quite a few other impressive folks hailed from this town. You know all about the Curwood Festival and what it celebrates, I presume, since you just took the Curwood Castle tour?" he asked.

"Yes, we got a lot of information about the festival. Now we know why, and who, we're celebrating."

Our little town has a lot to celebrate. Our citizens were also very involved in the antislavery movement and supporting the Underground Railroad. Not to mention the actual railroad over on Washington Street. Back in the day, it was critical to this town.

"Well then, I think that about does it for my knowledge on the history of Owosso. Do you have any questions?"

"Gosh, you know so much, my head is swimming with information. I can't think of any questions right now."

"If you have any later, swing on by. If I can't answer them, I'll ring my friends at the historical society, and we'll find an answer for you."

"You've been so helpful. I can't tell you how much I appreciate you taking the time to talk with me and share your knowledge. Nell will be so excited with all the information. I think I'll take your advice about the walking tour. It sounds cool." She sat back for a moment and tried to digest the new information.

"Wow, I've taken up a lot of your time today. My mom's going to wonder where I've been. I'd better get back home now," she said, forcing herself to stand. "Thank you again."

"Anytime. I enjoy the company," he said with a smile. "Tell your mother and father I said hello."

"I will. See you soon," Sam answered. A smile covered her face the entire walk home. She could feel that they were getting closer to the next clue. She just needed to process all that she had learned today.

As soon as she got home, Sam called Nell and relayed the conversation with Mr. Miller. She tried to tell it word for word, but there was so much to remember she found herself interrupting her tale each time she remembered another detail.

Nell was thrilled with the news. "What a great idea, talking to Mr. Miller," she said again. "He's a wealth of information. It's neat that the town's original families are still living here. It also seems like there are tons of places of interest that might hold our next clue. I wonder where we should go next. We could scope out the places of business for the founders or we could go on the walking tour, she said as her voice trailed off. What are you thinking?"

"It's hard to know where to begin," Sam answered. "I think maybe I would start with the walking tour. It's probably the best way to get into some of the homes and learn about our town's history. Plus, we might gain more information that could lead us to the next clue." She read Nell the tour times from the back of the pamphlet.

"Okay, I'm game. Hey, did you tell Mr. Miller anything about what we found?" Nell asked.

"Absolutely not!" Sam nearly yelled. "You and I—and Dean, I guess—are the sole secret keepers."

"I figured. I was just curious. Do you think we should show the star to Mr. Miller? You know, not tell him where we found it, but see if he can tell us anything about it?"

Sam thought for a moment. "No, I don't think we should show it to him. I have this feeling that no one would recognize it. Let's just keep it to ourselves, at least for now."

"Okay. Well, Curwood Festival starts on Thursday," Nell noted. "How about if you come over on Wednesday so we can do the tour thing? My dad will love it. Then we can enjoy the festival on Thursday, Friday, and Saturday."

"I think that's a good plan. Will your folks be ok with it? They did just get rid of me after all."

"Hey, it's Curwood Days. They don't have a choice," Nell immediately responded. "Will your parents let you come back so soon?"

"Oh, I'm sure that I will get some talk about how I can be a burden to your folks, but I'm pretty sure I can swing it. I'll wait to hear from you that your parents have given the okay before I deal with mine."

"Okay, I'll call you later today or tomorrow to confirm," Nell said.

It took Sam a long time to fall asleep that night. She laid in bed for hours, her mind racing. Ever present in her mind were Fred's face and his plea. The clues they'd found to date and the information they'd obtained added to the mix and swirled in her mind until they became such a jumbled mess that she couldn't think anymore.

Then Dean's face popped into her mind. He was very

good-looking and, she had to admit, very nice. Why was she annoyed with him? She realized she liked him. She just wished she didn't feel so strange around him. She would have to work on that. Finally, she fell into a fitful slumber.

In the middle of the night, Sam awoke from a sound sleep. She bolted upright in bed as the idea came to her. Mr. Miller and Pastor Dan had each said that Edward Gray fought in the Civil War. The secret compartment in the bell tower opened when she'd entered the combination 1865.

She turned to her nightstand where she had placed the walking tour map, pulled out her reading light, and began to look at the map with renewed interest. She located the Edward Gray house and stared at the dot marking its location for several minutes. Then she looked at the house in relation to the other structures she had learned about today.

She was looking at the dot marking the stone church when she saw it—Edward's house was located at the end of Weston Street. Weston and Gray; the windows honored Weston and Gray. They were considered founders of the town. The windows gave the location of the next clue. The next clue had to be at Edward's house!

Being the middle of the night, there was no way she could call Nell without severe repercussions. It was killing her to wait until morning, but she had no other choice. To occupy herself, she read the walking tour pamphlet over and over again until she'd nearly memorized it in its entirety.

As Mr. Miller had said, the pamphlet listed the historical sites around town. After each address was listed a short description of the house in question as well as the original or well-known owner. Sam was surprised at the number of historical sites. She even noted that Owosso had had coal mines at one point. Exhausted, she looked over at her clock and saw that it was just after 5:00 a.m. She closed her eyes, hoping for rest.

She woke up after 9:00 a.m. Finally, she could call Nell. She walked out into the hallway and picked up the phone. She carried it back into her room to dial. Thankfully, the phone had a long extension cord. She didn't want to risk her mother hearing and declaring it too early for phone calls. The line rang and rang. Sam held her breath, hoping that Nell would be the one to answer. Finally, to her relief, she heard Nell's voice.

"Hello?"

"Hey, Nell, it's Sam."

"What's up? It's early," she said.

"Listen, Nell, I think I've figured it out," Sam said breathlessly. She proceeded to walk Nell through her analysis of the clues they found so far and why she believed that the next clue was waiting for them at Edward Gray's house. "And I—don't laugh ..."

"I won't," Nell promised.

"I, uh, I think that the treasure has something to do with Edward Gray. I mean, the secret drawer opened when I entered 1865, the year the Civil War ended; he fought in the Civil War; the windows point to his house."

"Hmm," was all that Nell replied at first.

"Well?" Sam said after a minute or two. "What are you thinking?"

"Well, I understand where you are coming from, but ..."

"But what?"

"It's just that the windows were dedicated in 1892. That's well after the war ended. Plus, didn't you say that Edward died in like 1870 or 1880? Why would the windows lead us to a dead man's home? I mean, it could have been sold or torn down over the years. It wasn't donated to the town like the Adam Gray house."

"Oh." Sam's heart plummeted. "I'd forgotten about that." However, after a moment, she said, "So what? We still don't know what we are looking for and who hid it. I don't know why the windows are leading us to Edward's house, but my instincts are telling me that we need to check it out."

"I'm sorry. I didn't mean to sound negative," Nell apologized. "I sounded like my mother. You might have to kill me. I think I'm just tired right now, and I'm a little discouraged. We will totally check it out. Is the Edward Gray house on the walking tour?"

"It looks like it, but only for a limited number of hours, and I can't tell whether it's open on Wednesday."

"Well, the good news is that I have the green light to invite you over on Wednesday, and you can stay all weekend if you want. My dad is super excited that we are becoming so interested in local history."

"Great, I'll talk to my mom this morning. I'll head down now. Call you later."

9

◇

The Tour

As expected, Sam's mother had reservations about yet another stay with Nell's family so soon. She clearly insinuated that Sam was some sort of a burden on Aunt Sue and Uncle Hank.

"But, Mom, for years Nell has stayed with us for weeks at a time. Aunt Sue was okay with that. Plus, we are really having a good time learning about the town. They have a walking tour of some of the older homes in town, and we wanted to go on Wednesday. Then the festival starts on Thursday. We go every year. This year, I'll just be staying at Nell's house."

Eventually, her mother agreed, and Sam promptly called Nell to tell her the good news. She also wanted to confirm the plans before her mother could change her mind.

As Sam hung up the phone with Nell, she felt a small sense of accomplishment. It seemed that they were making headway in their search. Although something Nell said still bothered her. If the windows in the stone church were the next clue, how was it that they were created after Edward's death?

Without really intending to, Sam found herself walking down the driveway. She stopped at the end, wondering what she should do next. Then it came to her: she needed to make another little visit to Mr. Miller.

Just then, her mother came out of the house heading for the backyard. Sam called out that she was going for a walk around the block and would be back soon. This time, however, she headed directly for Mr. Miller's house.

She was several houses away from the Miller's when she saw, to her delight, that Mr. Miller was out front, watering flowers. He waved as he saw her, and she waved in return. Sunny trotted over to Sam and licked her hand. Sam reached down and patted Sunny's head and back. She cut across the lawn to where Mr. Miller was standing.

"Hi, kiddo. What's new?" He asked.

"Nell and I decided to take the walking tour like you suggested. We are hoping to go this Wednesday. Then we're going to the festival on Thursday, Friday, and Saturday. We're really looking forward to eating the carnival food and losing our money playing those games no one can win."

"That's great. I think you girls will have a nice time. Just remember that most of the homes on the tour don't have air-conditioning, so dress in cool clothes."

"Thanks for the tip; we will. Hey, I did want to ask you another question."

"Okay, shoot."

"I was telling Nell all of the information you gave me, and she actually raised a question about the stained-glass windows at the stone church. Pastor Dan said that the windows were dedicated in 1892 to honor the Weston and Gray families. I think you mentioned that Edward Gray died in 1870 or 1880. We were just wondering if you knew why the windows were dedicated so long after he died."

"Well, things sometimes just work out that way. You know the old saying, 'You don't know what you have until it's gone'? It is often very true."

"Oh," Sam murmured.

"But in this case," Mr. Miller continued, "I know that there was talk long before Edward died about the church doing some sort of dedication. I heard that Edward left a provision in his will describing that the windows should honor both the Weston and Gray families, and setting aside money to pay for the construction and installation. He had a rather large estate, and it reportedly took quite a while to administer it all. I think his brother Adam lived for several years after Edward died, and I believe he handled the estate. Anyway, it probably took a while to coordinate things. Why do you ask?"

"No reason really. Nell and I were just curious. Thanks again for the information. You're gonna want to start avoiding me now, what will all my questions."

"Not a chance," he replied. "I enjoy your company, and I'm happy to talk with you anytime. Let me know what you think of the walking tour."

"I will," Sam answered. "Have a nice day," she said as she walked back to the street. Although she wanted to rush home and call Nell, she thought it might look strange if she made a beeline for the Miller home and then returned home. She therefore decided to complete the circle around the block.

She used the time to think about why Edward Gray would leave money to pay for the church windows in his will, rather than just giving them the money. The bell had been given to the church outright. Realizing that she had to stop trying to read something into everything, she tried to put it out of her mind.

For the remainder of the day, she relaxed in the pool and read a book. She turned in early that night, wanting to be well rested for the next day's tour. She awoke Wednesday morning refreshed and excited to find out what she might uncover that day. She showered, dressed, and quickly packed a backpack. When she arrived downstairs, she found her mother doing some ironing in the kitchen.

"Hey, Mom, is there anything you need me to do before I go to Nell's?" (She wanted to start off with a thoughtful gesture.) Before her mother had a chance to answer, Sam said, "I'm really looking forward to this tour. The homes sound beautiful. Actually, I've seen the Adam Gray house forever, and I've always wondered what it looked like inside."

"No, there's nothing I need you to do before you go, but thank you for asking," her mother replied.

Sam could tell that her mother wasn't really listening, but she didn't care. "Mom, can you take me over to Nell's, or would you like me to ride my bike?"

"Ride your bike? All the way up Hickory? Of course not, I'll take you. When does the tour start?"

Sam informed her mother that the tour started at 1:00 p.m. but that she and Nell wanted to be there a little early. After being assured that Aunt Sue was aware of the plan, Sam's mother put down her ironing, and they headed for the car.

Arriving at Nell's house, Sam hopped out of the car, bringing her bag with her in one fell swoop.

"Thanks for the ride, Mom," she said, closing the car door. She waved and headed to the front door. She was hoping that this would discourage her mother from coming inside. Her hopes were answered when her mom gave a quick wave and backed out of the driveway.

Nell met her at the door and ushered them back to her bedroom. Behind closed doors, they discussed the plan for the walking tour.

"Hey, you're not going to like what I have to tell you," Nell said.

"What?

"The Edward Gray house is not going to be on today's tour."

"How do you know?"

"My dad called to find out where to drop me off, and the lady answering the phone told him. She said that some pamphlets were printed with old information. I guess since the house is privately owned and has been turned into a bed-and-breakfast they can't always guarantee that it is on the tour."

"Oh no! Now that you mention it, I think Mr. Miller mentioned that it was a bed-and-breakfast. What do we do now?"

"Well, I have a thought. I'm not sure that you're going to like it at first, but I think it's our best alternative."

"All right, let's hear it," Sam said, narrowing her eyes at Nell and bracing herself.

"We call Dean. He just might be able to get us access, you know, because of his mom's connections."

"Dean? I mean, I'll admit he's not as annoying as I thought at first, and he did come through for us at the church, but I don't like bringing other people into our little search."

"I know. I knew you'd say that. But I kind of like Dean. I think he really likes you. I also think we can trust him. More importantly, I think we need him."

Sam scowled, tugged on her hair and paced up and down Nell's room. "This sucks," she grumbled, knowing that Nell was right. "Fine, call him."

"Okay," Nell replied, jumping into action. She grabbed a phone off her dresser.

"You have your own phone now?" Sam said with obvious envy.

"Yeah, remember, my parents gave me one for my birthday? We just found it in one of the moving boxes."

"I so want to change parents with you sometimes," Sam said.

"Ah, but then you'd have to deal with my mother. Be careful what you wish for," she said with a warning look. "I've got my own issues over here, as you know."

"So true," Sam answered. "So true."

"Nell had dialed the number to Dean's house. After exchanging a few pleasantries, she told him about the tour and their desire to visit the Edward Gray house. After a moment of silence, she smiled and gave Sam the thumbs-up sign. She thanked him and arranged to meet at the start of the tour.

"He's going on the tour with us?" Sam exclaimed.

"Well, he sorta invited himself," Nell replied.

"I'm sorry," Nell apologized. "What could I do? Tell him we want your help, but we want to spend the least amount of time with you as possible? He really is nice, and he sounded excited about going on the tour with us."

"Great," Sam said, her voice dripping with sarcasm. "When and where are we meeting him?"

"One o'clock at Fayette Park, where the tour starts. He suggested that we take the tour and then go to the Edward Gray house afterward. It sounded like he was going to have his mom arrange for us to see it or something. He said that the owners are not particularly interested in having the home open to the public this year but that his mother has a good relationship with them."

"Well, this day started out promising," Sam said with a sour tone. Inwardly, she felt a flutter in her stomach.

"I know it's not how we discussed it, but, hey, we found the star with him. Maybe he's our good-luck charm."

"I doubt it," Sam retorted. "Well, it is what it is. We'll just have to go with it. Hey, did you find out anything more about the stone church?"

"Not really, they have a website, and it pretty much just states the stuff that Pastor Dan told us. I couldn't find much else out on the internet about the church other than the basics."

Sam filled Nell in on Edward's will and the money left to pay for the windows at the stone church.

"That's interesting," Nell said. "If the windows at the church really are a clue, do you think that Edward was involved in hiding the treasure?"

"I think that there's some connection with Edward Gray, I just don't know what. I haven't really thought that far ahead," Sam said, her eyebrows arching as she contemplated the thought. "Although things *are* starting to form a pattern. Edward attended the stone church. He paid for the church windows, which led back to his house. He was a Civil War hero. Well, okay, we don't know if was a hero, but he fought in the war. The combination lock in the bell tower opened to the year the Civil War ended. Yeah, it's starting to make sense. Hopefully we'll know more after we get inside his house."

"If his house is no longer owned by the Gray family, Edward certainly took a risk that any clue inside would remain there. What about his brother Adam?" Nell asked. "Do you think he was involved?"

"Good question," Sam admitted. "Who knows? If he handled Edward's estate, maybe he was fulfilling his brother's wishes. Maybe they were working together. Maybe Edward's house was supposed to be dedicated to the public like Adam's. Of course, maybe there is no treasure, no clues, and we are just creating an adventure that doesn't exist."

"Do you believe that?" Nell asked in shock.

"No," Sam admitted, "But I'm trying, key word *trying*, to be objective. I really think that we are following actual clues, but I need to prepare myself for the alternative. What do you think about all of this?"

"You have always had a better imagination than me, Sam, and I have always been a little envious of how you can create a world of possibilities. My adventures are totally due to your imagination. It does seem like we're meant to follow a trail. I'm not sure of what we will find or even if we will find anything. But you have me convinced that we are on to something."

"Okay then, we are two girls on a mission that we acknowledge may be imaginary. How very grown up of us," Sam joked.

"Commendable in fact," Nell added.

"Well, actually I guess it's not really imaginary. We must be on the hunt for something, since it was so important to Fred. You know, Nell, the killer could be out there looking for it too. I mean, he murdered Fred. I guess he wouldn't just give up after that. I think I wanted to believe that he was gone, but he's still out there. We don't know where he is or what he wants," Sam said. She looked at Nell and saw the intense look of concern on her face.

"I'm sorry. I didn't mean to be such a downer. Let's just take one thing at a time and focus on the tour today."

Before Nell could respond, Sam continued talking, mostly to distract her cousin. "I thought I'd bring along the walking tour map Mr. Miller gave me," Sam told Nell. I figure we can also use that. I'm debating on whether we should take the star. I'm deathly afraid of losing it, and I don't want anyone else to see it and ask about it."

"We could hide it in my room," Nell offered. "But what if we end up wanting to look at it for some reason?"

"Good point," Sam noted. "Okay, we'll take it, but we keep it guarded at all times."

Sam and Nell had a quick lunch of yogurt and fruit while they loaded a few water bottles into Nell's backpack.

Nell's mother grumbled about carting them around, but reluctantly followed them out to the car.

Sam and Nell were inside the car while Aunt Sue was still fishing for her keys. Nell rolled her eyes as she imitated her mother in a whisper. "'Where are you going again?' Honestly, like she didn't remember. Everything with my mom is such an ordeal. It's like she is always waiting for me to say or do the wrong thing. She sucks all the fun out of everything."

"She is a bit ... intense," Sam agreed. "But at least you have your dad. He is so nice, super laid-back and so supportive of your interests. Both of my parents are nearly devoid of emotion, at least when it comes to me, and I can't really talk to either of them. They're just so focused on everything and everyone else. They can't really be bothered to take an interest in me. Last year, my mom didn't even attend student honors night at school because she had her card club."

"Yeah, my dad is great, and I can always talk to him. Your parents aren't so bad. Your mom's not nearly as crazy as mine, and your dad's okay. He's super good at fixing everything you can imagine, and he takes you boating and stuff."

"It could be worse," Sam agreed.

Nell's mother finally entered the car, and they were on their way. "Dad gave me his cell phone and said to call you when we were ready to be picked up," Nell said. "When he talked to the lady at the historical society, he said it sounded like the tour varies depending on the amount of people that show up."

"Well, I won't necessarily be able to drop what I'm doing on a moment's notice when you call. Also, remember that phone is not a toy," Aunt Sue replied.

"No problem, Mom, we'll just hang out and wait for you, and I'll only use the phone to call you," Nell responded, refusing to be goaded into an argument. She gave Sam a subtle nudge to call attention to her mother's behavior. Luckily, they reached the park a few moments later. Fearing more questions, they quickly thanked Nell's mom for the ride and waved goodbye as they climbed out of the car. The girls could see people milling around, but it was difficult to tell whether they were there for the tour or just hanging out.

"Hey, guys," called a voice coming from over by one of the benches. Dean waved and started walking toward them.

"Thanks for letting me tag along today. My mother wanted me to catalog books at the library today. I think she's trying to torture me," he said with laugh.

"Hi, Dean," Sam and Nell replied together. "Yeah, uh, no problem. Thanks for agreeing to help us with the, um, other thing," Nell said.

"No worries. It's all set up. As I mentioned on the phone, the owner's not a huge fan of large tour groups traipsing over the property when she has the place booked, but my mom secured the okay for us to look around the house a little."

"What did you tell your mother?" Sam asked.

"You can relax," Dean said reassuringly. "Don't worry. Mom's cool. I just told her you guys were into old houses. She thought it was actually pretty funny."

Anyway, my mom, ever the preservationist, was impressed that you guys are undertaking such a project over the summer, and she wanted to help. She even mentioned that it would be nice to have some young people as members of the society. So, if she makes me join, I'll have to kill you two," he said jokingly. "Plus, you guys should probably hide from my mother unless you want to be drafted for the job."

"Okay, okay, we appreciate your efforts," Sam said, rolling her eyes at Nell.

Dean then brought up the topic of the Curwood Festival starting the next day. They all agreed that they were looking forward to it, and they discussed their favorite parts of the event. Nell and Sam talked about the food and trying out some of the rides. This year, Dean was determined to win at the basketball free-throw booth.

"I think I've figured out how to make it in the net, despite all the tricks they use," he told them.

As Sam was starting to tease Dean for striving to master a carnie game, she saw a woman holding up her hands and announcing, "Historical walking tour over here."

"Oh, it's starting," Nell said, "let's go."

The three quickly made their way to the woman, anxious for the tour to begin.

"Hello, everyone, my name is Janet, and I will be leading the walking tour today." Janet was tiny. She couldn't have been more than five feet tall, and her frame was so petite she looked like a pixie. Adding to the effect was that she had dark hair cut close to her small face, and she was bubbling with enthusiasm. She reminded Sam of Tinkerbell, except with dark hair.

"Everyone interested in talking the tour, please stand over here," she said, pointing to an area next to the Fayette Square Park sign. "Oh, hi, Dean, so nice to see you." She motioned to him.

"It's my mother's fault that she knows me," Dean muttered a little sheepishly.

Janet continued. "Okay, it's a little after one. I want to explain a few things to you before we start the tour, and I also want to give everyone a couple of minutes' leeway in case anyone is running behind. Okay, here are your maps, which list each of the buildings we will be visiting today," she said as she began distributing a stack of papers.

Sam took a pamphlet and began surveying the document. For the most part, it looked like the one Mr. Miller had given her. However, the Edward Gray house was noticeably absent.

Janet was discussing the tour route. Sam tried to focus on Janet's introduction, but she soon became bored. She was reminding everyone not to touch anything, to be respectful, and so on. As the group made its way to the first house, she wondered whether the tour would be a waste of time.

"Any questions? No, well, then it looks like we have a nice size group here. I count twenty-four people. Nice turnout." Janet seemed pleased.

Sam felt a flutter in her chest Janet led the group forward. Sam was walking next to Nell, with Dean walking slightly behind them. Christ Episcopal Church, the first stop, was striking. Janet explained that the church had been built in 1859 in the Roman style of architecture. The land had been donated by the Weston brothers, one of Owosso's first families. According to Janet, it was the oldest church in town still occupied by the same denomination.

The entire time they were in the church, Sam's thoughts were on the stone church. She couldn't help making comparisons between the two buildings. She also wondered if the fact that the land for this church had been donated by one of the founders was some sort of a sign. With that in mind, she gave close attention to both Janet's lecture and the details of the church. However, by the time the group began to leave the church, Sam had decided that the next clue was waiting elsewhere. She didn't know why, but she just knew.

Sam was startled when Dean whispered in her ear that Janet was almost as enthusiastic as Pastor Dan.

They toured a home, and then they came to the Adam Gray house. Sam and Nell gave each other a knowing look. Wanting to make sure they could hear, they made their way to the front of the group. Dean followed suit and stood by Sam's side. It was distracting, and Sam felt awkward.

Janet began discussing the Italian-style architecture of the building as they walked up the sidewalk. Sam took in the house and the grounds. The home was grand, and it was positioned squarely in the middle of a large rolling green lawn. It certainly was impressive.

Once inside the house, Janet continued to point out architectural details of the home. Looking out one of the windows, Sam could see that the landscape was remarkable by itself. The bushes were expertly trimmed to create a maze-like effect. Flowers of every shape and color surrounded the grounds. Near the back of the yard was a long, large arch over which grew hundreds of roses. Sam had the strongest urge to run through the rose-covered path until she remembered her severe allergy to bee stings, and the fantasy was cut short. Irritated with herself for her momentary lapse of attention, she refocused on Janet's lecture.

Janet was in the middle of a discussion about Adam Gray, and she obviously thought very highly of him. She mentioned many of the things Sam had heard from Pastor Dan and from Mr. Miller. She spent a long time telling tales of Adam's great accomplishments in the legal arena. According to her, he had rarely lost a case, and he had tried and won many of the notable cases of his time. Janet described him as a tireless advocate for truth, fairness, and justice. He was an inspiration to all, she informed them with pride.

Sam's favorite room in the house was the study. With its floor-to-ceiling bookcases stuffed with leather-bound books, Sam could picture Adam Gray sitting at the desk, reading books about law, art, or perhaps literature. She couldn't help but wonder whether Fred had spent time here.

Dean commented that it was stuffy and could use some air-conditioning.

"I can hear my mother now," Nell said, "I'd hate to be the one who has to dust all of this wood."

Sam and Dean burst into laughter. Several of the people from the group laughed as well.

They had been through all the rooms in the house and it was clear that the tour was coming to an end. However, Sam noted to herself that Janet hadn't revealed any potential secret hiding places. After quick whispering session with Nell, Sam nodded, and Nell raised her hand.

"Yes? Do you have a question?" Janet asked Nell.

"I've heard rumors that this house was used in the Underground Railroad to help Southern slaves escape to Canada. I was wondering whether that was true and if there's a tunnel under the house."

Sam noticed a tall blond man standing on the fringe of the group look over at Nell with surprise. Something about him seemed creepy.

"Ah, a very interesting question, thank you," Janet complimented. "Yes, it has long been believed that Adam Gray was involved in the Underground Railroad. The First Congregational Church, of which Adam was a member, was vehemently opposed to slavery. Adam himself, was quite outspoken on this subject. Many people believe that this house was used to hide people and aid them in their quest for freedom. Naturally, the house has been thoroughly searched by the historical society. Unfortunately, no secret hiding places or tunnels have been found. Too bad really— it would be great fun to add secret passages to the tour."

As Janet turned to the next question, Sam had already stopped listening. She wanted to discuss the house with Nell in greater detail, but she didn't dare with Dean hanging around. She half resented his presence, and yet she found him increasingly attractive. Despite his easygoing demeanor, she wasn't ready to share any more information with him, but she didn't exactly want him to leave either. Realizing that she didn't want to be rude, Sam asked Dean whether he knew anything else about the house. Apparently, Dean had been in the home many times but didn't have any information not already covered by Janet.

Now back outside in the blazing sun, Sam retrieved water bottles from the backpack and shared with Nell and Dean. She was struggling to think of something to say to Dean. Before she could utter a word, Janet signaled that the tour was resuming. She was relieved.

The next stop was St. John's United Church of Christ. Janet informed the group that the church was a New England–style church and was built in 1856 by Methodists. "Notably, it is the oldest church still standing in town," she said with great enthusiasm.

"Oh, I'll have to remember to tell my mother that—she loves anything to do with Methodists," Nell said with a grin.

"You are so bad," Sam said with a note of approval in her voice.

"Consider yourself lucky," Dean said. "My mom loves everything with any kind of history whatsoever." He rolled his eyes.

"Excuse me, I hate to interrupt," said a voice directly behind Sam. She turned and saw the tall blond man she had noticed earlier inside the Adam Gray house.

"I was wondering whether either of you happened to see a cell phone on the ground anywhere?" he asked. "I seem to have lost mine."

The man directed his question to Sam and Nell. He wasn't bad looking, but something about him made Sam feel on edge—very on edge. The tour group was talking rather loudly, which made it somewhat difficult to her him, but something about him bothered her.

"Gosh, no," Nell replied.

Sam also replied that she had not seen one but would keep her eyes open.

"Okay, thanks." The man returned to the other side of the group without giving Dean so much as a glance.

"That was weird," Sam observed. "I didn't hear him ask anyone else about his phone."

"He gave me the creeps," Nell added.

"I think I've seen him before," Dean said. "I just can't remember where."

"There *was* something familiar about him," Sam said. "He gave me the creeps too, and his voice sounded very familiar to me."

Janet summoned their attention, and soon the man was all but forgotten as Sam followed the group on to the homes originally owned by the Weston brothers, which were located side by side. Sam tried to pay close attention to Janet's lecture as she led them through the large homes. Although they were both beautiful, she could find no clues to help the search. After they had toured the last of the rooms, Janet gathered everyone back into the foyer for Q and A.

Sam stood off to one side and whispered into Nell's ear.

Dean moved closer to Sam. "What's up?"

"Nothing."

He leaned in closer. "What are you whispering about?" Dean pulled Sam and Nell back and away from earshot of the group. "All right, spill it. What are you two after?" he demanded, giving them a strange look.

"What are you talking about?" Sam answered dismissively.

"I'm not an idiot."

"Keep your voice down," Sam admonished. "We were just wondering whether this house has any secret passages."

"Why don't you go ask Janet?" Dean asked mystified.

"Because Nell already asked about the Gray house. We feel funny posing a similar question here," Sam answered. "We're just curious, you know with the Gray and Weston families being thought of as the founders of the town and the rumors that the Gray family helped the Underground Railroad. It's intriguing."

"Oh, I'll do it," he said, walking over to rejoin the group. Sam and Nell followed close behind.

Janet responded to several more questions before Dean was able to speak.

"Janet, I was wondering, since the Gray and the Weston families were reportedly so close, was there any talk that the Weston brothers were also involved in the Underground Railroad? Or perhaps, bootlegging?" he added with a chuckle.

"I love it; we have some true history buffs in the making here," Janet said, clapping her hands together. "I like the imagery, but sadly no, I have not heard any rumors to that effect."

"Also," Dean continued, "I've read that back in the 1800s people often built secret compartments to safeguard their valuables when they traveled. Do any of the homes on the tour have such features?"

"Not that we are able to show on the tour," Janet answered. "A number of the homes contain safes that are hidden from view. The homes that have these are privately owned, and the families may still use the safes, so they have asked us not to show them to the public. I'm sure you can understand their concerns."

"Absolutely, I've apparently been reading too many books," Dean said in effort to mock himself.

Another fruitless search, Sam thought.

"Thank you for the questions. You can join my tour anytime," Janet said to Dean, beaming at him.

Janet motioned the group outside and led them to the Thomas E. Dewey house. Sam saw that Janet was beaming with pride as she talked about Thomas Dewey being elected governor of New York, running for president of the United States twice, and about the apparently infamous *Dewey Defeats Truman* newspaper headline. Her voice became a distant buzz in Sam's ears. Another dead-end.

As they filed in to the Elizabeth Gray Adams house, Janet informed them that Elizabeth was the sister of Adam and Edward Gray and that her brothers had built the house for her. Sam had stopped listening again. She was frustrated that they hadn't learned anything on the tour that would help them in the search for the treasure.

"My legs are starting to ache," Nell complained.

"I know what you mean," Sam agreed, rubbing her neck. "Plus, I'm so hot I would kill for a shower."

"You little old ladies just need to make it through two more houses, and then we're free," Dean teased.

Hot and tired, both girls gave him a dirty look.

Dean seemed to get the hint and stopped talking.

Sam was happy that the final house was smaller, and the tour was less than fifteen minutes later. The group lingered outside on the sidewalk to thank Janet and to discuss their thoughts on the various homes and churches.

"Did you guys hear Janet mention that there is also a tour of some of the local businesses with historical backgrounds?" Dean asked.

"I don't want to hear the word *tour* anytime soon," Sam said rubbing her calves. "I should have worn better shoes."

Realizing that she was being unnecessarily cross with Dean,

she added, "Check back in a week or so after I've had time to recoup."

"Okay, duly noted," he replied. "When you guys are ready, let me know, and we can head over to our last stop," Dean said with a wink.

10

◇

Edward Gray's House

As excited as she was to see the Edward Gray house, Sam was tired of walking.

"We're not far," Dean said. "The house is down about two blocks and across M-52."

"That walk I can handle," Sam said. "I'm dreading the walk back to the park."

"Well, as luck would have it, you don't have to walk back," Dean responded.

"I won't?" Sam said with a confused expression.

"Yeah, I guess we could call my mom and have her pick us up," Nell offered without enthusiasm.

"What happens if your mother finds out that the official tour ended over on Oliver Street, and we crossed the *highway* on our own to look at another house?" Sam warned.

"She'll probably be livid, but my dad will understand," Nell said, clearly trying to convince herself.

"Wrong," Dean said, interrupting the girls' back-and-forth. "Actually, I parked my car over here, so we could drive back after we're done. My mom dropped me off at the park."

"Your car?" Both girls said.

"Yup, just got my license last month. I had saved up some money, so my parents let me buy a car. It's a Chevy. Nothing fancy, but it gets me where I need to go."

"That's great!" Sam exclaimed.

"Oh, *now* you like me," Dean said, pretending to be hurt.

"No, no, we're sorry," Sam replied. "It's just that I'm exhausted. I get crabby when I'm tired. Come to think of it, sometimes I'm crabby even when I'm not tired," she said a little sheepishly. "Dean, you're a life saver. Thank you."

"You're forgiven, and you're welcome. Now, are we ready to go?"

"We're ready!" Sam said in unison with Nell. The news that Dean had a car and they didn't have to walk back to the park gave Sam her second wind. She felt refreshed and rejuvenated.

"All right then," Dean said. "Okay, here's the deal. As you know, the house is now a bed-and-breakfast, so we may not be able to see all of the rooms. I'll do my best, but I can't make any promises."

"We understand," they responded.

As they approached the house, Sam realized how large it was. The pillars in front, the two-story balcony and the ornately carved entrance were amazing. It seemed to be a mix of Italian and Southern architecture, and it was easily Sam's favorite.

Sam trailed behind Dan and Nell as they ascended the large wide steps leading up to the front door. As Dean led the way inside, Sam was surprised by the somewhat small foyer area. It was small in comparison to some of the other homes. There was a large living room off to the right-hand side. Straight ahead was a spectacular wooden staircase leading to the second floor.

Sam's thoughts again turned to Fred. It was difficult not to think about him while she was walking in his family's home and talking about their past. Sam heard the tinkle of a bell as Dean closed the door. A moment later, they were met by a middle-aged woman who introduced herself as the owner.

Dean escorted Sam and Nell into the house. The owner, a

middle-aged woman named Linda, said they could have the run of the place, except for the occupied rooms.

"These are my friends, Sam and Nell," Dean added. "Thank you very much for allowing us to tour this beautiful home."

"You're quite welcome. Your mother is one of my favorite people. When she told me that you young people were taking in the local historic sites, well, I couldn't refuse. I'm sorry to say that I can't stay with you for very long. I have nearly a full house this week, and I'll need to start preparing dinner shortly."

Linda looked to be in her thirties, and had a kind but matronly face. She was of average height and a little on the chubby side. Her light-brown hair was cropped in a bob style, and it bounced as she talked. Sam noticed that Linda had a hectic look about her, as if she was always in a rush.

"We completely understand," Dean replied smoothly. "We didn't give you much notice. We greatly appreciate any time you can give us."

"Yes, thank you," Sam added. "I had an old pamphlet that indicated this house was on the tour. We were so disappointed to find out it wasn't this year. It's the most beautiful house in town if you ask me," she said in her most complimentary voice.

"You are quite welcome, and thank you very much for your compliments on the home. Yes, some years it is difficult to balance the tours with our guests."

"I can imagine," Sam said, hoping that she hadn't offended her.

"Well, let's see how much we can fit in before duty calls," Linda replied. "Let's start in the living room."

She led them through the first doorway on the right, the one Sam had noticed moments earlier. The site was truly breathtaking. The only word to describe the room was *grand*, like old movie grand. The entire room was filled with exquisitely detailed crown molding everywhere the eye could see. The windows reached almost from floor to ceiling, a striking feature since the ceiling seemed to be at least twelve feet high. Crimson draperies flowed from the top of each window and curled in luxurious pools of velvet fabric on the wooden floor.

The centerpiece of the room was clearly the marble fireplace and the larger-than-life oil painting that hung above. An over-stuffed sofa and a couple of sitting chairs were placed facing the fireplace. On the other side of the room, a pair of velvet sofas faced each other, flanked by two high-backed chairs and separated by a low wooden coffee table. The wall behind the chairs was decorated with a large painting of the house. Underneath this grouping of furniture was placed a thick woolen rug bearing the Italian style of decorating Sam had come to recognize from the tour that day. The chocolate-brown, caramel, and cream colors in the rug, the dark wood floor, and the rich red drapes made the room elegant, inviting, and relaxing all at the same time.

Linda began by pointing out various pieces of furniture. She explained that most of the pieces were not original to the home, but that all, with the exception of the kitchen, were authentic to the period in which the home was built.

"The rug is, we believe, original to the home," Linda said with air of importance. "We are thrilled that it has been so well preserved and that we are able to continue using it in our home. The painting you see over the seating area on this wall" —she motioned with her hand— "was commission by a prior owner of the home sometime in the 1900s. We think that it's a lovely representation of the structure.

"Also, we were fortunate enough to be able to obtain the painting of Edward Gray hanging over the fireplace."

As she spoke Sam, Nell, and Dean followed her gaze to the huge fireplace. The fireplace surround was made of white marble carved with beautiful Italian designs. The painting of Edward Gray was one of the largest the girls had ever seen. It portrayed a man in what must have been a Civil War uniform, staring off to the side as if he were lost in some deep thought.

His hair was dark black and cut short. His black mustache was neatly trimmed and fit his face perfectly. The man in the portrait looked serious, intense, and intelligent, yet kind. His eyes, however, looked sad somehow. Sam pictured him riding a horse off into battle.

"Edward Gray was an amazing man," Linda was saying. "By all accounts, he was brilliant, honest, loving, and generous."

She discussed his achievements in the law, many of which Sam had already heard from one source or another.

"He was also a passionate abolitionist, an advocate against slavery," Linda said. "His strong beliefs are what led him to fight in the war. He believed in freedom for all. He was wounded in battle, but he returned home to Owosso where he continued to practice law with his brother Adam for many years thereafter. They were very close. As a matter of fact, we have several photographs of Edward and Adam together. A few of the photographs came with the house. Several others were donated by, or purchased by us from, the Gray family. As you can see from the photos, Edward was very close with his brother Adam. Edward had many accomplishments, and he was held in very high esteem by all of the town's inhabitants, then as well as now."

As Linda talked, Sam's mind was running wild. Was there a clue here? Where would the *it* be? Here in this room? Or would Edward have hidden a clue in a private place like his bedroom? That's the place where Sam would keep personal items. Would they even be able to see his bedroom? The question would no doubt sound creepy coming from her, so she would just have to wait and see.

"Okay, let's move on to the study," Linda said, moving the group toward a second set of doors on the other side of the room. She turned to the right and led them down the hall and into a room located on the left side of the hallway.

In the middle of the room sat a large wooden desk. The desk was obviously old, bore elegant carving, and showed signs of many years of use. In the middle of the desk was a dark-green desk pad. In the upper right-hand corner, an ink well and pen stood ready for use. The wood was polished to a high sheen, and it looked as if it was waiting to accommodate someone important. Sam was admiring the desk and looking for a clue or hidden compartment at the same time.

Linda must have noticed Sam's interest in the desk. "I see that you like the desk, Sam. This is the actual desk used by Edward in his law practice. It used to sit in his office over on Main Street. My husband and I were thrilled when we were able to purchase this several years ago. It is our understanding that the original desk Edward used in this house was, unfortunately, destroyed. Stories dating back to when Edward lived here say that he spent many hours thinking, reading and writing here in this room. I can understand why—this room has a very calming atmosphere about it."

"It is beautiful," Sam said. "Did you happen to find any old papers in it?" Sensing that the question probably sounded odd coming from a girl her age, Sam continued on saying, "My neighbor volunteers with the historical society, and he mentioned that sometimes they find antique furniture with love letters or other old documents inside and that it's always really exciting when they do."

"Oh, yes, it would have been nice to find some of Edward's old papers, but unfortunately, the desk was empty. Empty or not, it is one of my favorite pieces in the home," Linda declared with obvious admiration.

Linda then turned her attention to the bookcases that encased the room and covered the walls from floor to ceiling. They were jam-packed with books. "Several of the books in this room date back to the 1800s," Linda informed them. "However, most of them were written much more recently. We like to keep a supply of current books on hand for our guests to read and enjoy. The old ones tend to put them to sleep."

Sam noticed that Dean seemed to be paying more attention to her than to what Linda was telling them. She started to feel a little guilty that she wasn't confiding in him. After all, he had done nothing but help them.

Linda led the way out of the study then and down the hallway. On the right side was an exquisite dining room that looked like was straight out of a Civil War movie. It was covered in the same beautiful molding that trimmed the living room and the heavy, ivory, floor-to-ceiling curtains were every bit as elegant. Two French-style doors opened to the lower level of a two-story porch. Linda led them just outside the doors and pointed out the grounds. The view was breathtaking. In light of her time restrictions, she only let them take in the sight for a moment before ushering them inside.

Sam was anxious to get back to the search, and in her haste, she tripped over Dean. Embarrassed and irritated with herself, she scowled and made a beeline for the stairs.

As they walked, Sam listen to Linda as she pointed out the kitchen, which was located behind the stairs. It was on the small side, but had apparently been updated with modern appliances. Sam very much doubted any clues would be found there, and was happy when Linda suggested that they head upstairs.

Sam was elated when Linda informed them that the one room available for them to see had been Edward's. Sam knew that Nell would be just as excited as she was to explore the room. Sam was so excited she could barely contain herself. She noticed that Dean was looking at her with a grin. Was he mocking her?

"This staircase is a really nice piece of craftsmanship," Dean commented, running his hand along the banister. "It seems so solid. Many of the homes we saw today had narrow stairs with little detail. This one looks like a lot of thought and work went into building it. I see why my mom loves this house so much."

Sam guessed that he added the last statement for Linda's benefit.

"Dean, you sound just like your mother," Linda said, blushing. "I appreciate your observations. Yes, the staircase does seem to be very well made. It is my understanding that Edward Gray himself was very involved in designing and constructing the home. If you look on the side of the stairs, you will see a number of designs carved into or affixed to the wood. For example, there are carvings of a young man and woman in period clothing, a young man in a military uniform, and the US flag, as it existed in 1865, among other things. Also, if you look underneath this step, she said touching a step a third of the way up, you will see Edward's signature. He must have signed it after it was completed."

Sam stopped to take a closer look at the signature on the stairs.

"Okay, I have to hurry us a bit," Linda said, climbing the stairs.

Nell, Dean, and Sam dutifully followed her, with Sam bringing up the rear.

"Hey, are these metal stair plates original to the house?" Nell asked. "I've never seen anything like them. They are very interesting."

"I'm sorry. I've been in such a rush it seems I'm not the best tour guide today," she said coming to a stop. "Yes, the metal risers are original to the house. They are visible in several of the old photographs we have in our possession that were taken in the house shortly after it was built. They are not very common, and we are not really certain of the purpose for using metal. As you can see, the risers each are decorated with stars and stripes. It is well known that Edward loved his country and served proudly in the army. It may be that Edward wanted the decoration and figured that metal would last longer than wood. We just don't know."

The stairs were nice, but Sam's mind was on Edward's bedroom upstairs. She could feel that they were running out of time, and Linda was droning on about the stairs. Finally, Linda resumed climbing. In her excitement, Sam lunged forward and fell up the stairs. Her hands stopped her head from striking the stairs. However, her right knee slammed into the second stair, and she suddenly felt a sharp pain in her left thigh.

"Are you okay?" Nell exclaimed, rushing back down to Sam's side.

Fearful that Linda was going to discover their true intensions, Sam took a deep breath and tried to calm down.

"Oh man, am I clumsy," Sam answered. "But yes, I'm fine. Sorry for the commotion." She rubbed her knee. "Only I can fall *up* a flight of stairs."

"Are you sure you aren't hurt?" Linda inquired.

"Honestly, I'm fine. Sorry for the interruption. Please continue." The pain in her thigh lessened as she stood up, but she still felt like she had been stabbed. She climbed the stairs carefully this time, holding on to the railing the entire time.

At the top of the stairs, Linda showed them a small sitting area with a small fireplace and four chairs. "This seating area is also original to the house. It is a nice, cozy area to talk, read, or just relax. It is one of my favorite spots in the home. Plus, it is directly over the dining room and the doors here lead out to the upper level of the porch. On a nice summer day with a breeze blowing, I could stay out there for hours," she said.

Finally, Linda brought them to the end of the hallway and announced that they were now at the bedroom used by Edward Gray when he'd lived in the house. As Linda was describing the furniture, Sam looked around the room. In addition to the bed and two dressers, a fireplace also graced the room on the wall opposite of the bed. Sam wanted a chance to poke around a little. She just wasn't sure how that was going to happen.

"Okay," Linda said. "Well, then, I'm sorry to say that I have to bring our tour to an end here. I have to get down to the kitchen and get dinner started or my guests will be eating at midnight." The girls knew it was an obvious exaggeration.

Sam was in a panic. She couldn't leave, not yet. She looked over at Nell in time to see her nudge Dean. He seemed a little surprised, but quickly caught himself.

"Linda, my mother was right when she said that this house is one of the town's most precious gems. It really is one of a kind. I can't thank you enough for your time today. And contrary to your protests, you are an excellent tour guide."

"Oh, now Dean, you're going to make me blush again," Linda said, actually turning a little pink in the cheeks. "I was more than happy to help, I'm just sorry that I don't have more time." She made her way to the door.

"I wouldn't dream of imposing on you for a moment longer," Dean responded. "But I wonder, would it be asking too much for us to spend a few more minutes here in this room? We won't be any trouble, I promise, and we will show ourselves out."

"Well, I ... I ... I ...," Linda stuttered. Dean, Nell, and Sam all had their eyes glued on her, trying to look as innocent as possible and silently begging her to grant them additional time.

"Oh, sure. You take your time and enjoy the house. Feel free to take a look at the grounds from the porch as well, just make sure not to go into any of the other bedrooms since I have guests there. You kids are certainly good for my ego. It makes me so happy to see people appreciating this house. I've really got to run now. So nice to meet all of you."

"Same here," Sam replied.

"Me too," Nell said.

Dean said, "Thank you again."

As soon as she was out the door and safely down the hallway, Dean turned around to face Sam. "All right, what's going on here? Why did you guys really want to come here?"

"What are you talking about?" Sam snapped. "You spent the entire day with us touring historic homes."

"That's not why you wanted to come here."

"Why else would we want to come here? You said it yourself: your own mother loves this house."

"I may have embellished a little again," Dean confessed. "I know you guys were up to something, and I'm trying to help. However, it's difficult when you keep me in the dark. Remember who was with you when you found the star."

"Shhhh!" Sam hissed.

"Well, that just confirmed any doubts I might have had that you are up to something. Are you trying to find a connection between the star and this house?"

"You're crazy," Sam retorted.

"Oh, I'm crazy?" Dean's voice was rising now. "You nearly kill yourself trying to get upstairs, and once we get here, your face gets all flushed. You are obviously all wound up about something. You're on the hunt for something. What is it?"

"I'm a little winded from all of our walking and climbing today, that's all. Apparently, I'm a little out of shape. Plus, my leg is still throbbing from my fall."

"Either you two come clean with me right now, or we're leaving," Dean demanded. "I'm not kidding."

Sam and Nell stood mute.

"Fine, I'm going downstairs to tell Linda that I'm leaving. I suspect that if she finds the two of you still here later, she is going to wondering what is going on, but I'll leave you to sort that out." He turned and walked out the door.

"Wait!" Sam called as quietly as possible. "Come back."

Dean pivoted on the spot and returned to the room as quickly as he had left. The look on his face had softened. "Honestly, guys, you can trust me," he said in earnest.

"Okay, we think that this house may have a secret compartment like the one in the bell tower," Sam admitted.

"Why would you think that?" Dean questioned.

Sam took a deep breath. She knew that Nell wanted to tell Dean the whole story, and now seemed to be as good a time as any. "So, Dean, did you hear about the murder that happened off of M-52?" Sam asked.

"Um, yeah, everyone has," he responded.

"Well, we sort of witnessed it." Dean appeared to be dumbfounded as Sam told him about what Fred said before he died and the clues they had found so far.

"You can understand why we have to do this, right?" Sam asked.

Dean was clearly unnerved. "Wow. God. No wonder you guys didn't want to talk about it. I can't believe you had to see something so like that. Thank you for trusting me enough to tell me. It means a lot."

"Actually, it kind of feels good to be able to share it with someone our own age," Sam admitted.

"Yeah," Nell agreed. "My mother just keeps looking at me as if she is trying to decide whether I need some sort of counseling. I'm glad we told you."

"But, Dean, we don't really want people to know," Sam cautioned. "I mean, the killer is still out there somewhere."

"I understand completely," he said reassuringly. "I won't say a word. But I want to help." What now?"

Sam was relieved to have confided in Dean. He was definitely growing on her. Man, he was very cute.

"Look," Sam replied. "Linda said that the only three items in this room that were here when Edward owned the house are the bed, the fireplace, and the closet. I think we need to go over them with a fine-tooth comb and see if we can find any clue or a compartment of any kind. Dean, check out the bed. See if you notice anything unusual." She quickly reminded them of how she had discovered the secret compartment in the bell tower. "Run your hands over everything so you can feel any variations that might reveal a hiding spot."

"Nell, do you want to take the fireplace or the closet?"

"Um, closet."

"I'll take the fireplace," Sam stated.

The three of them quickly got to work. Each of them poked and prodded their respective targets. The room echoed softly with the sound of tapping as each of them tried to identify any hidden compartment. The search revealed no secrets.

Sam was dejected. "Come on. Let's get out of her," she said.

Nell gasped, "Sam, you're bleeding!"

"What? Where?"

"There, on your left leg," Nell responded pointing.

Sam looked down and saw a large dark spot on her shorts. Her shorts were dark, masking the blood. Except for the bit of blood trickling underneath, it looked like she had spilled something on herself. "That's weird," Sam said. She touched her hand to the spot and felt a bulge just above the stain. "Oh, I must have done it when I fell on the stairs."

"How on earth did you do that?" Dean asked in shock.

Sam reached into her pocket and pulled out the metal star. She opened her hand to show the star to Dean and Nell. "I think that *this* jabbed into my leg when I fell. I had no idea that I was packing a weapon," she said, trying to lighten the mood. "I'm fine, Nell. I'm sure it looks worse than it is. Come on. Let's go."

Sam descended the stairs behind Dean, taking care to watch where she was going. However, her mind was somewhere else. Mindlessly, she turned the star over and over in her hand.

Dean reached the bottom of the stairs first. Sam followed.

"Hey, Sam, that star looks like the ones on this staircase," Dean observed in a hushed tone.

"Oh my God, you're right, it does," Sam said.

150

Nell looked over her shoulder. "Actually, it looks *exactly* like the stars on the risers."

Another ridiculous idea was forming in Sam's mind. "Nell, do you mind going over and standing by the kitchen door in case Linda comes out? I want to look at something."

"No problem."

Dean stood at the end of the stairs, his arms resting on the banister. "What are you thinking Sam?"

"I'm thinking that it's not a coincidence that the star we found is an exact match for the stars running along this staircase."

She walked over to the foot of the stairs and looked up. Each riser looked the same; a metal plate imprinted with stars the same size, shape, and color as the one sitting in her hand. Puzzled, she walked back over to the side of the stairs. She paid close attention to the various designs adorning the side. Gently, but firmly, she tried to manipulate the designs that protruded from the wood. Everything seemed firmly in place.

Finally, she turned her attention to the flag design carved into the side of the staircase level with the third stair.

She noticed for the first time that on the side of each step was a metal star. Each star was also the exact size, shape, and color as the one in her hand. She ran her eyes up and down the stair case. The third step from the bottom was missing its star. There was a star-shaped hole where the star should be.

Sam was suddenly acutely aware of noises coming from the kitchen. She could hear Linda talking with someone and the sound of pots and pans clanging on the stove. The door to the kitchen had frosted glass on the top half. Sam stopped breathing for a moment when she saw Linda heading for the door. She looked at Nell in desperation. Nell swung around to face the door clearly prepared to try and block Linda from observing their activities. Luckily, they saw Linda reach into a cupboard and then disappear deeper into the kitchen.

Sam turned her attention back to the stairs. She could feel sweat on her upper lip, and her hands were trembling. She wiped off her lip, crouched down, and peered into the hole where the missing star should be. She closed her eyes for a moment to calm her nerves. She held the star up to the hole. It looked like a perfect match. Slowly she pressed it into the hole. It fit perfectly. Nothing happened.

"Well?" Dean asked.

"Nothing. I thought I might have been on to something," Sam whispered.

He leaned around the banister to look at her. She just pointed to the star she had inserted.

"It fits perfectly," he said. "Here." He drove the star into the hole with his thumb.

Clank.

11

◇

The Conductor's Path

Sam stiffened at the sound she'd just heard. It was metal on metal, almost like a spring lock had been released.

"What was that?" Nell said anxiously.

"Guys, get over here," Dean said, motioning them to come over to the front of the stairs.

Sam and Nell joined him at the foot of the stairs. To Sam's utter shock, she saw that the riser three steps up had opened to reveal a hidden compartment. Sam looked around to make sure no one was watching. Certain that they were alone, she reached into the compartment. Inside, was a small, rectangular metal box. After she had removed the box, she inspected the area. The compartment did not come out, and there were no other markings or clues on or around the area.

Suddenly, they heard the front door open. A couple entered, laughing and talking. Sam kicked the compartment shut with her foot. The couple must have been guests, because they merely smiled at Sam, Nell, and Dean and proceeded up the stairs. Sam's heart was pounding so hard she felt like she was going to pass out. She wanted to open the box and see what was inside, but she couldn't risk Linda finding out and claiming the box for herself.

Before anyone could say a word, the kitchen door opened, and Linda walked out. "Oh, you guys are still here?"

"We're so sorry," Dean said, walking toward Linda. "We're just leaving. Sam was feeling a little woozy after her fall, so we got a little air on the porch as you suggested. Sorry to startle you. Thank you again for your hospitality." Dean nearly shoved Sam out the front door, waving and smiling at Janet.

"What are you doing?" Sam demanded. "I left the star back there. What if we need it again?"

"Well, lucky for us that I grabbed it on the way out," he said, holding it up and handing it to Sam.

"How did you get it out? It looked really wedged in there," Sam asked once they were outside.

"Pried it out with my car key. Now let's get out of here."

"Dean, I think you're starting to grow on me," Sam said in effort to say she was sorry. She instantly felt sorry for saying it since it was so close to her true feelings.

"To hell with that. Dean, you were our hero today!" Nell proclaimed. She lowered her voice. "But come on. Let's get in your car so we can open the box."

The three of them walked side by side down the stairs, across the sidewalk, and over to where Dean's car was parked. They had to force themselves to keep a normal pace and not run like children. He opened the door for the girls and circled around to the driver's side. Everyone piled in the front seat.

Finally alone, Sam pulled out the metal box. It was small, but sturdy. Her hands trembled, and her initial efforts to open the box were unsuccessful.

"Here, let me try," Dean suggested. "Hmm, it's really stuck." He used one of the keys from his key ring and gently forced the top open. "Here you go," he said, handing it back to Sam.

Inside was a piece of paper folded in quarters. It looked old and delicate, much like the first clue. Gingerly, Sam opened the paper and held it so they all could read.

The conductor's path was clear
A walk in his footsteps
will lead you there
That which was hidden was
done with pure heart
So any seeker must so start

They sat in the car, dumbfounded. Nell was the first one to speak. "Another clue that gives us more questions than answers," she commented. "One thing is clear, though; this note was written by Edward Gray. This is the same handwriting as his name on the stairs."

"Are you sure?" Sam asked.

"Pretty sure. The signature on the stairs had the same nearly perfect penmanship as this note. It's formal, manly, and neat, not flowery like a girl would write."

"Well, you haven't paid much attention to my terrible handwriting then," Sam said with a laugh.

"Yeah, you know, I think Nell is right," Dean chimed in. "It looks like a perfect match."

"Okay, so Edward wrote the note," Sam said. "What was he trying to tell us?"

"The note refers to the conductor," Dean noted. "That obviously means a train conductor, right?"

"I would assume so," Sam agreed.

"Dean, did you ever hear anything about Edward Gray being a train conductor?" Nell asked.

"Nope, but I've never really asked anyone."

"I think we need to do a bit more research on Edward Gray," Nell proposed.

"Good idea. We should fire up your computer tonight," Sam agreed.

"I wonder what the part about the pure heart is all about," Nell added.

"Me too, it's a little weird," Sam noted.

"This whole thing is a little weird," Dean added.

"Hey, you asked to tag along," Sam sniped.

"I know. I know," he replied. "Weird is better than boring."

"Let's just try to identify the *conductor* first, then we can worry about the pure heart," Sam suggested.

"Agreed," said Nell and Dean at the same time.

"Man, look at the time!" Nell exclaimed, pointing to the clock on the dashboard. "I'd better call my mom before she sends out a search party. Dean, can you still drive us back to the park?"

"No problem," he answered, starting the car and putting it into gear.

"Okay, everyone quiet," Nell instructed sternly. "If my mother finds out I'm in a car with a *strange* boy, I won't see the light of day for weeks."

Dean and Sam did as they were told while Nell called. As expected, Nell apologized several times before confirming her mother's agreement to pick them up.

"How mad was she?" Sam asked.

"Slightly more miffed than usual. It is after five. I'm lucky that she's not waiting at the park now. We need to get there before she does."

"I'll have you guys there sitting outside on a bench before she pulls up, I promise. We're only a few blocks away," Dean reassured them.

They reached the park a few short minutes later, and the girls had their door open before the car had come to a complete stop.

Nell nearly pushed Sam out of the car. When everyone was out of the car and standing on the grass, Nell's face finally relaxed, and she let out a deep sigh.

"Hey, let's go wait for your mom over on that bench," Sam suggested. The three of them made their wait over to the bench where they had met before the tour. Once they were seated, the tension seemed to lift.

"Thanks for giving us a lift," said Nell. "And for your help today."

"Yeah, thanks," Sam agreed.

"You're welcome. It's nice to know I bring something to the table," he said and grinned. "Maybe I'm not quite the third wheel you thought."

"We never thought that," Nell objected.

Dean burst into laughter. "I was just joking, although you guys did protest a little loudly. Maybe I hit a nerve."

"Please understand that this whole thing is just as strange to us as it is to you, and we just hadn't intended to trust anyone with our information," Sam explained.

"I understand, and I'm not offended," Dean responded. "Do you trust me now?"

"Absolutely," the Nell immediately answered.

"Yeah," Sam agreed.

"All right, then, that's all I need to know."

"Hey," he said, gently changing the subject, "Nell's mom will be here any second. Before she does, I was wondering what your plans were for Curwood Festival and whether you might want to meet up at some point and tackle the food, rides, and games together."

"That sounds like fun," Nell said after getting the silent okay from Sam. "My parents usually have us attend some of the family events on Thursday, but we should be on our own Friday and Saturday. Let me check with them, and we'll call you later."

"Yeah, that sounds fun," Sam agreed. She suddenly liked the idea of having him around.

"Great, thanks," Dean responded with genuine excitement.

"That's weird," Sam said. "Don't look now, but that guy from the tour today who asked if we found his phone, I think he followed us from the Edward Gray house. He just parked his car down the street."

"Are you sure?" Nell said with concern.

"I'm certain now," Sam replied. "I remember the car. It's a black Yukon, like my uncle's."

"Why would he be following us?" Dean wondered out loud.

"I don't know. But I swear that I've seen that car several times recently. Maybe it's just a coincidence. Maybe I'm imagining things. It's been a long, hot, strange day," Sam answered.

A clear and distinct car horn jolted the girls to their feet. "That's my mom," Nell uttered, instantly turning to wave in the direction of the honking. "See you later, Dean."

"Bye," Sam added, quickly following after Nell.

12

◇

Curwood Festival

They were barely inside Aunt Sue's car when the assault of questions began. First and foremost, Nell's mother wanted to know who the *strange* boy was with whom they'd been sitting.

As Nell explained that Dean's mother was the director of the library, Sam thought about how ridiculous it was that their mothers constantly grilled them. It had been like that for years. They always seemed to be trying to catch Sam and Nell doing something wrong. Up until they'd seen Fred killed, the most exciting thing they'd done was cross the highway. Sam tuned out as her aunt continued the inquisition.

At dinner, the girls learned that Nell's parents did, in fact, have plans for them on the next day. They were apparently going, along with Sam's parents, to the music festival and arts and crafts exhibition. Sam found the festival music, which was generally played by local performers, to be loud and a little too country for her taste. Unfortunately, it was the price you paid for enjoying the rest of Curwood days.

Although tomorrow was unlikely to be much fun, Nell had confirmed that the girls would be allowed to spend Friday and Saturday enjoying the festival on their own. Nell and Sam had each received a small amount of funds from their parents to use during the event. Nell's dad had given her a little extra, unbeknownst to her mother. The girls had each been admonished by their respective parents that when the money was gone, it was gone and not to ask for more. They needn't have bothered. Sam's parent in particular were rather frugal, and she knew better than to ask for more. Luckily, Sam had saved up some of money and was pleased with her haul.

That night, they spent several hours researching Edward Gray, including whether he had been a train conductor. Having Nell's computer and the high-speed internet made researching much faster, and more enjoyable than trudging to the library. Unfortunately, the search was a bust. No connection with Edward Gray, any railroad, or conductors in Owosso's history.

Later that night, Nell called Dean, and everyone agreed to meet Friday afternoon at 1:00 p.m. near the Ferris wheel. Nell also filled Dean in on their failed research efforts, and Dean agreed to see if he could find out any information on the subject from his mother.

Thursday was uneventful. As Sam had expected, the street music was terrible, well, at least very mediocre. Sam longed for something with a little more linguistic complexity. Her taste in music gravitated toward what she understood was called alternative. Her favorite band was REM, a band she could only hear by having the guy at the music store special order for her. She wished that the festival would play any music that didn't make her want to pull her ears off.

When they finally were able to pry the parents away from the music, the mothers headed straight for the arts and crafts. That part may have been worse. Far too many things made out of yarn.

Finally, Friday arrived. Sam took a shower and ready to go at lightning speed. Shortly before noon, Nell's mother dropped them off on Washington Street a few blocks away from the carnival rides and games. As usual, the streets were closed in the vicinity of the rides, which meant walking for everyone. The upside was that parents were forced to part with their kids far away from the actual festivities. Sam smirked with happiness, thinking how it was nearly impossible for her parents to monitor her. That was the one upside to not having her own cell phone. With a happy wave, the girls left Aunt Sue's car and made a beeline for the rides.

Given Sam's historically weak stomach, they had agreed to try out several rides *before* eating lunch. Better to be safe than humiliated Sam thought. They decided to ride the Roundabout ride first. Sam had recently conquered this ride, so the girls thought that it would be a good way to kick things off.

They buckled into the safety harnesses, and the ride began spinning and rising a few moments later. For the first few seconds of the ride, Sam had knots in her stomach. Luckily, they soon passed as she enjoyed the speed of the ride and the wind in her hair.

They next tackled the "salt-and-pepper-shaker" ride. Sam's stomach felt queasy, and for a moment, she worried that she was going to throw up. Thank god, Dean wasn't there to see her condition. As they got off the ride, Sam felt wobbly but pulled herself together when she saw Dean. She took several deep breaths to clear her head after the rides, happy as ever that she hadn't puked. She flashed a big, proud smile at Nell. Then she saw Dean emerge from the crowd.

"Hey, guys!" he said.

"Hi," they both responded waving.

"Was that you in the salt-and-pepper ride?"

"It was," said Nell proudly.

"Well done," he proclaimed. "I've only ridden it once, and I felt like I was going to puke."

"Really?" Sam said. "I didn't think it was that bad."

Nell stifled a giggle.

"Okay, what do you guys want to do?" Dean asked.

Wanting to give her stomach a few moments to settle down,

Sam suggested that they try a few games. Dean was excited to try his hand at the basketball free-throw booth, so they started there first. He was rather good. Despite the obvious challenges posed by the slanted hoop and small rim, Dean managed to win a good-sized stuffed animal. He handed the cute, stuffed green turtle to the girls.

After that, they each tried their hand at water-gun racing, dart throwing, ring tossing, and—Sam's favorite—the duck game. She realized that there was no skill or challenge involved with the last game, but she just couldn't resist the little yellow ducks floating around in the circle. She played it every year without fail.

Feeling stronger, Sam suggested that they grab lunch. They loaded up on hot dogs, fries, and sodas and miraculously found an empty bench on the perimeter of the action. They sat, ate, and discussed their luck with the games so far. When they finished with their lunch, the girls eyed the stand that sold elephant ears and funnel cakes. To their surprise and delight, Dean fetched several of the tasty treats, and everyone ate until they were stuffed.

"Thank goodness this carnival only comes once a year," Sam moaned. "I can barely move I'm so full."

"Ugh! Me too," Nell groaned. "I ate way too much."

"You girls certainly can handle your food," Dean said with admiration.

"I'm choosing to take that as a compliment," Sam said.

"You should," Dean responded.

After the food was gone, conversation turned to the latest clue. In a hushed tone, Dean informed the girls that he had spoken with his mother but had been unable to find a link between Edward Gray and a train conductor. They went over the wording of the clue again, but none of them could offer a convincing explanation that would lead the way to the next step in their search to unravel the clues Fred led them to.

Finally, they gave up and agreed to put it out of their minds for the time being and just enjoy themselves. They rode the Ferris wheel and a few of the tamer rides, then they played a few more games. Dean won another stuffed animal, a large white bear, and smiled and handed it directly to Sam. She gleefully accepted it.

As Dean stopped to say hello to someone, Nell jabbed her in the ribs, whispering, "I told you he likes you. Cute couple alert." She had an annoying twinkle in her eye, clearly happy that Sam had a potential love interest.

"Zip it," Sam said.

"Hey, by any chance are you girls up for the old-fashioned photo booth? It might be fun," Dean proposed as he turned back to the girls.

"It's one of our favorite things about the festival. I love looking at the pictures they create," said Sam. "I'm in."

"Me too," Nell agreed.

They left the heart of the carnival and made their way one block over to the antique photo booth. It took some time to pick out just the right costumes. Dean had to find just the right hat and gun to look menacing, and Sam and Nell wanted to find hats that didn't make them look ridiculous. When they were all satisfied with their outfits, the photographer placed them in front of some period appropriate props and started clicking. Dean was having fun with his toy gun, and the girls were busy brandishing theirs, much to Dean's dismay.

"I'm supposed to have the gun, so it looks like I'm protecting you," he complained.

"Well maybe we're protecting you," Sam teased him.

Dean groaned and rolled his eyes.

When their session came to an end, they were all a little disappointed. As they waited for the pictures to develop, they talked about their plans for the next day. They agreed to meet at noon at the same place.

A short time later, the photographer handed them their photos.

"These are awesome!" Dean exclaimed.

"They are pretty funny," Sam agreed.

"You look great," Nell said to Dean and Sam.

"So do you," they said.

Happy but tired, they were ready to head home.

"I can give you guys a ride home if you want," Dean offered. "My mom scored me a parking spot not too far from here."

"Let me just call my mom and make sure it's okay," Nell said. "Such a surprise could just send her over the edge."

She called her mother, and after several awkward minutes of Nell explaining yet again who Dean was, she apparently got the okay to ride home with him.

"Everything is a big drama with my mother," Nell grumbled after she ended the call. "But I got the okay. I heard my dad in the background tell her to let me. Lead the way."

They followed Dean to his car and sank into the front seat, exhausted.

"Whew! All this play is really tiring," Sam said and laughed.

"We better get a good rest tonight if we hope to survive tomorrow," said Nell, doing her best impression of her mother.

"Do you want me to pick you guys up tomorrow?" Dean offered.

"Let's not tempt my mother's sanity," Nell said with a smile. "I'll have my dad drop us off."

A few minutes later, Dean pulled into Nell's driveway. Sam and Nell thanked him again for the ride and got out of the car. Sam could see Aunt Sue standing in the window, watching.

Dean waved goodbye, backed out of the driveway, and slowly drove away. Sam was happy that Dean was a responsible driver. He didn't give Aunt Sue anything to complain about.

She was wrong. They were no sooner inside Nell's house when the barrage of questions commenced. Nell's mother again asked about Dean, who he was, how they had met him, and so on. Next, Aunt Sue turned her attention to his car.

"That car looks awfully fast," she said sourly.

Sam wasn't sure how her aunt could make that deduction, but she wasn't about to ask.

"Well, he doesn't drive fast," Sam interjected in her sweetest voice. She felt sorry that Nell had to deal with her mother's perpetual negativity. "And look at the cute stuffed animals he won for us!"

Sam used the stuffed bear she was holding and pretended to chase Nell down the hallway to the bedroom. She let the stuff animal land on the floor and flung herself on top of it like a chair.

"Dean is a lot of fun to be around," Sam admitted.

"I agree," Nell responded. "He's super nice, thoughtful, funny, and a total doll."

"Hmm, it sounds like you've got quite the crush on him," Sam teased.

"I like him but not that way. Besides, he's obviously got a thing for you."

"You're crazy," Sam said, chucking one of the stuffed animals Dean had won at her.

"We'll see," said Nell. "If you let yourself, I know you'll like him too."

Sam didn't reply, but she knew that Nell was right. She liked Dean more than she cared to admit.

At dinner, while Nell recited their day's activities for Nell's parents, Sam observed her aunt. While Aunt Sue seemed to scrutinize every comment, Uncle Hank was all smiles, and bent over with laughter as they described their experience on the rides and the photo shoot. Nell's dad thought the pictures were hysterical, while her mother noted the dresses had low necklines and was uncomfortable with the guns.

Back in Nell's room after dinner, Sam turned her attention to the latest clue. She still couldn't seem to make heads or tails out of it.

"How can we possibly figure out who the conductor is?" Sam groaned. "Plus, how could we ever find his path? I mean, wouldn't his path be the railroad tracks? It would take us years to search every inch of track."

Nell agreed that it was a daunting task. Then she reminded Sam about how much her brothers loved trains and attended the Owosso train festival every year.

Nell checked her computer and informed Sam that the station was located on Washington Street south of Main Street.

"Let's head over there tomorrow and poke around a little," Sam suggested. "It's actually not far from the rides."

At that moment, there was a knock on the door. Nell hit the power button on her computer and faced the door. The door opened, and Nell's father poked his head in.

"Your mother wanted me to tell you that it's getting late and it's time for you guys to turn in," he said looking somewhat embarrassed.

"Thanks, Dad. We were just saying the same thing. Good night."

Sam girls slept soundly that night. No nightmares, which was nice. She woke a little later than intended and had to scramble to get showered and dressed before they left. Nell's father was chipper as usual, and he chatted with them all the way into town. Sam was proud of Nell when she heard her get permission from him to ride home with Dean. He dropped them off as close to the rides as possible, and they waved goodbye and thanked him for the ride.

They found Dean standing in the same spot as the day before. They pulled him over toward the benches and quietly filled him in on their plan to visit the station.

"That's a great idea. I've been there before so I know the way. Do you want to head over their now?"

"Sure," the girls agreed.

"Let's grab some food to eat on the way," Dean suggested.

They purchased an assortment of cotton candy, caramel apples, popcorn, and sodas. As they walked, they discussed strategy.

"Okay, I'll take the lead with whoever is working at the station," Dean offered. "I'll find out whether Edward Gray was a conductor and whether his family had any connection with the railway. I think it will seem less odd coming from me since I'm a boy. No offense."

"None taken," Sam replied. "Since we don't speak train, you've got the job."

"Nell and I will look around the station for any clues," Sam said.

"Looks like you are going to have your work cut out for you," Dean stated. "Look at that. I'd forgotten how big it was."

Sam looked up and saw the station looming ahead. The few photographs they had found on the internet did not do it justice. It was huge for a town of this size. From Sam's estimation, it was the size of three Adam Gray mansions put together. It even had what looked like turrets in several spots.

"Oh, great. Why can't anything be easy?" Sam complained. "Nell, it looks like we will need to divide and conquer like we did with Curwood Castle."

"You were investigating the castle?" Dean said with surprise.

"Don't ask. We didn't find anything," Sam said, closing the discussion. "Dean, can you check out the inside for any clues?"

"Sure thing. Let's meet back here when we're done," he said, climbing the steps to the station entrance.

"Okay, good luck," they each whispered as they split up.

Desperately hoping to find a clue, Sam was determined to inspect every minute detail of the station. She slowly made her way around the building, being careful to take in every detail. It was rather tall, and the roof cast a large shadow. The cover felt good after walking in the blazing sun, but it made inspecting the grounds slightly more difficult.

Sam was trying to survey the premises without looking as if

she were bent in half staring at the ground. She would have preferred to hurry up and get out of there, but the station was so large she had to move at a snail's pace in order to take in everything. Adding to her stress was the fact that she felt like she was wearing a sign that read "Trying to find a hidden treasure." Sam felt incredibly self-conscious. She acted as casual as she could and hoped that it was enough.

She past the midway point of the station and saw Nell standing ten feet away, talking to a portly, balding, middle-aged man. She quickened her pace to join her cousin. As she approached, she heard Nell explain that they were here with a friend who loved trains. She looked up, saw Sam, and smiled with relief.

"This is my cousin Sam," Nell said, pointing in Sam's direction.

"Hi there, nice to meet you. My name's Bob," he said as he chewed on a toothpick. "I was just wondering what brought your cousin Nell out here. Usually it's just a bunch of us old-timers. I'm here checking out the trains myself, lovely specimens. They always bring in a few extra ones during the Curwood Days."

"I was telling Bob that we're more into architecture than trains, so we were enjoying this beautiful station," Nell summarized.

"Yeah, we thought we'd give our friend some time to talk train talk or whatever," Sam added. "We didn't want to rush him."

"Very kind of you two. Oh, there's my buddy. Well, I'd better hustle. Nice to meet you both."

"Same here," they called back.

When the man was out of earshot, Sam began firing questions at Nell. "What was his deal? Where did he come from?"

"I have no idea!" Nell said exasperated. "He showed up and then started following me. I thought that if I kept walking, he'd leave, but it didn't work. He seemed nice enough, but I was so happy to see you."

"Nothing is ever easy," they said in unison. They finished checking the remaining portion of the building and then slowly made their way back to the front of the station. Sam looked at her watch. Dean had been inside for nearly thirty minutes.

"I know we agreed to meet back here, but should we go inside and see how he is doing?" Nell asked.

"I think we should," Sam replied.

They opened the heavy front doors and stepped inside. The interior was open and spacious. Sam looked around and spotted Dean standing at the opposite end of the building, talking to a tall middle-aged man. They walked toward him slowly, trying to catch his eye. He didn't notice them until they were nearly on top of him. At that point, he smiled and motioned toward the man to introduce Nell and Sam.

"Wayne, these are my friends, Sam and Nell."

"Howdy, girls, nice to meet you."

"Nice to meet you too," they replied.

"Wayne here was nice enough to take the time to show me around the station and tell me the history of this place. It certainly has an interesting past. It's nice to hear that this station still gets some use."

"Yup, this place is mostly used for historical tours and train shows, but it is still an operating rail station. We are quite proud of it," Wayne said. "Well, Dean, any other questions?"

"Nope, you were a great tour guide," Dean responded. "I can't thank you enough for your time."

"Anytime. I guess I'd better get back to the front desk. Nice meeting you all. Enjoy the festival," he said as he walked away.

"Well?" Sam said. "What did you find out?"

"No connection that he knows of between any member of the Gray family and the station or the railway. Not so much as a donation as far as he is aware."

"What about the building? Have you had the chance to look around?" Nell inquired.

"He was quite the long talker, so I had a lot of time to look, point and ask questions," Dean answered. "I didn't see so much as random graffiti. I even asked him if there were any historical markers in or around the station. He told me that the only marker is the sign near the front steps. I looked at in on the way in. It's just your standard standing sign on a small metal post. Nothing unusual there."

Sam looked around the space. There was so much to take in. "What about over there?" she said, pointing to a wall near the front of the entrance.

"Looked and nothing," Dean responded.

"And over there?" she asked.

"Ditto."

"Did you ask about the building from an architectural perspective?" Nell asked.

"I did, and I still came up with nothing."

"Honest, I swear I was thorough," Dean assured them. "That guy told me more than I ever wanted to know, and I still asked him questions. I don't think there's anything here."

"Is there anyone else we could talk to?" Sam pressed.

"Probably, but Wayne has worked here for nearly twenty years, and his father worked here before him. I hate to say it, but I don't think this place holds the answers we are looking for."

"Fine, it was a long shot anyway," Sam said, relenting.

"Let's head back to the carnival and drown our sorrows in some ice cream," Dean proposed.

"That sounds fantastic," Nell responded.

Sam just nodded, too disappointed to speak.

As they were about to exit the front doors, Wayne called out another goodbye to them. All three of them smiled and waved. They picked up their pace to ensure a clean getaway. Sam was the first one out of the door. She was looking at the ground, and she bumped into someone. Looking up to apologize, she saw the creepy tall, lanky man with blond hair from the home tour.

"I'm sorry," she said to the man.

"Don't worry about it," he replied.

How do I know that voice? Sam thought.

"We seem to have the same interests," Dean said to the man.

"Pardon?"

"I remember seeing you at the home tour the other day," Dean observed.

"Oh, er, yes, that's right. Nice to see you again," he said acting a little uncomfortable.

"Well, we'd better be off," Dean said. "It's not a full day unless these girls ride the Ferris wheel a minimum of five times."

Sam was initially irritated at the jab, and she turned away to start the walk back to the carnival. What she heard next made the hair on the back of her neck stand up straight. It was a laugh, coming from the man she had just bumped into. It was the *exact* same laugh she had heard in the woods that night.

Before she could think, she realized that she had pivoted on the spot and was now staring at the stranger. The same stranger whose voice, she was sure, had been in the woods that night. The stranger who had been on the home tour, followed them back to the park, and was now here. Staring at him, she also realized that he was the same man that she had nearly collided with that day outside the bowling alley after she had located the first clue.

"You!" Sam said, choking on the words.

Dean and Nell looked at her like she was possessed.

"Sam? What is it?" asked Nell. Before Sam could respond, Nell had obviously figured it out. Her mouth dropped open, and the color instantly drained from her face.

"What am I missing?" Dean said with a worried look on his face.

The man was now leering at the girls, his lip turned up at the corner in what looked like a snarl.

"The woods," Nell whispered.

Dean's eyes widened in shock.

The man moved his hand toward his belt, and they saw a knife strapped to his belt.

Sam looked around. The grounds were empty but for the four of them. Sam looked at her watch. It was two o'clock and the parade had started. She could hear band music emanating from Main Street. Everyone was at the parade. She looked at the station door, and saw that the man was blocking the entrance. She felt like screaming, but she knew no one would hear them.

"Run!" Sam suddenly ordered.

Sam sprinted off the front steps as if catapulted by a giant slingshot, and launched herself onto the grass below. She heard Nell and Dean behind her, and they all started running toward the parade route.

13

◇

The Chase

The stranger snarled like a tiger and lunged toward them.

"You can run, but you can't hide," the stranger called.

The grass turned into gravel, and Sam, Nell, and Dean struggled to maintain their balance as they bolted for the road. Their shoes slid in the loose stones, and dirt was flying everywhere. Sam could hear the stranger behind them, huffing and puffing. She knew he was close behind, but she didn't dare look back for fear of losing speed. He was shouting something, but she couldn't hear the words. She heard a yell and then a thud. She chanced a look back and saw that he had tripped and fallen in the gravel. She was thankful for the extra distance now between them.

Although she was running with all of her might, it seemed as if she was moving in slow motion. Finally, her feet made contact with the road and the hard surface enabled her legs to propel her faster. It felt like they were running through a ghost town. They just needed to make it to the parade. Running long distances had never been a favorite past time for Sam. Now she could feel her chest and throat burning. It felt like her insides were on fire.

She recalled that Nell had run track last year, and she envied her for the training which hopefully was making this experience easier for her. Main Street was still a block away, and Sam didn't know how she was going to make it. She was afraid that the stranger would close in on them, and she was terrified as she pictured what he might do if he caught up to them.

Finally, the people lined up for the parade were just up ahead. Main Street was lined with crowds of people yelling and cheering. She could see parade floats rolling by, and the high school band was marching in front of them. Sam looked back, hoping to see that the stranger had given up. She couldn't believe her eyes when she saw that he was still coming at them full steam. His face was beet red, and his eyes where shiny and bloodshot. The look on his face was deadly.

Sam saw Nell and Dean slowing down.

Without a second thought, Sam grabbed Nell and pulled her through the crowd and directly into the parade route. Dean followed suit. They caught the tail end of the band, and Sam had to swerve to miss the kid holding the tuba. There were shouts of confusion and laugher coming from the onlookers. Sam didn't stop. She pulled them through the crowd on the opposite side of the street where she ran headfirst into Officer Mike.

"Oomph!" All the air was knocked out of her as Sam hit Mike and crumbled to the ground. Nell and Dean tripped over Sam and ended up on the ground next to her. Mike looked at them with a mixture of surprise and confusion.

"What the?" Mike began as he lifted Sam to her feet.

"Mike, you've got to help us! He's after us," said Sam, gasping for breath.

"He's got a knife, and he was chasing us," Nell said, coming to her feet but doubled over in effort to catch her breath.

"I think that guy was trying to kill us!" Dean said between gasps of air.

"What in the devil are you talking about?" Mike demanded. "What man? Why would anyone be trying to kill you?" Sam saw that as Mike asked the question, he was scanning the crowd. Sam followed his gaze. There was no sign of the stranger in the crowd.

"Mike, the guy in the woods, the one that killed Fred, we found him. He knows that we know who he is, and he's trying to kill us."

"Come over here," Mike ordered the three of them sternly, using Sam's elbow to steer her down the side street and away from the crowd of people. He came to a stop glared at each of them, then pointed his finger at Sam. "You told me that you never got a look at the killer's face. How could you possibly identify him now?"

"His laugh," Sam said with absolute certainty.

"His laugh?" Mike repeated with skepticism.

"Yes, his laugh," Sam said, slightly offended by the question. "I've been trying so hard not to think about what happened in the woods. Fred's last moments. I wanted to drown out the voices inside my head. In my dreams. But just before the guy killed Fred, he laughed. His laugh was distinctive, and I will never forget the sound."

"Look, I know you guys witnessed a gruesome scene, and that can be traumatic."

"I'm not imagining things, if that's what you're implying," Sam said interrupted haughtily.

"She's really good at identifying voices," Nell offered. "She's been that way since she was little. Plus, I remembered his laugh too. It's him."

"We're wasting time," Dean said with exasperation. "He's here. Let's get him."

"What ... I ... what's he wearing? Give me a description," Mike stammered.

Sam, Nell, and Dean all started talking at once, describing his hair, height, build and clothes, down to his white shirt and jeans.

"Stay here," Mike growled and headed for the crowd.

Sam, Nell, and Dean leaned up against a building and waited for Mike to return. They were standing in the area between the parade and the parking lot that hosted the arts and crafts booths. They were surrounded by people, but they kept their eyes peeled for the stranger.

When Sam was able to catch her breath, she turned to look at Nell and Dean. "I'm so sorry."

"What for?" They asked with confusion.

"For being an idiot," she answered. "I was so shocked and angry when I realized who he was that I didn't think. I should have kept it to myself. Now he knows who we are and that we can identify him. I've put us all in danger. Worse yet, I'm a complete moron for not recognizing his voice earlier—at the tour."

"The man's a killer," Dean said, trying to console her. "He killed someone in front of you and has apparently been following us around. You were scared, and you have nothing to apologize for. Besides, if he has been following us around, he probably knew who you were already."

"Dean's right. You have absolutely nothing to feel sorry for," Nell said in agreement as she put her arm around her cousin.

A few minutes later, Mike returned to them.

"Well? Did you find him?" Dean asked.

"No, and no one saw or heard anything except you three lunatics running into the middle of the parade. Everyone was watching the parade, the music was loud, and his physical description matches half of the people in town. I'm sorry. However, I have a sense that there's more you're not telling me."

Sam started to tell Mike about seeing the killer around town, but stopped herself. She had a feeling that telling him that a murderer had followed her to bowling alley, on the tour, and to the train station would result in her being quarantined in her house for the remainder of the summer. It was at that moment she realized he'd been outside the morgue too. It was him. She knew it now.

Oh my god. He really has been following us. Bone-chilling terror coursed through her entire body. She felt week in the knees. This was far more serious than she had ever thought possible. How stupid she was, thinking that her role in the murder could have truly been kept secret.

"I can't believe you waited this long to tell me all of this," Mike was saying with obvious irritation. "I have half a mind to throttle you all. Anyway, I should probably have you come down to the station and give a statement."

"No way!" Sam objected. "Our parents will kill us!"

"Oh, please don't. My mother will never let me out of the house again," Nell exclaimed in horror.

"We didn't do anything wrong, but I'm not dying to have my mother find out about this either," Dean chimed in.

"What exactly do you propose that I do?" Mike asked.

"We've told our parents what we know so far," Sam lied. But give us a day or so to find a way to tell our parents about today," Sam begged.

"If this guy is after you, I can't just do nothing," Mike argued.

Sam was desperate to keep this incident from her parents. If they found out, neither she nor Nell would be able to continue their search.

"Ya know, now that I'm standing here, I realize that it's possible I overreacted," Sam lied. "I have been on edge lately. If someone really wanted to get us, a lousy parade wouldn't have stopped him. Plus, he couldn't know where we live." Sam said this last with more confidence than she felt. "He certainly has no reason to know where I live. Fred was killed acres away from my home, and Nell and I made certain we weren't followed that day. Plus, you said yourself that you sealed the witness records." The last part was added for Mike's benefit. She felt strongly that it wasn't a true statement, but she really needed to buy some time to think.

"Oh, yeah, and we would have noticed if he had been to my house. My mother is always on the lookout for cars loitering in the area," Nell offered in support of their position.

"Plus, we did have a lot of sugar today," Dean said, coming to Sam's side. "We were pretty amped up."

Mike was looking at her intensely. "Then why do you think he has been following you?" Mike questioned.

Sam paused for a moment. "I don't know. It could just be in my head." She still wasn't ready to fill Mike in on the mystery and she needed to buy some time.

"Something doesn't add up," said Mike, looking at her with suspicion. "You guys can confide in me. But I can't help you unless I know all of the facts."

"We know," Sam responded. "Please trust us right now."

"It's against my better judgment, but I won't say anything to your parents—yet. But I am going issue a BOLO alert for this guy. And I'm going to set up a time for you guys to meet with a sketch artist ASAP. It may take a day or two. In the meantime, you need to tell your parents about it, stay home and don't go wandering off by yourselves. If you see this guy again, you had better call me or the station immediately. Also," he continued, "I am going to send a car by each of your houses for the next few nights as a precaution. I will be keeping my eye on you."

"Okay, thank you, Mike. We really appreciate everything you have done for us," Sam said with sincerity.

"You're welcome. You guys should go directly home. Do you need a ride?"

"I have my car," Dean piped up, "I'll drive them home."

"Fine," Mike responded. "But I'm going to following in my car just to make sure you get home."

"Okay," Sam begrudgingly agreed. "But *please* don't let Nell's parents see your cruiser."

They made their way to Dean's car without talking. Nell was visibly shaken, and Dean looked intense. The group got in his car, and he maneuvered his vehicle to where Mike had indicated his car was parked. They sat in silence and waited for Mike to get in to his vehicle and start the engine before Dean turned the car around and headed for Nell's house.

Once they were on the road, Nell informed them that she was completely freaked out.

"I know, Nell. I'm so sorry. That was crazy," Sam said. Look, I don't want to freak you out any more, but despite what I told Mike, I do think we're being followed. In fact, I'm sure of it."

"Why did you lie to him?" Nell asked.

"Because, otherwise you and I would be on total lockdown and we'd never solve this thing."

Sam turned to Dean and said, "If you don't want to hang out with us anymore, I understand. Things have gotten out of hand."

"I'm never bored with you two. That's for sure," he replied. "But I have fun with you guys. Plus, there's no way that I'm leaving you guys alone with that psycho out there. We need to figure out the next clue because the railway station was a complete bust. Well, except for the fact that we found the killer."

"Are you sure you guys are still up for this?" Sam asked. "I will understand if this is too much. I mean, I'm terrified by what just happened. But I just can't give up. I just can't."

After a moment of silence, both Nell and Dean agreed that they had to continue.

"But we need to be a lot more careful from now on," Dean said.

"Sam, maybe you could talk with your neighbor again and ask him about any connection between a train conductor and the Gray family," Nell suggested. Her voice was soft. Sam could tell that she was trying to be brave.

"Yeah, I could," she replied. "He is quite the talker. He proba-bly ..." Her voice stopped midsentence. Her eyes narrowed to slits, and her forehead creased. "But I ... I may not need to."

"Why?" Nell asked.

"When I talked to Mr. Miller, he told me about how Adam Gray was supposed to be very active in the Underground Railroad," Sam said. "He said some stuff about stations and conductors that didn't seem that important at the time. Plus, remember we asked the tour guide and she confirmed that his house has long been rumored to have been used to aid the Underground Railroad?"

"Yes, and I found a few articles online discussing the same thing. You think that the note we found in Edward's house was referring to the Underground Railroad?" Nell asked.

"Yes, and I think Adam Gray may be the *conductor,*" Sam announced. "I don't know. That may be a stretch," Nell responded, pondering the thought.

"Yeah, it is, but Linda did say that Edward and Adam were very close," Dean recounted. "And there were a lot of pictures of them hanging out together. It's not the most far-fetched idea I've heard."

"Mr. Miller told me that people here were really into supporting the Underground Railroad and, well, hiding bootleg booze too," Sam continued. "There were rumored to be tunnels hiding places all over town. The clue doesn't point to an actual train conductor, but it may be a reference to the Underground Railroad or some other underground effort. I'm an idiot. I don't know why I didn't put it together before. I'll bet that one of those hiding places were used to store lots of very valuable stuff. Maybe even a treasure."

"Guys, we have to find the treasure, or whatever it is that we are looking for, before the killer does," Sam stated emphatically. "We can't let Fred die in vain. We have to finish what he started. More importantly, I have to live up to my promise to him. We are running out of time. Dean, can you get us back in the Adam Gray house?"

"I think so, when?"

"Tomorrow," Sam replied. "It's really important that we find the next clue before Mike tells our parents about it."

"That might be tough. The house is closed tomorrow, but I'll do my best. I will call you later to confirm." Dean promised.

Their conversation made the ride fly by, and they were at Nell's home before they realized it. Dean pulled into Nell's driveway and put the car in park. "Do you want me to walk you to the door?" he offered.

"No, we're fine," Nell answered. She looked in the rear-view mirror. "Thank goodness Mike stopped his car down the block. I can just hear my mother's outburst if she thought we had a police escort."

The girls slowly climbed out of the car and headed inside. The clock on the wall read almost four.

"Well, you girls are home earlier than expected," proclaimed Uncle Hank.

"It seems that we have had our fill of food, rides, and games," Nell offered weakly. "Lots of excitement condensed into two days."

"I could hear the parade from here. How was it?" he asked.

"It was loud," Nell responded.

"The high school band sounded good," Sam added. "Very quick on their feet." She had to suppress a giggle now, imagining the sight of them crashing the parade. She felt a little punchy. It was strange how she tended to make jokes when she was really stressed out.

"Dad, we're pooped. We thought that we would just relax and do some reading until dinner," Nell said. "Is that okay?"

"Sure, sure, I'll tell your mother, and I think I'll do the same. I'll let you know when dinner is ready."

"If we can do anything to help, please let us know," Sam asked.

"Will do, but you guys just relax. You have certainly had a lot of excitement and more than a little stress lately. It's no wonder that you're tired. Go kick back for a while."

If he only knew, Sam thought.

They nodded gratefully and walked down the hall to Nell's room. As soon as they were inside, and the door was securely closed, Nell turned to Sam.

"Okay, I admit that I was skeptical at first, but now that I've had time to think about it, I think that you might be on to something," Nell said. "But I don't know how we are going to find the next clue in a house that is open to the public and has been searched multiple times."

"I know it sounds crazy, and I don't know how we should go about it. But on the other hand, look at how far we've come, you know, being as inept as we are."

Nell laughed. "I know; it just all seems like a dream," she said as she lowered herself on to her bed.

"If Dean gets us back in the house, how do we get permission to go? Sam inquired. "I mean, if we ask to go back to a house we just saw, I think your parents will get suspicious."

"Well, we're in luck there," Nell responded. "My parents are going to some church picnic. My dad agreed that I could skip church this week, and they would go without me. That will give us a few hours at least."

"Thank heaven for small favors," Sam said, sighing. "But what do we do when we get there?" She considered her options silently before continuing. "If we get inside the house, we are going to need to be prepared."

"For what?" Nell asked. "I don't know how we prepare ourselves for finding some unknown clue."

"I can't stop thinking about that house, and I still believe that it has a secret tunnel," Sam responded.

"But you heard the tour guide: the house has been searched many times, and no tunnel was ever found."

"If there is a secret passageway, I bet it's sealed off somehow and not visible. That's why it hasn't been found yet. The Gray family probably doesn't want the public to know so they hid it. It's even possible that the living members of the family don't even know that it's there."

"We can't go busting open walls in a historical home," Nell cautioned.

"I know. I wasn't implying that we pack a sledgehammer or dynamite."

"What do you think we need?" Nell inquired.

"I'm thinking strong flashlights, screwdrivers, and a crowbar," Sam said.

"It's that last one that has me worried," said Nell. "In any event, you know my dad doesn't have any tools. He always borrows what he needs from your dad. I've got the flashlights, though. Really good ones from the time my dad took me through those caves up north."

"Right, well, maybe Dean will be able to help."

"Okay, we can call him after dinner. I can hear my mom banging around in the kitchen. It sounds like supper's almost ready." As if on cue, Nell's dad knocked on her door to let them know that "grub was on."

Dinner that night was uncomfortable. Uncle Hank wanted to hear everything about their carnival adventures. He even offered to take them back that night so they could ride the Ferris wheel in the dark with the colored lights blazing.

As much as Sam would have normally liked to take a few more turns on the Ferris wheel or ride the bumper cars, she had absolutely no desire to go there now. They couldn't risk running into the killer again, or Mike for that matter. Sam thanked Nell's father profusely, but told him they were simply too exhausted to handle any more of the carnival.

"I think all of those hot dogs and cotton candy have gotten to me," Sam said, rubbing her stomach. "I feel like I've had my fill of carnie food for another year."

"That food is pure sugar and grease," Aunt Sue complained. "I don't know how anyone can consume such garbage."

"It's part of the festival experience," her husband reminded her. "Plus, I seem to recall that you enjoyed the kettle corn we ate on Thursday." His eyes were twinkling.

"Yes, well, popcorn is different. It's a low-calorie food."

Uncle Hank chuckled.

Sam thanked her aunt for a great meal and managed to fend off her negativity by insisting on the kitchen. Her aunt hovered nearby as the girls cleared the table, stored the leftovers in the fridge, and loaded the dishwasher. Aunt Sue apparently didn't trust them to wipe off the table and counters, for she shooed them off to their room with a murmur of thanks for their efforts.

They had just reentered Nell's room when her phone rang. Nell picked up the receiver.

"Hi, Dean. Yup, we're okay. You? Good. You did? Great. My parents will head off to church by nine thirty for ten o'clock services. Sam and I will be free until at least one or two. Sure, if you don't mind picking us up, that would be perfect." Sam shot her a look. "Say, can you bring a, uh, a screwdriver and a crowbar? Sam is thinking that we need to bring a few tools in case we find a secret entrance. Yeah, bring whatever else you think we might need. Okay, see you then." She hung up the phone and turned to Sam.

"Dean is going to pick us up tomorrow at 10:00. He said that the house is closed to the public tomorrow, so it'll be empty."

"How are we getting in?" Sam asked.

"He didn't say, and I didn't ask," Nell responded. "I'm not sure that I want to know."

"Right."

Before they went to bed that night, they made sure Nell's backpack was loaded with supplies including three flashlights. Nell's bedroom faced the backyard. Sam made several trips out to the kitchen, so she could look through the family room and outside the picture window. To her relief, she didn't see any cars lurking in the area.

Sleep was elusive for Sam. In the darkness, she thought she heard car doors creaking open. The wind in the trees sounded like someone walking under the window. A tree branch crackled, and Sam jumped off her beds. She got up and closed and locked her window. The fireworks from the carnival area were the worst of all. It mimicked gunfire, and the sound transported Sam back to that day in the woods. Sam wondered whether the killer would ever leave town.

Flashes of light, screams, and loud music swirled together as Sam ran faster and faster. She was running through the festival, being chased by the killer. He was laughing. She shouted for someone to help her, but it was like she was invisible. No one paid any attention to her cries. Everyone was laughing and dancing. She ran and ran until she ended up in an empty alley. She had reached a dead-end. She turned and was face-to-face with the blond man.

The killer came closer and closer. "There you are. I told you: you can run, but you can't hide!" He reached out, and she closed her eyes waiting for the inevitable.

Sam gasped and sat bolt upright. She'd been having a nightmare. She could still hear the sound of loud music in her head. Her heart was drumming in her ears. She realized that she was awake. Something was holding on to her. She looked up to see that Nell was holding her arm.

"It sounded like you were having a bad dream," Nell said with concern.

"Nightmare," Sam reported. "Sorry if I woke you. My nightmares came back."

"You're having nightmares?" Why didn't you tell me?

"I didn't want you to worry," Sam replied. "Did I wake you up?"

"No, I was awake. I can't stop thinking about the killer. I feel like my heart has been racing for days. And I have a knot in my stomach like I swallowed a humungous wad of gum."

"Do you want to tell our parents?" Sam asked.

Nell paused for a moment before responding. "You know, no, I don't. At least not yet anyway. I'm not ready to deal with my mother. She will go crazy. I might never be allowed out of my room again. Plus, I keep thinking about Fred and his request. I want us to do what he asked. Why? Do you want to tell our parents?"

"Part of me wants to tell them. But no, I'm not ready either. I can't explain why, but something tells me we should wait and see what we find tomorrow, well, I guess I mean today. If we find another clue or a tunnel, it may help us convince people that there is a treasure out there and that they need to take us seriously. Or at least finish what Fred started. And listen, I've been thinking about everything we know so far. We know that Edward Gray wrote at least one of the clues. We also know that he fought in the Civil War. And we agree that these clues seem to be leading us toward some type of a treasure, right?"

"Right," Nell agreed tentatively.

"If there is a treasure, then it must date back to the Civil War," Sam concluded. "It's really rather incredible if you think about it."

"I hadn't really stopped to think about it like that, but you're right: it is incredible to think that a treasure was buried somewhere in town and that it has been sitting there waiting to be discovered all this time. If there really is a treasure, what do you think it is?"

"I've been laying here wondering that very thing," Sam replied.

"I remember watching a show with my dad about the Civil War, and it said that during the war, a shipment of Confederate gold went missing," Nell recalled. "It was never found, and the theory was that the North intercepted it and hid it somewhere."

"How much was the gold worth?"

"The show said that no one really knows, but it would be worth at least a few million in today's dollars. Plus, the show mentioned that lots of artwork and other valuables were seized or looted from private homes and never recovered. So, the treasure could be anything."

Sam let out a low whistle. "Can you imagine finding a pile of gold here in Owosso? Maybe then I could buy a phone and my own computer," she said with a chuckle.

"Yeah, imagine all the things we could do with the money."

"If I do that now, I'll never get to sleep. I'd better save those thoughts for later."

"It is getting late. It's after two," Nell said, stifling a yawn.

"Okay, go to sleep. I'll try to keep my dreams to myself this time," Sam mumbled with embarrassment.

14

◇

Adam Gray's House

Morning came early. Sam was exhausted from lack of sleep but grateful that the night was over. Sam had just returned from the bathroom when Nell scurried into the bedroom with two cans of soda.

"I figured we could use the caffeine today," Nell stated.

"You are the greatest; thank you," Sam praised, cracking open the can and guzzling.

They were able to successfully evade Nell's mom while they got ready. Sam couldn't wait for them to leave. She was so afraid that Mike would spill the beans to their parents before they had a chance to finish their search.

Shortly before nine thirty, Uncle Hank knocked on the bedroom door to tell them goodbye.

"Are you sure you guys don't want to come to the picnic?" He asked.

"No thanks, Dad," Nell responded. "But thanks for asking. You and mom go and enjoy yourselves."

"Okay, see you guys later," he responded. "Have fun."

They heard Nell's parents leave a few minutes later. They waited until they heard the garage door opened and closed before they ventured out of the bedroom. Sam's stomach was rolling. She felt anxious, queasy, and a little light-headed. Nell commented that she felt like she needed to throw up. They grabbed a few slices of toast to settle their stomachs and polished off the rest of their sodas. Nell grabbed three apples, some crackers, and three bottles of water to add to the backpack. They didn't know how long they would be gone, but they figured that it made sense to pack something to eat.

Dean picked them up right on time. As they got in to his car, everyone looked a little nervous.

"I made sure I wasn't followed," Dean informed them once the door was shut. "Also, I brought along the stuff you asked for and a few other tools. I didn't know what we might need."

"Thanks, Dean," said Sam.

"No problem. How are you guys doing? I had some wicked nightmares last night," Dean said.

"We're in the same condition," Sam said, answering for the both of them. She could hardly sit still. She felt a sense of urgency to search the house, but she was also terrified that the killer would find them. At least, they would be safe in the house away from public view. She wouldn't have to worry about looking over her shoulder to see if she was being followed as she was doing now.

"Listen, I did some research on the Underground Railroad last night," Dean said. "It turns out that some houses had secret compartments, just large enough to fit a few people. I also read that lots of homes and buildings had tunnels underneath to hide booze. Since no tunnel has been found, I'm thinking that if we are searching for the next clue, then we should be looking for a compartment of some sort. The articles I read described the secret areas as often being hidden in the floor under a rug or in the wall behind a bookcase or something like that."

"Oh great, there must be a thousand potential spots like that in the Adam Gray house," Sam groaned.

"I know. I was thinking that too," Dean said, sharing her look of concern. "I figure that we'll have to split up and tackle the house in divisions."

"Okay, are you sure that the house is closed to the public today?" Nell questioned nervously.

"I'm sure. No one will know that we're there," Dean assured her.

"Um, I'm not comfortable breaking in," Nell objected.

"We're not breaking in. I have a key," Dean informed her. "My mother's."

"I'm not sure that's much better, Dean," Nell admonished.

"I'm allowed on the premises. I just didn't mention the nature of my visit today. Anyway, do you want to find the next clue or not?" he asked.

"Yes, yes, I do. It's just that I wish we could do it another way."

"Any ideas?" Dean asked her.

"No. I think we have to do it your way," she replied.

"All right, so I think that we leave the car down the road a little and walk over to the Adam Gray house," Dean continued. "The hedges in the back hide the back door, so I think we should enter there. Everyone needs to keep a look out for that guy and/or his car."

"Where are your tools?" Nell asked. "We can't look obvious."

"They're in my backpack," Dean said. "We won't look obvious. We just need to try and relax. Okay, we're here. Grab your stuff."

Dean had parked the car a few houses down from the Gray mansion and across from the park. Sam took another look around to see if they had been tailed. She saw no signs of the blond killer or his black SUV. The three of them got out of the car and started walking down the sidewalk as nonchalantly as possible.

She wanted to sprint toward the house, but knew that would only call attention to them. None of them spoke as they made their way along the sidewalk and around to the side of the house. Dean led the way up the driveway and to the back door. He quickly unlocked the door and ushered the girls inside.

Sam furtively glanced outside in all directions but saw no one.

"Okay, so far, so good. I didn't see any sign that we were followed," she told them.

"Are you sure that the house is empty?" Nell asked again. Her voice quivered.

"Yes," Dean said.

"How do you know for sure that no one will be coming here today?" Nell pressed.

"The house is typically closed on Sundays, and I also overheard my mother talking with one of the members from the historical society. Everything's fine, relax. You're making me even more nervous. We need to get right to work. I was thinking that we should focus on the library/office first, any objection?"

"No," Sam and Nell answered.

"I bet that any hidden compartment will be either in the library or the basement," Dean speculated.

"What about the bedrooms and the attic?" Nell questioned.

"The attic would be the first place people would look," Dean answered. "So I don't think the Grays would have used it as a hiding place."

"Plus, the stories about this house center on it having some sort of a passage between it and another house nearby," Sam added. "It makes more sense that the secret passage would be off the main level of the house like the library or the basement. Personally, I have a feeling that the basement is the key."

"I guess you're both right," Nell added. "Those areas do make the most sense."

"I say that we all work together in the library, and if we don't find anything after, say, a half hour, we move down to the basement," Dean suggested.

"Okay," said Sam and Nell.

The three of them walked down the hallway and into the library. As they walked down a hallway, a floorboard creaked. "Ah!" Sam screamed. "I'm sorry, I'm wound up." She added.

In the library, Sam took a wall and began the process of inspecting it inch by inch. The others did the same. Since the room was nearly wall-to-wall bookcases, they moved very slowly. Where there was bare wall, it seemed to be solid and intact. They could not find any seams or gaps to indicate any compartment, opening or passageway. Tapping on the walls produced low-toned thuds, which, according to Dean, meant that that area was solid.

Inspecting the bookshelves was more challenging. They all had watched movies in which what seemed to be a solid and permanent bookshelf that was transformed into a doorway by moving the right book. They visually inspected the top, bottom, and sides of the shelves. The shelves seemed normal. They then began the tedious process of moving each book, one by one, to see whether they could locate the key to unlocking any hidden door. The last book was pulled out and replaced without any movement by the shelves. They checked the floor as well and were unable to find evidence of a secret opening.

"We've been at this for more than forty-five minutes," Sam said.

"I didn't realize how long it had been. Down to the basement now?" Dean asked.

"Yes," Sam answered with enthusiasm.

"Sure," Nell responded with trepidation.

"Okay, follow me," instructed Dean.

Since the basement had not been on the tour, Sam pointed to Dean to lead the way and followed closely behind him. He led them back down the hallway and toward the kitchen. At the end of the hallway, just outside the entrance to the kitchen, was a door which Sam had not noticed before.

"Get out your flashlights," Dean said as he grabbed his own from his pack. He opened the door and began descending the wooden stairs. Nell followed Dean and Sam brought up the rear, closing the door behind her.

"I hate old basements," Nell muttered.

"I kind of like them," Dean said.

"It smells like feet down here," Nell responded.

"Who have you been hanging out with that have feet that smell like this?" Sam asked, teasing her. "If you say me, I'll have to kill myself." She giggled.

"If your feet smelled like this, I'd have to kill you," Nell said and giggled as well. The laughter helped Sam relax. She quickly reached the bottom of the stairs.

"It's creepy down here," Sam said.

"Here," Dean said, flipping on a light switch. Four single light bulbs came to life revealing, a large basement.

For a moment, they stood there, looking around the large space.

Sam looked around her. The basement was large. To the left, she saw what was obviously the laundry area. It had washer, drawer, and clothesline. The furnace was located further back near the corner. Off the right side of the staircase, along the east wall, Sam observed rows of shelves bearing jars of canned food. Farther down the wall, more shelves held boxes and plastic storage containers. Straight ahead, on the far end of the basement, the wall was lined with a massive wine storage area. Hundreds of bottles of wine were nested in wooden shelves that rose from the floor to ceiling. The ceiling itself was unfinished with wooden beams running across the entire basement.

"Look at the wine," Dean said with awe. "My mom said that the Grays had an impressive wine collection."

"Man, there is a lot of stuff down here," Sam observed.

"There sure is," Nell agreed. "It's difficult to know where to start."

"In the movies, the secret passages always seem to be behind a bookcase, a painting, or something similar," Dean noted. "I think we should check out the wine racks first.

"That's a good idea," Sam responded. "Although if there is a secret door behind the wine, wouldn't it be kinda hard to open it without wine bottles falling out and breaking?"

"Excellent point," Dean answered, rubbing his chin and looking dejected.

"Don't get me wrong. I still think it's a good idea," Sam said, trying not to sound negative. "I just think we need to be careful. It's bad enough that we are poking around in a historic house without permission. I don't want to make matters worse by destroying a priceless wine collection. By the way, why is there wine down here if the house is owed by the historical society?"

"I think that the Grays gifted the house and the contents, including the wine. My mom said that the family had such a huge wine collection they gifted these to the society. They're used for charity events. Mom said there must have been some tax benefit," Dean told them.

"Oh," Sam responded. "In any event, given my history of clumsiness, how about if you and Nell start checking the wine rack area and I start looking at the area behind these shelves?"

"Okay, sounds good," Dean replied.

"Okay by me," Nell added.

As Sam eyed the storage area, she instantly regretted her decision to stay away from the wine area. The shelving seemed endless and riddled with cobwebs. She decided to start at the far end of the basement, close to where Nell and Dean were working. At first, she was certain that, at any minute, Nell or Dean would call out that they had found a secret door. However, after several minutes, she became engrossed in her own work.

The shelves were filled with everything from Christmas decorations to what looked like old pieces of machinery. To properly search, she needed to not only inspect the shelving itself, but the wall behind it as well. This meant that she had to shift heavy boxes and other items from side to side so that she could have a clear view of the wall. It was slow, backbreaking work. Soon her arms, legs and back were aching and she felt filthy.

"How are you guys coming?" she called out.

"Very slow," Nell responded. "You have me paranoid that I'm going to knock one of these bottles of wine onto the floor."

"Sorry," Sam said apologetically. "I didn't mean to psych you out; I just know my own tendencies. You'll be fine. You are much more graceful than I could ever be."

"The wine rack *seems* to be permanently attached to the wall, but I'm looking for anything unusual which might indicate that it is moveable or anything that looks like a lever or a latch," Dean said, updating them.

"Do you think we should start removing the bottles one by one to see if they trigger a secret compartment?" From the look on her face, Sam could tell that Nell did not relish the thought.

"You guess is as good as mine, but it probably can't hurt," Sam answered. "As soon as I'm done with these shelves, I'll come over and help."

"Somehow, I knew it was going to come to this," Nell mumbled.

"I can't help it if you have excellent ideas," Sam said smiling.

"Yeah, yeah, yeah," Nell said, blowing off Sam's mocking.

Sam continued with her assigned task. Behind her, she could hear faint clinking sounds as Nell and Dean removed and replaced the bottles.

"Wow, there are some really old bottles of wine down here!" Dean exclaimed. "Some of the labels date back to before the civil war."

"Well then, for sure don't drop those bottles," Sam said with a chuckle.

"Great, now I'm the one who's getting psyched out," Dean muttered.

Sam thought she heard a creak overhead. For a moment, she

froze until she remembered that the house was closed to the public today. "Man, I'm paranoid," She muttered.

Sam continued on with her work. It felt like the shelves would never end. The most difficult part was being able to clear enough space to reach through them to the wall behind. The stored items were packed on the shelves and left little room to maneuver. It was hard to make enough space to allow her arm to move around and test the solidness of the wall by tapping on it as they had done upstairs.

Since the walls were made of brick, she used the back of a screwdriver to test for any hollow spots. Several times, the screwdriver popped out of her hand, and she had to fish around to locate it. So far, the wall seemed solid as a rock. She found a number of cracks, but none appeared anything more than the usual ones found in any Michigan basement.

There was one crack which ran nearly the full distance from floor to ceiling. Sam's excitement got the best of her, and she called Dean over to take a look. They cleared the shelves in that area and examined that portion of the wall in earnest. Unfortunately, it soon became obvious that the crack was just that. Dean returned to his inspection of the wine racks, looking disappointed.

Finally, Sam had come to the end of the shelves, which held boxes and storage containers. To her dismay, she saw the rows and rows of canned food that now awaited her review. Oh great, she thought, how many jars of preserves will I send to their death today? Dean had explained that the canned food was made by the historical society members and sold at various fundraisers to help pay for maintenance on the house. She didn't know how much they actually sold, but they certainly had a lot of jars.

She looked back to the end of the basement and saw that Dean and Nell were a little more than halfway through the wine. Nell's eyes met her glaze and told her, without words, that their search was so far fruitless.

Sam took a deep breath and started in on the jars. The good thing about this section of the basement was that she could see through and behind most of the containers. Thankfully, this meant much less pushing and shoving. Of course, the wall tapping portion of the inspection was still tense. Since everything here was breakable, her movements had to be precise and perfectly aimed. Not her best skills. To top it off, she kept thinking she heard footsteps. However, every time she stopped tapping, the sound stopped. She knew that her imagination was getting the best of her.

Sam worked in silence now. Hunched over the rows of canned goods, Sam's back started to throb again. She extracted her head and arms from the shelves to stretch. As she stood upright, her right elbow clipped a jar of preserves, and it toppled over the side of the shelf.

"Ah!" she cried out. She grabbed for the container, and with uncommon agility, she caught the jar in her left hand.

"What?" Nell and Dean yelled, rushing toward her.

"I knocked this off the shelf," she said, holding up the jar. "Luckily, I caught it before it hit the floor."

"Oh man!" Nell said, letting out a deep sigh. "I thought you had found something."

"Me too," Dean said, looking slightly annoyed.

"I'm sorry," Sam said, now disappointed too. "I guess I sort of panicked. I wish I *had* found something."

"That's okay," Nell responded. "I think that we are all a little tired and on edge right now. We've been down here for almost an hour. We didn't find anything in the wine rack," she added.

"Yeah, those racks aren't going anywhere," Dean said.

"Hey, what if more than one bottle needs to be moved to activate a hidden lock?" Sam inquired.

"I don't know. I guess it's possible," Dean responded, staring back at the wall of wine. "But I wouldn't have a clue where to start."

"It's an intriguing thought," Nell said, with renewed excitement.

She paused for a moment before continuing. "I'm thinking about how you were able to open the compartment in the bell tower. What if somehow the dates on the bottles here are significant. But I'm not sure what dates we could combine which would be important to the Gray family."

"Hmm," Sam said looking at the floor. "The only things that I can think of would be the dates we tried in the bell tower including the years covered by the Civil War. Did you find bottles for each of those years?"

"I'll go back and check," Nell answered.

"Okay, I'll finish the canned food. Ew, gross, it looks like they can meat here. Ugh!" Sam said with mock gagging.

Sam finished her inspection and called out to Nell.

"Anything?"

"Nope. That didn't work," Nell answered.

"Okay," Sam responded. She was standing just off the right side of the staircase. Straight ahead was a wooden work table filled with tools. A few wooden barrels and a box of wires were sitting on the floor. She looked under the stairs and saw several more boxes piled one on top of another.

She turned back to the work table and eyed the objects cluttering the top. It reminded her of her own father's work bench, which he kept in their basement. Nothing seemed unusual about the table, and there was definitely no hidden button or switch either on, in or behind the table. She checked the barrels, but they were just filled with old clothes. She knew that she should check under the stairs, but she didn't quite have the energy to start tackling that project just yet.

She lowered herself on to one a wooden box and let her eyes glaze over in thought. This basement held the key to finding the next clue. She could feel it. According to the historical society, this house had been used in the Underground Railroad and was rumored to be connected to another house. Maybe for bootlegging. *Who knew?* Some sort of passageway had to be here—it just had to.

Sam let her eyes roam around the room. On the other side of the basement, was the laundry area. Sam didn't think that a secret passage would be hidden in that section of the basement. There would be too much traffic. Someone would have found a door by now. Of course, maybe the Gray family had always known the location of the entrance but chose to keep it a secret. That would be reasonable from a security perspective Sam thought. If the owners were open about the location, they could risk someone tunneling into the house. If the Gray's did know about the tunnel, then they would have had to have concealed the opening, so it couldn't be found by accident.

"Well, that was a bust," Dean said as he and Nell made their way back to Sam. "Let's just hope that no one notices fingerprints on every bottle of wine."

"I'm pooped," Nell said as she walked over and leaned against a barrel next to Sam.

"Well, there's not much left," Dean offered in effort to be encouraging.

"I know. That's what has me depressed," Sam replied. "I was just so sure that a secret tunnel entrance was down here. I mean, I—" Her voice abruptly cut off and her eyes were locked on the wall behind were Dean was standing.

"What?" Nell asked.

"Look," Sam answered, pointing at the wall.

"What are you looking at," Dean asked, turning to follow Sam's finger. "All I see is the wall."

"No, look there at that little metal door in the wall," Sam responded.

"That's just a fireplace cleanout," Dean said with disinterest.

"Look at the door," Sam instructed. "It reads 'Heart Engineering.'"

"And ..." Dean prompted.

"Oh!" Nell exclaimed. "Do you think?"

"I think," Sam replied excitedly.

"Will someone fill me in?" Dean begged.

"The clue, remember," Sam started, but was too excited to continue.

Nell picked up where Sam left off. "The clue said:

> The conductor's path was clear
> A walk in his footsteps will lead you there
> That which was hidden was done with pure heart
> So any seeker must so start"

"Pure Heart. Heart Engineering." Sam looked at Dean and waited for the meaning to sink in.

"Fireplace cleanouts are common," he stated wearily. "Plus, I think this area of the basement is under the library which, if you remember, has a fireplace."

"I understand that," Sam said. "I just think the clue was leading us here." She walked over to the wall and pulled on the metal door. Nothing happened. "I can't open it. Dean can you give it a try?"

"Sure." Dean walked over and tugged on the door, but it remained closed tight. "Hang on," he said. He fished around in his backpack for a moment and retrieved a screwdriver. He inserted the tip in to the door and pried. The door flew open, and ashes burst into the air leaving a momentary black cloud.

The girls coughed and waved in the air, trying to fend off the soot.

As Dean went to grab something to clean up the mess, Sam peered into the door. It was filthy.

"Looks like an ordinary cleanout door to me," Dean said returning with a bucket.

Undeterred, Sam narrowed her eyes and surveyed the small opening. She put her hand inside and began to feel around. Suddenly, she cocked her head to the side and began rubbing on the inside wall of the clean out. "Dean, can you hand me a paintbrush from that table?" Sam asked without looking up.

"Sure," Dean answered with a confused expression. He grabbed a brush and placed it into Sam's waiting hand.

Sam began brushing the interior wall with focused intensity. "Look, there," she said. Her face was beaming with excitement. She had soot on her face and in her hair, but she couldn't have cared less.

Nell pressed her face closer inside the opening. "A star!"

"Can you believe it?" Sam asked out of breath from the excitement. She reached into her pocket and pulled out the metal star they had found in the bell tower. The same star that had been the key to finding the clue at the Edward Gray house.

"No way!" Dean yelled.

"Way!" Sam yelled back.

On the left side of the clean out was a depression in the shape of a star. It was the same size and design of the star Sam held in her hand. She held the star out and reached inside the opening.

A floorboard creaked over their heads, and everyone jumped. Looks of terror froze on each of their faces. Sam pivoted and looked at Dean as they listened for any other sound. After several moments glued in their places, they began to relax. No other sounds had emanated from upstairs.

"Would you stop it? No one is coming to the house today," Dean reminded them, trying to calm everyone's nerves. "I have the information straight from my mom. This house is old, and we are all a little jumpy. Our imaginations are running wild."

"I know you're right. It's just that it really sounded like someone was walking just above us," Nell said, exhaling deeply.

Sam returned to the opening, holding the star up to compare the designs. It seemed to be the perfect size. Gently, she pressed the star into the depression. It clicked into place, but nothing happened. Sam looked up at Nell and Dean.

"Can you turn it?" Nell inquired.

Sam grunted as she attempted to turn the star. "Nope."

"Can I try?" Dean asked.

"Yeah, sure," Sam answered.

They switched places. Dean reached in, grabbed the star, and rotated his hand. Nothing happened.

"Wait, you rotated to the right," Sam observed. "Try going to the left."

Dean nodded his head. He grabbed the star. He secured his hold and turned to the left as hard as he could. The metal bottom of the compartment popped up. Dean lifted the metal up and shined his flashlight inside. Under the metal bottom, they saw a small black switch.

"Does that come with your standard fireplace cleanout?" Sam said to Dean with a mocking tone.

"Uh, no," he admitted.

"Pull the switch," Sam ordered Dean.

"Okay, here it goes," he said. He grabbed the switch and yanked it. They heard a clank, then a loud popping sound, and then what sounded like cracking. Dean pulled his hand out of the opening as if he had been electrocuted.

"Are you okay? Nell asked him.

"Yeah, fine," he said, staring at the door. "All that and nothing happened."

"I wouldn't say nothing," Sam corrected. "Look at the wall." She pointed to the wall. Several large cracks were visible in the brick wall in the shape of a doorway. The floor now was covered with a light dusting of powder.

"It's an entrance," Sam said in almost a whispered. She walked closer and felt around for a handle. Unable to locate one, she began pushing and pulling on the wall. Dean and Nell came to assist her.

"I think this section is stuck," Dean said. He reached back into his bag and brought out a hammer and a chisel. He lightly tapped the wall in several places. With a final whack of his hammer, a chunk of mortar fell to the floor and the wall of brick swung toward them.

For several seconds Sam didn't realize what was happening, and she jumped backward trying to avoid being hit by falling debris. It took her several more seconds to realize that the bricks were not falling but rather opening. The bricks had been laid over a hidden door. Behind the door, a tunnel was visible.

They had found the secret passageway.

"Yes!" Sam screamed. "I knew it!"

"Finally!" Nell added. She was jumping up and down. Then she flung her arms around Sam and started hugging her.

"Holy shit!" Dean exclaimed, looking dazed.

"Yes, yes, well done indeed," said a voice on the stairs.

Sam's stomach twisted, and she knew instantly that they were in a lot of trouble. Absolute terror set in as she saw Fred's murderer was standing on the steps smirking down at them. It felt as though some kind of poisonous venom was coursing through her veins paralyzing her from head to toe. She was rooted to the spot, her head was tingling, and she couldn't think. She thought of Fred and suddenly she was filled with unbridled anger.

"What the hell are you doing here?" Sam demanded.

"I might ask the same of you," the killer retorted.

"You need to leave the premises immediately," Dean ordered.

"Oh, I don't think so," the killer replied. "I have the same right to be here as you do. Or do you have permission from the historical society to be digging up their basement? No? I didn't think so."

"The cleaning crew will be here any minute now," Nell lied.

The killer just laughed. "Oh, don't worry. I called earlier this week. No one is scheduled to be here until tomorrow at the earliest. That gives us plenty of time."

The killer made his way down the stairs and came to a stop a few feet away from them.

"Well, we don't take orders from you," Dean said. He walked toward the killer placing himself in front of the girls.

It happened so fast that everything was a blur. The killer punched Dean in the face with such force that Dean was knocked off his feet, landing on the floor in a seated position. Once Dean was on the ground, the killer withdrew a 9mm handgun from his waist and struck Dean on the head. A trickle of blood ran down Dean's face. He appeared to be unconscious but breathing.

"No!" Sam shouted, turning to help Dean.

"Stay where you are, or I'll kill him," the killer ordered. "Here, take this rope and tape and tie him up. Tie him up nice and tight, or I'll shoot him so he can't move."

"What the hell did you do that for?" Sam demanded.

"You are the feisty one, aren't you?" he observed. "He would only be in our way. We want to make good time, now don't we? Get to work. Or do I need to remind you that I have no problem firing a gun? Trust me, with this old basement, no one would hear a thing."

"Okay, okay," Sam responded, still glaring at him. She was livid and petrified at the same time. She picked up the rope, knelt down alongside Dean, and started tying his hands together. Nell kneeled beside her, looking like she was going to cry.

"Tape his mouth shut too," the killer said with a snicker.

"Is that really necessary?" Sam asked.

"It is unless you just want me to shoot him," he responded.

Sam tore off a piece of the duct tape the killer had provided and gently covered Dean's mouth.

"Now shove him underneath the stairs," he ordered.

Sam glared at him again. The gun was pointed directly at Dean's chest. She was trembling with both fear and hatred. She wished that she had the courage to grab the gun and cram it down his throat. She had handled and fired guns with her father plenty of times. However, at the moment her hands were shaking so hard she knew that she was in no position to try anything. She couldn't risk Dean's or Nell's life.

"Come on, Nell. Grab his feet," Sam said softly. With much effort, they dragged Dean and carefully laid him under the stairs. They propped his head up on his backpack, hoping that would help. While Nell had her back to the killer and was blocking his view, Sam removed a screwdriver from Dean's backpack and slipped it inside her waistband. She also carefully slid a wrench out of Dean's bag and into her own.

"We're going to get help. Don't worry," Sam whispered in Dean's ear as she brushed a strand of hair out of his eye.

15

◇

The Passage

Sam and Nell didn't have much time with Dean before the killer started issuing orders.

"All right then, let's check out this secret passage you industrious kids found," the killer instructed.

"We're not kids," Sam corrected him.

"Please just let us go," Nell begged with tears in her eyes. Sam could tell that she was worried about Dean and more than a little worried for the two of them.

He simply laughed in return.

"Why are you doing this?" Sam asked in spite of herself.

"Well, my partner and I were looking for a lost Civil War treasure before his untimely death, and I intend to find it."

"Don't you mean before you killed him?" Sam demanded. She didn't know what had come over her. She knew that she should keep her mouth shut, but the blinding rage she felt was consuming her.

"Well, yes, that was unfortunate," the killer replied. "However, he had become uncooperative. Plus, he was a whiner, 'Oh Clay, no one understands or respects me.' Give me a break. He was a fool, and he couldn't keep his mouth shut. Knowing what I do about

Fred, and based on the way you've been scurrying around town,, it's my guess that he told you something before you died. The shock she felt, must have registered on her face, since Clay looked at her and laughed.

"Yeah, I've been following you since your little trip to the morgue." Plus, this town's a rumor mill. Two kids witness a murder and you two show up there on a Sunday. It wasn't that hard to figure out. So? The first clue perhaps? That belonged to me as his partner."

"You've been following us?" Sam asked in shock. She felt like someone had smacked her in the face.

"Oh my God! You're him! You're the guy Fred wrote about in his journal!"

"I'm flattered," Clay replied with a smile.

Nell gave her a befuddled look.

"Nell, the little black book we found. It was Fred's, and he wrote about Clay offering to help look for some lost items. You're from the Davis family. It was your crazy family from the South that kept bothering the Gray family, insisting that they had something of yours." She instantly regretted using the term *crazy*, but her nervousness made her keep talking.

"My family is not crazy!" he roared back. "They're the victims here. They were only trying to get back what is rightfully theirs. What was taken from by those thieving Grays."

"Man, I'm such an idiot," Sam said. "I should have paid more attention to Fred's journal. It just seemed to random. But now it all makes sense. You targeted poor Fred and latched on to him."

"Poor Fred, my ass," Clay retorted. "His family stole from my family and countless others. They are complete frauds. Acting like they are benevolent benefactors when all the while they knew they had cherished heirlooms. They've been hoarding a treasure since the war. It makes me sick."

"Well, Clay," Sam began, emphasizing his name, "how did you

learn about the treasure in the first place?" She'd read something about establishing a connection with a kidnapper so maybe using his name would help.

"I am a person with a vested interest. However, let's save that discussion for another time. Sam, why don't you lead the way into the tunnel," he said, brandishing the gun.

Sam didn't like the idea of Nell being so close to Clay, but she did as she was told and walked toward the entrance. She wondered why he was keeping them around now that they had located the hidden door. However, she figured that it was wiser not to ask that question.

The entrance was covered in cobwebs. Despite her fear of Clay, Sam was still creeped out by spiders. She looked around to make sure none were visible before clearing the webs away and wiping her hands on her pants. She picked up her backpack and, holding her flashlight, entered the tunnel. Nell clicked on her flashlight and followed Sam inside the tunnel. Clay was right behind Nell.

Once they were all inside, Clay pulled the door shut behind them. She heard the click of a lock. It was a frightening sound. Sam was about to ask him why he needed to close the door, but she didn't really want the answer. They were trapped. He motioned for Sam to continue, and she slowly began making her way forward.

The tunnel seemed to have been dug out of pure rock. The ceiling was only a few feet taller than Sam and was just barely wide enough for her to walk side by side with Nell. Overhead, here and there, Sam could see some wiring and piping. There must have been some lighting in the tunnel. Now, it was dark but for the light emitted by the girls' flashlights. The air was cool, and it felt eerie walking underground. Sam wondered what they would find at the end of the tunnel. She also dreaded coming to the end of the tunnel.

"Clay, what makes you think that there is any treasure buried here. I mean, you were on the tour. If there was a treasure down here, someone would have found it by now. This tunnel is probably just tunnel."

"Well, since we're on a first-name basis, Sam, I'll tell you. I know some things about you too," he said with a wicked grin. "My family passed down stories about the Yankees who looted Southern homes during the Civil War and how those items were never returned after the war ended. My family lost a fortune."

"What does that have to do with the Gray family or Owosso?" Nell asked timidly.

"One name kept resurfacing, a colonel from Owosso, Michigan. He stole huge quantities of valuables from the South and hid them."

"Edward Gray?" Sam asked, although she already knew the answer.

"Very good," Clay responded. "Yes, that colonel was Edward Gray."

"Based on everything that we've heard and read, Edward Gray seemed to be a good man," Nell offered. "He doesn't sound like the kind of man who would steal things."

"Those are all lies!" It's time for family to have their belongings returned to them."

"You're doing all this to get some silverware back?" Nell said with amazement.

Clay looked like he was going to explode. Instead, he took a deep breath and ordered them to keep walking. After a moment, he started talking again.

"For your information little miss naive, Mr. Gray took quite haul of valuables from the South—gold, silver, and artwork. Rumor has it that he hijacked a million-dollar shipment of Confederate gold."

Sam was stunned by the stuff Clay seemed to think was down here. He seemed to be becoming increasingly agitated, but she thought she should keep him talking. Maybe it would distract him. "Why not seek help through the legal system?" Sam questioned.

"Ha! Don't make me laugh. Boy, you are dumb. The courts would never force the Gray family to do anything. That family can do no wrong in this town."

"If you find a treasure, how are you going to figure out which items belong to which families?" Nell inquired.

"Now you sound like Fred. I assure you I won't need to divide anything up. I've tracked down this treasure, and I'm entitled to whatever I find."

"You're not even going to donate any items to a museum?" Nell said in shock.

Clay looked at her with a mixture of amusement and irritation. "A museum? I don't think so. I intend to take care of myself and restore my family's reputation."

"I don't think that assault, battery, and kidnapping are going to restore your family's reputation, unless they have a history of this sort of thing," Sam said.

"What are you, a budding lawyer? Don't get snotty with me," Clay said through clenched teeth. "You don't know what you're talking about."

"You said that you have been looking for the treasure for a long time," Nell interrupted in a neutral tone. Sam suspected that Nell was trying to ease the tension and calm Clay down. "What have you been doing?"

"My family's account after the war is supported by my research. Hell, one of Gray's own people backed up the story."

"If all of this is true, did anyone approach the Gray family directly?" Nell asked.

"Like it made any difference. The entire Gray family played dumb, and denied having any information. My family actually requested assistance from the Owosso Police Department, but they never took the claim seriously. Edward Gray was seen as a 'war hero,'" he said in a mocking tone. "Hell, he had near sainthood status. That was the end of it. After that, we took matters into our own hands. You can figure out the rest."

"Fred's journal mentioned something about being worried about some fires that were set around town. That was you, wasn't it?" Sam asked. It was all coming together in her mind now.

"That's right, that was me." Clay seemed pleased with himself. He also looked, dangerous. Very dangerous.

Sam knew that she needed to keep her mouth shut for a moment, to make sure that she didn't say the wrong thing. She proceeded carefully, trying to think, and trying not to trip on the rough floor of the tunnel. Her surroundings smelled musty and felt damp. She aimed her light up toward the ceiling. Water wet the rock. She realized that they must be well under the water table.

"This tunnel might not be safe," she said, turning to Clay. "See? The rock is crumbling. See the chunks all over the place? "Keep moving," Clay said.

Sam fought back against the overwhelming fear she felt.

"Stop talking and pick up the pace," Clay continued. "We need to find out where this tunnel leads."

So far, the tunnel seemed to be an endless black hole surrounded by rock and dirt and the faint smell of mold. The tunnel generally seemed to head straight west as far as Sam could tell, but she had no concept of how far they had traveled. They continued to walk, now in silence. Clay's presence lurking behind them was a constant reminder of the immense danger they were facing.

Although Sam was anxious to find out what was at the end of the tunnel, the fact that Dean was now lying unconscious and bleeding, and that she and Nell were likely in mortal danger, had altered her perspective considerably. She still wanted to find the treasure. However, she was fairly confident that Clay was going to kill them and leave them in the tunnel regardless of what they found.

Still, she couldn't help but wonder, if they did find the treasure,

what was it going to be? What if it really was stolen from innocent families? She wasn't sure how the answers to those questions
would affect how she felt about what they might find. Her confidence started to wane. Her mind came back to the fact that she was
only fifteen years old. How had she gotten this far on such a crazy
quest? More importantly, if there were more clues ahead, how were
she and Nell going to solve them? In reality, she, Nell and Dean and
worked together and had been incredibly lucky in stumbling on
the clues. She wasn't sure how much longer that luck would hold.

16

◇

The Second Door

She lifted her flashlight higher and strained her eyes into the darkness. Thank god Uncle Hank insisted on buying high-intensity
flash lights. The beam from her flashlight bounced off metal.
Straight ahead was a large metal door. It caught Sam off guard,
and she slowed her pace.

"Why are you stopping?" Clay growled.

Sam hand shook as she pointed ahead. She aimed the flashlight
at the door and approached it slowly, dreading the fact that if Clay
got what he wanted, he wouldn't need her and Nell anymore. She
could hear Nell and Clay behind her.

Upon closer inspection, the door looked like a bank vault, except that it had no handle or other obvious method of opening it.
Embedded in the door, were a series of designs. Sam could make
out stars, shields, a coat of arms and several crosses. In the center of
the design was an eagle in flight, below the eagle was a triangular
depression, and below that was a single star. The center design was
encircled by a ring of stars.

The tunnel here was wider. To the right of the door, Sam observed another tunnel that she hadn't initially noticed. It only went

a few yards and looked like it had been sealed. She flashed her light into the darkness.

"I bet that tunnel used to lead to another house," she said to Nell. "Maybe even the Underground Railroad."

"I think it might lead to Adam's sister's house," Nell said. "Remember that Edward and Adam built her a house."

"Oh yeah, that's right," Sam replied. "She only lived a few houses down from Adam. But I bet it's sealed off now."

"Enough chatter!" Clay snapped. "Open the door!"

Sam scanned the area. Off to the left side of the door, there sat a small metal table. On it lay several flags folded and encased in traditional triangular preservation containers. Each was covered in a thick layer of dust.

"Well? What are you waiting for?" Clay demanded. "Open it up already!"

"If you haven't noticed, there isn't a handle," Sam retorted angrily. "You go and open it." She was panicking, and the words flew out of her mouth before she could stop them.

"I didn't think that you were going to outlive your usefulness this quickly," Clay responded menacingly, brandishing his gun.

"Give me a break. I've never seen anything like this before. I have no idea where to start," Sam replied, realizing that she needed to dial it down and stay calm.

"Let's just calm down and figure this out like we have with the other clues," Nell advised her in a reassuring tone. "We can do this. I know we can. First, let's look to see whether there are any more written clues hidden down here."

"Now your cousin is much more enjoyable to be around," Clay said, reaching out to touch her hair.

"Don't touch her!" Sam shouted.

Clay laughed. "Why don't you give me something else to focus on?"

"Okay, okay." Sam looked up at the ceiling and then at the walls of the tunnel. Quickly noting the absence of any obvious written clues, she directed her attention back to the metal door. She began to stare at it in earnest now, willing her brain to make sense of the images.

Nell walked over to the table and began inspecting the flag cases. She gently brushed off the dust to reveal the contents with more clarity. She let out a loud sneeze. She turned to Clay, addressing him more cautiously.

"Do you have any insight which can make sense of this stuff?"

He looked from her to Sam, then slowly walked over to the table eyeing the objects. "Not that I can think of. They just look like flags. How did you find the other clues?"

Sam looked over at Nell and cautioned her with her eyes.

"Mostly by accident," Nell responded. "Why don't you look under the table and see whether there is a note or anything else under there."

"Why don't you do it?" he said with distrust.

"Because I'm examining these cases," she responded with mild irritation. Sam was glad to see that Nell was overcoming some of her fear of Clay. It somehow made her feel better.

Sam turned to look at Clay. He was still standing motionless next to Nell. She was very protective of her cousin and he made her very uncomfortable standing so close to Nell. Whatever she did, she needed to keep his focus off Nell.

"Clay, if you want to take credit for finding a treasure, you need to actually help." She saw the gun twitch in his hand and added, "Look, we need to work together if we want to figure this out."

That seemed to do the trick. He got down on his knees, the gun still tightly gripped in his hand, and looked up at the underside of the table.

"No note, or anything else," he reported.

"Do you see anything unusual or that seems out of place?" Sam prompted.

"No, just metal." He stood back up and brushed off his pants. "Now what?"

"Nell, anything there?" Sam asked.

"Well, all of these containers have an American flag inside. The only difference seems to be in the number of stars visible through the glass."

"Do the containers open?" Sam questioned.

"Nope, they all seem pretty well sealed shut."

"We could break the glass," Clay suggested.

"I don't think that we should destroy these. I mean, they're antiques," Nell countered.

Clay took a step closer to Nell. Sam noted his movement with concern. "Let's hold off breaking the glass for the time being," she said.

Sam returned her attention to the metal door. "Wait a minute, Nell. Come over here. Do these crosses mean anything to you?"

Nell was at her side in an instant. "Hmm, not really. Different churches use different crosses. There seems to be several different versions here."

"What do you make of the eagle, the triangle, and the star," Sam said in a whisper.

Nell leaned closer to the door. "The eagle looks like the one you see on money," she said softly. "I think I read somewhere that it was chosen for our nation's symbol because it represents courage, strength and freedom. The triangle, on the other hand …"

"Why are you guys whispering?" Clay demanded. "Don't even think about trying anything funny. I can put a bullet in each one of you before you can take a step."

Sam's back stiffened in response to his harsh voice.

"We're trying to figure out what we're supposed to learn from these symbols."

"Well?" he demanded again.

"We won't be able to work any faster if you keep stressing us out," Sam retorted. "We're doing the best we can."

"Does that star you used back at the house work on this door?" Clay suggested, this time slightly less aggressively. "I heard you heard you talking about it," he added when they looked at him.

"I was wondering that," Sam admitted. She removed the star from her pocket and held it up to the door. She eyed the star impression in the center of the door for a moment before trying to insert her star. They did seem to be the same size. She pressed the star into the similarly shaped cavity, but nothing happened.

Remembering what had happened before, when she had not pushed hard enough, she used her thumb to drive the star into the door. A faint click could be heard, but Sam couldn't tell whether it was the sound of the star sliding into place or the sound that something else was going on. In any event, nothing else happened.

"Okay, Nell what next?"

"Thirty-five," Nell murmured.

"What?" Sam asked.

"There are thirty-five stars on the door surrounding the eagle, the triangle and the larger star," Nell responded.

"At the end of the Civil War, there were thirty-five states," Clay informed them.

"I wonder ..." Nell said, turning to look back at the table. She walked back over to the table, and began looking through the cases again. Finally, she picked one up and brought it over to Sam. It's hard to tell since the flags are all folded in the cases, but this flag seems to have more stars than the rest of them. "The case looks like it will fit in the triangle under the eagle."

"The flag is the most important symbol for the United States," Sam said quietly. "I bet it was special to Edward Gray."

She looked down at the flag case, over to the door and back to Nell. Could it be that easy? she wondered.

"Go ahead. Try it," she urged Nell.

"All right," Nell said, her face flushed with nerves. She grasped the case and delicately laid it into the triangle-shaped impression in the door.

"You have to press more firmly," Sam suggested with encouragement. "Here, I'll help." She placed her hands next to Nell's on the case and pressed.

There was a loud popping and cracking sound. Sam thought they had cracked the case for the flag. She looked down expecting to see shards of glass, but the container was intact. Still trying to identify the sound, it took Sam a moment to realize that the door was now swinging inward.

"Oh my gosh, it worked!" Nell exclaimed with shock and excitement.

"I was beginning to think your luck had run out," Clay said. He was obviously excited but doing his best to hide his emotions.

His voice sent shivers down Sam's back. His excitement likely signaled bad things for her and Nell. "Come on! You're not done yet. Open it," Clay demanded without offering any assistance.

The door was incredibly heavy, and it took considerable effort to force it completely open. Finally, Sam was in. She peered into the darkness. Nell came to her side and held her hand. Clay yanked the flashlight from Sam's hand and held it up high. With a mixture of relief and confusion, Sam saw that another tunnel lay in their path. No treasure. With a grunt of dissatisfaction, Clay shoved the flashlight back into her hand.

"Well, keep moving. We don't have time to stand around and do nothing."

Sam was more afraid than she had ever been in her life. However, anger was also bubbling inside her. She had several things she wished she could say to him, among them was the observation that *he* was, in fact, standing around and doing absolutely nothing. But given his elevated agitation, she realized that she would be better off keeping her mouth shut. She took hold of Nell's arm and urged her forward.

Why would that fancy door be there if a treasure wasn't on the other side? Sam thought.

"Where's the blasted treasure?" Clay growled. "We should be under the school now. We must be close."

Sam kept her eyes peeled for any sign or clue. The walls in the tunnel seemed to be slightly larger now. Sam appreciated the extra room. Although she wasn't claustrophobic that she knew of, the longer they were down there, the more conscience she was becoming of the small space in which they were traveling.

They continued walking in silence. Clay kept them moving at a steady pace, nudging them in the back when he felt that their pace was too slow. After a particularly sharp jab in her back from Clay, Sam decided that perhaps if she could get him talking again, he would be distracted by the conversation and she could buy some more time.

"Clay," she began, "you said that your family started many of the fires in Owosso. How did they decide on the locations?"

"Well, that was an ingenious idea, if I do say so myself," he replied. "My family focused on places where the Grays were involved. They been especially involved in rebuilding and expanding the grade school, so it seemed logical that the treasure was located somewhere on the grounds. All of the renovations seemed a little unusual for a small town. We were surprised when the fires we started at the school didn't expose the treasure."

"But people could have died," Nell said with surprise.

"People *did* die," Sam said.

"That's a small price to pay for what was done," Clay responded without any sign of emotion.

"I can't believe that Fred helped you break into people's homes and businesses," Nell said with sadness.

"Oh, for God's sake! None of this would have been necessary if the Gray family would have done the right thing and returned my family's property. But if it will make you stop whining, Fred was not involved in the break-ins. He was a bit of a goody-goody. His family apparently never paid very much attention to him. He never attended law or medical school. Apparently, if you're a male in the Gray family, that's a disappointment to the entire family heritage. He was thrilled that I wanted to be his friend. He was also looking for the treasure and knew he needed help."

"How did you get him to trust you?" Sam asked. She couldn't help herself.

"Slowly. Lots of talk about family legacies, lots of drinks. Eventually, I told him that I had heard a rumor about Civil War treasure being buried somewhere in town. He got really riled up about it. He mentioned that he had read an old journal belonging to Elizabeth Gray, Edward Gray's sister, which mentioned some 'crazy family' approaching the Grays after Edward's death and accusing Edward of stealing from them. When I asked him what he thought, Fred staunchly defended his family and was upset that anyone would accuse his family of 'stealing.' Of course, I never told him my real name just in case my family's name had been mentioned in the journal. He never would have talked to me then.

"Anyway, he slipped up and said that his great-grandfather had left some kind of clue in his will. Apparently, a message from Edward Gray was passed down to each member of the family when he or she turned twenty-one. Fred thought it was some sort of a test to determine who was worthy to head the Gray Foundation. I knew differently."

Sam elected not to ask how he had figured that out.

"What did Fred say about the message?" Nell asked, captivated by the story.

"Not a lot actually," Clay said. "He clammed up pretty quickly after he told me, and he never showed me the written clue. He would only say that the clue talked about something being preserved and about finding something for the nation, or something like that. Unfortunately, the more I asked, the less he said. He told me that Edward's Will admonished the family not to reveal its contents to non-family members. He did tell me that his family had not taken it very seriously."

"Why was Fred so interested in the message?" Nell asked.

"He wanted to live up to the *Gray family legacy*," Clay added with a scoff. "He wanted to do something to garner the praise he so desperately craved. I told him that I was underappreciated too, and I understood."

It felt like the tunnel was getting warmer. *Was it just her nerves?"* Sam wondered.

"How long before Fred was on to you?" Sam couldn't help but ask.

"Fred was very trusting. He didn't figure out anything at first. Eventually he connected break-ins to places we had talked about. He began asking a lot of questions about me and why I was really helping him. He became more and more suspicious."

"Why did you have to kill him?" Nell asked softly.

"I knew that he was going to ruin everything. He had started to talk to members of the historical society, and I knew it was only a matter of time before he brought them in on his quest. More importantly, I think that he was about to turn me into the police for the break-ins. I figured that they wouldn't have enough to prosecute me for the thefts. But if they arrested me and discovered my true identity, it would all be over for me. I would never have another chance in this town. I tried to reason with Fred, but he couldn't see beyond his own goals and his precious family name."

"He must have left his journal for someone to find in case anything happened to him," Sam said. It was a clear now. *Dammit*, she wished she would have paid more attention to that journal. They probably wouldn't be in this situation now.

"Yes, well. I didn't know about that, but I did know he had to go. He was just in the way. You know the rest of the story. I thought for sure I'd find clues at his house, but he was at least smart enough not to leave anything there."

"Why did you move his body?" Sam said with genuine curiosity.

"To get him out in to the open, let the rain wash away any evidence. I couldn't have anything tying me to his death."

"You've been following us ever since, haven't you?" Sam demanded. The thought made her shutter.

"No, actually, I had no idea that anyone else was in the woods until the next day. I heard that the police had found Fred's body, so I hung out in the parking lot of the station. This town is pretty dull, and the station doesn't seem to get a lot of action, so it seemed strange to see young kids going in on the weekend. I didn't see your faces, and I wasn't sure what to do, so I followed a clerk to the bar after her shift the next day and struck up a conversation. Eventually, we talked about the body found in the woods, and she mentioned that there were two witnesses, but that they couldn't identify the shooter. I figured that I was in the clear and decided not to worry about it."

"But you were at the bowling alley," Sam said.

"Coincidence." Clay replied. When you bumped into me, I didn't think much about it at first. But you seemed so ... stressed. You barreled out of there like you had been shot from a cannon. It seemed strange, but I was focused on where Fred would have hidden the clue."

"Then I started running into you two everywhere," Clay continued. "At the castle, the tour."

"You were in the parking lot at the church, weren't you?" Sam asked slowly.

"Yes. I saw you in the bell tower. It seemed odd to me. When you came out, all of you had the same look of shock on your faces. I knew then that you were up to something. I knew I needed to keep an eye on you. I didn't know your names or where you lived so mostly I drove around looking for you. This town's not that big."

"But how did you follow us on the walking tour?" Sam asked. "How could you have possibly known that we were going to take it?"

"I didn't. I decided that I needed to get inside the Gray family homes and look around for myself. When I saw you two in the tour group, I knew that you guys were definitely up to something. How many teenagers take historic home tours as a form of entertainment? I'll tell you, not many.

"Dean saw you outside when we were at the Edward Gray house too," Sam said

"Yes, well, I would have continued to stay in the background, but when you recognized me at the train station, I scrapped that approach. I wasn't about to let you two and that dumb kids screw up everything. Luckily, I was able to follow you home, and I've been watching you ever since."

Sam shuddered at the thought. He had been watching them. Shivers of fear made their way down her spine. Her thoughts immediately turned to Dean and Nell. She felt gut-wrenching guilt for dragging them both into this. She desperately hoped that Dean was okay, and that somehow, someone, would come and save them from this lunatic.

"Enough about me," Clay suddenly declared.

"Put it into high gear. We need to find the end of this tunnel."

He shoved the gun into Sam's back, prompting her to move faster. She started to panic. What if they found another clue? If they couldn't solve it, he would kill them for sure.

17

◇

The Third Door

Sam took a step back and looked at Clay. She felt sick as she looked at the gun. It was black, sleek, and lethal. Think fast, she thought.

"You don't want to do that, Clay," she said. "You still don't have the treasure. What if it's not down here? Then what?"

She felt the weight of the gun leave her back. Then, she saw it. The blackness took on a metallic gleam as a door emerged into view. It was haunting and beautiful at the same time.

"How many damn doors are we going to find down here?" Clay yelled.

Sam figured that his question was rhetorical and kept her mouth closed. Instinctively, she grabbed Nell's arm, and they approached the door together. It loomed in front of them massive and bold. The color of the metal was a deep chocolate. Details started popping out at her. It was a barrage of images. In the center, figures protruded outward.

It was a scene of sorts, depicting soldiers marching forward. A figure in the middle held onto a pole on which was affixed a large American flag. Above the flag an eagle soared clutching arrows and olive branches. Higher up, an angel floated over the figures below.

Scanning the lower portion, Sam saw a shield with the dates

1861–1865 engraved on it in the lower left-hand corner. Columns running down the sides of the door listed what appeared to be various military divisions along with several names of soldiers who had apparently lost their lives in the Civil War.

Sam probably wouldn't have been able to know what these were if it hadn't been for all of their research at the library. Toward the bottom of the door in the middle was an inscription that read:

> Behold this monument to those who gave their lives to protect this great nation. In their honor, that which was in mortal danger has been preserved. A show faith and humble appeal for a united people shall return our invaluable history.

Sam's mind was reeling. Her head was throbbing, and the back of her neck felt numb with fear. She stood back from the door to gain a different perspective.

"So? What's the key to opening this thing up?" Clay's voice cut through Sam's thoughts like a knife. "Where do we push? What do we turn?"

Sam turned to look at him. She was mentally and physically exhausted. Without caring, she shot him a look that clearly indicated she thought he was an idiot. The menacing look she received in return helped to snap her mind back into focus.

"Clay, this door is incredibly complex, and I'm tired. I just need to sit and think for a moment."

Without waiting for his permission, she plopped down on the ground to left side of the door and grabbed the water bottle out of her pack. She looked over at Nell, who quietly came to sit by her side, pulling out her own water as she sat down.

"Well, fine, but just for a minute," Clay said, capitulating. "This is it. I can feel it. Tell me about the clues you found so far," Clay demanded.

Sam quickly summarized the clues they had uncovered, including the note in Fred's locker. "Ha!" Clay snorted. "*Lost for preservation?* That's rich. More like stolen for the Gray family pocket book.

"Why didn't you just take your clues to the historical society?" he said, imitating Nell's voice.

"I don't appreciate the mocking tone," Sam replied. "For your information, we intended to stop if we found a hidden door and alert the historical society."

"*Sure*, you did," Clay said sarcastically.

"If you will recall," Sam interjected, "you were the one that forced us into the tunnel at gunpoint."

"I promise that I will shoot you right here and now if you don't shut up and open this door," Clay threatened, taking a step closer to Sam. "I don't need both of you. I'm sure your cousin here is smart enough to figure it out on her own."

Sam had to keep it together. If they didn't open this door soon, she was dead. She looked at the door again. It so elaborate; surely if a treasure existed, it must be stored behind it. That thought both terrified and motivated her to keep going. She didn't know where to begin to decode the mysteries this door.

Worse yet, she knew that the moment the treasure was found, Clay was going to kill them. She just knew from the look in his eye that he would not let them walk away; they had learned too much. It was for this reason that Sam was taking time to collect her thoughts. She needed to figure out a way for Nell and her to get out of this adventure alive.

If they attacked him, they risked getting shot. She could feel the mounting pressure pushing down on her like a heavy weight. She closed her eyes, leaned her head back on the wall and let out a deep sigh. When she opened her eyes, she noticed for the first time that to the left of the door the rock wall rose up high overhead.

As Sam continued to stare at it, she observed what looked like rungs of a ladder carved into the rock. Squinting into the darkness above, she saw a large metal plaque high above.

"What? What is it?" Clay asked.

"I'm not sure," Sam responded absentmindedly. "It might be a clue."

She didn't really believe it was a clue, but she needed to buy time. She climbed the rock ladder to get a better view of the plaque. Up close, she realized that the plaque was even larger than it looked from the floor below. It was a plain, rectangular shape.

At first, she couldn't read it. Then she realized that the images were backward as if it had been installed inside out. She was able to make out the words Central Elementary School and bell dedication. On the left side of the plaque, midway up, she saw a star-shaped imprint. It reminded her of the stars leading up the stairs in Edward Gray's house. There was nothing else visible, no clues.

She pressed her hand against the metal. It seemed to be firmly bolted in place. She thought it odd to have such an acknowledgment underground, but then again, she was in a subterranean walkway trying to find an unknown treasure. Something was bothering her about the plaque, but she couldn't put her finger on what it was.

"Well? What do you see?" Clay called.

"Not much," she replied. "Just a plaque commemorating the bell used by Central School."

"I bet we're under the school," Clay announced. "Then my family was right: Edward Gray did bury the treasure on the school property."

"Don't get too excited," Sam cautioned as she made her way down the wall. "We haven't found any treasure yet."

"Okay, you've had enough time to get your second wind," Clay announced. "Now get working on this door, or else. Time is ticking." He said, making a ticktock sound.

"What are your thoughts on the door and how we should open it?" Sam asked Clay as politely as she could muster.

"I don't have any idea," he answered. "I say we just start pushing and pulling on stuff until the door opens."

"The problem with that approach is that we might damage the door, and then we would never get in," Nell advised.

"How could you possibly know that?" Clay demanded.

"That's just it. We don't know anything about this door," Nell replied gently. "What if there is a booby trap or something?"

"Nell's right. We need to take a moment and do this the right way. You know, it would be a lot easier for us to figure this out if you weren't breathing down our necks and waving your gun at us."

"I'm not leaving you two alone," he snapped. "Besides, in case you hadn't noticed, we are in a tunnel. I don't have any where I could go even if I wanted to."

"You're right. We are in a tunnel, which means that Nell and I aren't going anywhere either. We just need some space, so we can try and figure out this thing. In case you hadn't noticed, we are two teenagers trying to follow clues that have been buried since long before we were ever borne. We're hot, we're tired, and we're stressed out. If you could just take a walk down the tunnel for a few minutes, I think it would really help us figure this out faster."

Clay stared at her for several seconds. He was glaring at her as if he were trying to read her mind. She could tell that he was assessing the risk of leaving the two of them to talk among themselves and whether she was trying to pull something. Finally, he seemed to have convinced himself that it was safe for him to accommodate her request.

"Fine," he said. "I'll stand over there. He pointed about ten feet away. "But if you try anything funny, I think you know what the outcome will be." He patted the gun now holstered at his side.

"Thank you," Sam replied with relief.

Once he was out of earshot, Nell began talking. "I am freaking out," she said under her breath but clearly in a panic. "What are we going to do? This is just so ... overwhelming."

"I know. Me too. That's why I had to ask him to give us some room. I can hardly think with him hovering over us. Now I feel like maybe you and I, together, can figure this thing out."

Sam could see just how petrified her cousin was.

"Nell, we are going to find a way out of this. I promise."

"I've been wondering why there are three doors down here," Sam said. "It seems like this monstrosity would be more than enough. It has to be because Edward wanted who ever found the treasure to understand its importance and why it was hidden.

"Think about the clues. The stars, the flag, they keep resurfacing. This door is trying to tell us a story, not just give us some random clues. Clay wants us to believe that Edward Gray stole a bunch of stuff for personal gain.

"But that just doesn't fit the man we have been learning about. Based on everything we have read and seen, it seems like Edward Gray was a very honorable man. Everyone we talked to said that he was a good man who loved his family and his country."

"You're right," Nell said. "Stealing doesn't fit his character. I mean, appearances can be deceiving, but I just can't believe that Edward Gray was a thief. Plus, if he took the treasure for personal gain, why would it still be locked up underground? He would have sold it, wouldn't he?

"That has to be it. Edward not only wants us to understand why he did it, but I think he also wants us to experience the same emotions he had. The clue said that 'the conductor's path was clear, a walk in his footsteps will lead you there.' It's sort of like the old adage that you never really know a person until you walk in their shoes."

"Exactly," Sam said. "He wanted us to walk in his shoes! Okay, let's break it down door by door. The first door was opened by using the star we found in the bell tower. What does that tell us?" Sam posed the question as she stared at the ceiling.

"Love," Nell said.

"What?"

"The first door was about love. Remember the clue said: 'That which was hidden was done with pure heart; so any seeker must so start.' Heart Engineering? I bet that wasn't even a real company."

"That actually makes sense. Gray certainly seemed to love his family, this country, and this town for that matter," Sam replied.

"The second door had an eagle, a flag, and stars," Sam recounted.

"An eagle is a noble bird, known for having a long life, great strength, majestic looks, and courage. I think that door represents freedom," Nell said.

"Hmm, maybe, Sam replied. "Nell, think back. Does the center image on the second door remind you of anything?"

"No, why?"

"Because now that I think about it, it reminds me of a war metal that Grandpa showed me once."

"Oh my gosh, you're right!" Nell exclaimed. "It looks like the National Medal of Honor given to soldiers who distinguish themselves for service to the country above and beyond the call of duty and in the face danger. The second door has to represent honor!"

"How do you know this stuff?" Sam uttered in amazement.

Nell blushed. "You recognized the symbols and tied them to the metal," Nell said, returning the compliment. "I just know what the metal was given for. I remember Grandpa showing that metal to me and my dad once. On the way home later, my dad gave me a long lecture on the history of the metal."

"All right, so if the first two doors symbolize love and honor, what does this door represent?" Nell asked aloud.

Sam stepped back to look at the door with fresh eyes. Sam finally broke the silence. "The soldiers look like they are wearing Civil War–era uniforms. The flag, the stars, the bald eagle, they are all symbols for the United States," she stated.

"I think you're right," Nell agreed. "The eagle must represent America. I remember my dad telling me that the Founding Fathers chose the bald eagle as this nation's symbol because it was unique to this part of the world. Ben Franklin wanted to use the turkey," she said with a nervous giggle.

"This door has to represent country," Sam said definitively. "It has to. Okay, so Edward's messages to us are love, honor, and country."

"That does seem in keeping with what we know about Edward Gray," Nell agreed excitedly. "You know the flag in the center of this door may stand for love of country and patriotism. Of course, it could also symbolize courage, safety, and protection. As for the stars, I read somewhere that some people believe that the stars on the American flag stand for God and heaven. Gosh, there is so much symbolism here. Oh, then there's the angel. I think the angel is there to watch over everything below."

Suddenly, Clay lurched toward them. "Enough already! I've about had it with you two. Open the damn door!"

"We're trying! Sam cried out, holding her hands up in a defensive manner. "Just give us a little more time."

"You are out of time. I heard what you said, and it seems like you have figured out the clues, so get crackin."

"Okay, okay," Sam said. The inscription must be the clue," Sam said aloud. "Mortal danger, what was in mortal danger? Other than us," Sam thought. "Okay, faith. Hmm. Nell, I think we need a little of that faith of yours. What do you think 'a *show of faith and humble appeal for a united people*' means?

"Well, faith is complete trust," Nell began. "Humble appeal, humble appeal," she repeated to herself. Be humble before ... I think that *humble appeal* means a prayer."

A lot of people pray on their knees. She pressed her hands together and knelt on the ground. Sam followed suit. In that position, Sam saw the door in a different perspective. The soldiers above now looked like two different groups marching toward each other, rather than marching as one. The flag seemed to be pointed by one group toward the other. She jumped to her feet.

"What do you think you're doing?" Clay shouted at her in surprise and brandishing the gun.

"I have an idea, she responded, grabbing the flag pole in the door, and wiggling it. It moved. She felt her heart beat faster. Slowly, she rotated the flag until it was flying straight up over both groups. When it clicked into position, the door gave a loud pop, and the two groups of soldiers in the door slid toward each other until they formed one group, now marching together.

"Is it open? Is it open?" Clay was now screaming in Sam's ear.

Sam looked at the door. It was still closed.

"It doesn't look like it," Sam responded breathlessly.

"Goddammit! Why not? What are you trying to pull?" Clay screamed, getting so close to Sam's face that she felt his hot breath.

"I swear that we're not hiding anything. We want to find this as much as you do," Sam said in as calm a tone as she could manage.

"Listen, there must be more than one lock to open. We must have triggered one of them." Sam said.

"What's next?" He demanded.

Sam chest felt like it was going to explode she was so anxious. She scrutinized the carvings on the door at eye level. On her knees, she was now able to appreciate the beauty of the lower part of the door. She noticed two round medallions of sorts, one in each corner of the lower half of the door. Each had tiny words engraved in a circle. The one on the left read: A citizen's duty is to preserve, protect, and defend our union. The one on the right read: God grant us all freedom from oppression.

Sam reached out and touched the medallion on the left. For a moment, she couldn't move. Fear and excitement swirled in her head. She closed her eyes, shook her head, and focused on the door. Slowly, she wrapped her hand around the medallion and pressed. It required more force than she had expected, but slowly the medallion turned. She rotated the dial until the word union was directly at the top of the circle. She heard a click.

Nell let out a gasp of breath behind her. Sam didn't dare look at her for fear that she would lose her train of thought. She turned now to the medallion on the right. She turned the dial until the word *freedom* was on top. Another loud click came from the door. This time, the medallion on the right popped open, revealing a small opening. Nell grabbed Sam's shoulders and squeezed. Sam was too excited for words.

"Nell, shine your flashlight into that hole," Sam said pointing. Sam saw a beam of light illuminate the small opening. It was just large enough for a hand to be inserted. Inside, sharp metal teeth protruded downward stopping just short of the bottom of the opening. Sam looked at Nell. "I take it someone has to put their hand in there?" She asked anxiously.

"Maybe that's where the show of faith comes in," Nell responded.

"Shit," Sam muttered.

"What are you waiting for?" Clay demanded. "Stick your damn hand in there and find the lever or whatever opens this door!"

"Clay, this is a pretty solid door. Maybe it would help to have a man's strength to manipulate whatever is in there," Sam suggested.

"Are you kidding me? Do I look stupid to you? I can see the daggers in there. No way I'm sticking my hand in there. Now get on with it, open that door! Otherwise, I will have to do it with your cold, dead hand."

Sam looked at Nell. "Nell, Clay's right this might end badly. I'll reach in there. It's just that ..." She paused.

"I'll do it," Nell offered, apparently sensing Sam's hesitation.

"No, I'm not asking you to do it," Sam responded. "It's just that the clue has me a little worried. It talks about faith and, well, you know I've never been very good at that. I'm a disaster at church. What if the door can ... well, sense that about me?"

"First of all, you don't have to attend church to have faith or to be a good person for that matter. You are a good person with plenty of faith. You just don't have blind faith," she said smiling.

"Get on with it already, or one of you won't live to see what's on the other side of this door!" Clay bellowed.

Nell leaned in front of Sam and slowly reached into the compartment. "Hmm. I can't get my hand all the way in. Those metal teeth are blocking me. Ouch!"

"What! What is it?" Sam asked anxiously.

"Nothing, sorry, I just scraped by hand on the metal."

Sam placed her hand on her heart and let out a deep breath. You just scared the crap out of me.

"Sorry, I didn't mean to."

"Wait a minute, Nell. You said that the clue *humble appeal* meant 'prayer.'"

"Yeah, that's what it means to me."

"Okay, look at your hands," Sam instructed. "How would you hold your hands in prayer?"

Nell looked down at her hand, then at Sam. She removed her hand from the door.

"Well at home I'd pray with my hands together like this," she said, pressing her hands together in the traditional prayer pose. "But at church, we pray with our palms facing up like this." She demonstrated. "Oh, I see what you mean."

Nell took a deep breath and placed her right hand back inside the door, this time palm side up.

"I feel something!" she exclaimed. "It's like a lever. Hang on, it's ... I can't quite reach it." She leaned into the door. "There, I've got it!"

With a groan she pulled on the lever. They heard a loud creaking coming from the door followed by multiple clinks and clunks. Nell quickly extracted her arm from the door. The air was filled with dust.

It took a moment for everyone to see through the murky air, but when they did, they all saw the same thing. The door had been opened. It now protruded a few inches into the tunnel.

"Don't just stand there!" Clay ordered. "Help me get this door open all the way." He was pressing his body against the door, but kept the gun pointed at them.

Sam and Nell jumped to his side and used their combined weight to pry the door open. Like the prior door, this one was built like a tank. It was several inches thick and incredibly heavy. It groaned as it inched open.

Clay wedged himself in the crack between the door and the rock wall. He let out a primal growl and slammed his body against the door, forcing it open.

They stood in the threshold staring into the darkness before them. Although it was pitch-black, it was obvious that they were standing in a large room.

"Give me that," Clay ordered, wrenching Nell's flashlight from her. He panned around the space. As the light made its way through the dark, it spotlighted what appeared to be rows of objects, and a few glimmers of gold.

Sam directed her flashlight to the wall nearest the door. She saw what looked like a switch to the left of the door. She walked over to it and flipped it up. The room burst to life. The lights were crudely constructed and like none Sam had ever seen. They obviously had been down there for a very long time.

Thanks to the illumination, they could now see that they were standing in a room the size of a school gymnasium. On one side of the room were rows and rows of paintings, all standing upright, neatly separated by what resembled bicycle racks. On the right side of the room, there were gathered various statutes, vases, and other objects. Sam was just noticing that the far wall was a pink color when she heard Clay yell.

"I knew it! That bastard took it all! But I found it, including the gold!"

Sam followed Clay's gaze and was stunned. In the center of the room was a huge pile of gold bars. "Do you think they're real?" She asked.

"Of course, they are real, you moron," Clay said smugly. "This is the shipment of Confederate gold that the Gray family stole. If it wouldn't have been for their thieving ways, the South would have won the war!" Clay ran down to the center of the room and began caressing the gold. "It's all here. I knew it!" Clay had the look of a madman. His eyes were bloodshot, and his whole body was shaking. Sam knew this was their chance.

She turned to Nell. but before she could speak, she noticed a small desk a few feet away from the door. It reminded her of the desk she had seen in the Edward Gray house. On the desk was an envelope marked 'To whom it may concern.'

Sam couldn't help herself. She made her way over to the desk trying not to make any sudden movements. She kept her eyes on Clay. Luckily, he was too busy conducting an inventory of the room. She grabbed the envelope and returned to Nell's side. Clay was muttering to himself. He wasn't making any sense, and his outbursts were becoming more animated. She wanted to open the envelope in the worst way, but she knew what they had to do if they wanted to get out of this alive.

"Nell, we've got to get out of here, now."

"What? How?" Nell asked, staring at her.

"We're only a few feet from the door. Trust me, and run," Sam said, grabbing Nell's arm and pulling.

At first, she felt dead weight, but then Nell began to run with her. They heard Clay's shrieking at them before they reached the door, but they kept running. Sam hoped that Clay had put down his gun to check out his loot and that they would have a few extra moments to escape. They were nearly to the door when gunshots rang out. Sam saw sparks as several rounds hit and bounced off the metal door. She heard a whizzing sound close to her head.

She shoved Nell over the threshold, whipped around, and grabbed for the door. They had to pull it closed behind them. Luckily, it was heavy enough that it had partly closed on its own while they were in the room. There was nothing to hold onto except the hole in which Nell had inserted her hand.

There was no time to think. She dropped to one knee, braced the other leg against the wall next to the door, plunged her hand into the opening, and pulled. She pulled with all of her strength, knowing that her life depended on it.

Sam felt a stabbing pain in her arm, but she kept pulling. Nell had dropped to her knees too and was pulling at the door. As if by some miracle, it closed. As she heard the click, Sam quickly began rotating the medallions on the door in the opposite direction that had caused it to open. Then she grabbed the screwdriver from her waistband and jammed in under the door as hard as she could. She hopped up and kicked the screwdriver hard, driving it deeper into the ground. She hoped that was enough to keep the door closed.

"That should keep it closed," Sam told Nell with more confidence than she actually felt. Nell's eyes were open wide, and she looked terrified. The dense door muffled the sound, but Sam could still make out the sound of gunfire coming from the other side of the door. She reached into her bag and pulled out the wrench she had taken from Dean's bag. She clenched it tightly in her hand, hoping that she wouldn't need to use it.

By now, Clay was pounding on the door. He was enraged and shrieking at them to open the door. He screamed louder and louder like a madman. His voice was muffled by the thick door, but Sam could certainly guess what he was saying. He wanted to kill them now more than ever.

"What are we going to do?" Nell asked frantically. "Oh my god, you're bleeding!"

"What?" Sam looked at her arm where Nell was pointing. Sure enough, blood was running down her arm. She looked closer and saw a gash on her arm a few inches above her right elbow.

"You were shot!" Nell yelled hysterically. Instantly she burst into tears.

Sam knew that she had to hold it together for Nell. If she didn't, they wouldn't make it out of here.

"Listen, I'm okay. It's not really that bad. It's not nearly as bad as that time a fell out of a tree behind the house. Let's just focus on getting out of here."

"How?" Nell asked.

"When I climbed up the wall and looked at that plaque, I saw something. I didn't realize it at the time, but I think that it's a way out. Here, take the star," she said, handing it to Nell. "Climb up the ladder in the wall. On the left side of the plaque, you will see a star-shaped depression. Press the star in there."

"But what are you going to do?" Nell asked.

"For now, I am going to stay here in case he's able to open the door. I'm handier with tools than you are," she joked. "I'm better suited for this job. Now go!"

They heard more gunshots. Clay was clearly shooting at the door again.

"Go!"

"Okay," Nell said, clearly unsure of the plan. With one more look at Sam and the door, she ran over to the wall and began climbing. In her haste, she slipped several times and nearly fell. After a few tries she made it to the top. "I'm here and I see the star. Here it goes."

Sam heard the now familiar sound of metal on metal.

"It worked! I had to turn the star, but it's open," Nell called down. "There's the road. Come on. Let's go."

"Listen, Nell, I need to stay here. You are a fast runner. Run to the nearest house and call the police."

"I can't just leave you here," Nell objected.

"Look, we're wasting time. If we both leave, and he gets away he'll come after us, and then both of our families will be at risk. This is the only way. Please go!"

"Fine," Nell said. "But I'll be right back." She scrambled up the remaining portion of the wall and was out of the hole in a flash.

The pounding and screaming continued from behind the door. Clay fired several more shots and continued hurling what Sam was certain were death threats.

Sam was reasonably sure that the metal door would stop the bullets. However, she had no idea how long it would be before Clay would find a way to force it open. She hoped that Nell would return in time.

18

◇

Edward's Explanation

It felt like Nell was gone for an eternity. What if she couldn't find help? What if Clay managed to open the door? It was silent on the other side of the wall, but she was sure that Clay hadn't given up. Her arm was throbbing. Bells started ringing. Where was the sound coming from? It felt like it was coming from over her head.

Then she heard it. A sound she never in a million years would have thought would have been so welcomed—Mike's voice.

"Mike? Is that you?" Sam called out. "I'm down here."

"Yes, it's me. You're safe now. I'm coming down," he said.

"Be careful. The ladder is carved into the wall, but it's kind of slick."

Mike had a more difficult time getting through the entrance. With his bulky police jacket, it was a snug fit. For a moment, Sam panicked and worried that he would get stuck and Clay would fling open the door and kill them both. At least Nell made it out safely, she thought. It felt like things were moving in slow motion, but eventually, Mike landed with a thud on the floor next to her.

She jumped up and hugged him as hard as she could. "I'm so happy to see you!"

"I'm happy to see you too, but you need to get out of here right

240

now," he instructed. "And trust me: I will be yelling at you for your boneheaded actions today."

"Okay," she said, "you don't have to tell me twice." She quickly filled him in on how to open the door, who was trapped behind it, and that he had a gun.

Then she hastily climbed the ladder, leaving the wrench behind, and popped out of the hole a moment later.

It was so dark outside. She knew they had been down in the tunnel for a while, but for some reason, she didn't expect the darkness.

"Thank God, you're okay," Nell exclaimed, flinging herself over Sam, nearly knocking her to the ground. "I hated leaving you like that!"

"It's a good thing that you were the one to get help. You were gone like thirty seconds before the cavalry arrived. Nice work!"

A paramedic introduced himself and started attending to her arm. He informed Sam that the bullet had only brushed the surface of her skin and that she was going to be fine, but she should follow up wither doctor in a few days. It was bandaged in no time. Sam was too excited to listen to what he was saying. She wanted to find out how Nell had done it.

"They were already on their way to find us," Nell informed her as she led her away from the tunnel entrance. She quickly filled Sam in on how she was able to get help and that she had given Mike the information on Dean, Clay, and the treasure. Sam could easily picture how Nell had grasped the bell to sound the alarm, then sprinted across the grounds and across the street. She could imagine the crowd that gathered to observe the flashing lights of a police car.

"They?" Sam looked up to see a crowd of people moving toward her. "Dean! You're okay!" She ran over to Dean and, without thinking, hugged him. Nell was still glued to her side.

Dean looked pale and was holding an ice pack to his head. "Oh,

I'm so sorry we had to leave you like that!" A new wave of guilt washed over her and without stopping to think, she gave him a bear hug.

"It's not like you had a choice," Dean reminded her. "You're hurt!" He pointed to her arm.

"It's nothing. How did you get free?" Sam asked.

"Luckily, one of the maintenance workers had left his tools by mistake, and he came back to the house to retrieve them. I heard someone upstairs, so I thrashed around knocking over everything I could until he came down and found me. I'm okay. I just have a bump on my head, no serious damage. However, my mom is pretty upset with me. They called her as soon as they found me. Actually, I think that she's more scared than mad, but I don't want to press the issue right now. More importantly, is it true that you found the treasure?"

"Yes! We found it, and it's amazing! But, oh Dean, I'm so sorry," Sam said. "Please, your mom has to know that it was all my fault, not yours."

"That's amazing! Way to go! Forget about the house. My mom will cool off. Especially when she hears about the find."

"Your mother may be understanding, but our parents are going to kill us," said Sam, with a quiver in her voice. No treasure could save her from her mother's wrath. She felt sick to her stomach. It was the same feeling she always had whenever she had done something she knew her parents wouldn't approve of.

"There's my mom now," Dean said under his breath as a woman approached.

"Dean, we really should get you to the hospital, so you can be properly examined," she said.

"Mom, these are the friends I was telling you about. This is Nell, and this is Sam," he said, gesturing.

"Hello," she responded stiffly, barely taking her eyes off her son.

Sirens filled the air as several more police cars screeched to a halt in front of the school. Out of the corner of her eye, Sam saw officers pouring out of their cars and heading for the entrance to the tunnel.

Sam faced Dean's mother. "We are so very sorry for all of this. Please don't blame Dean," Sam begged.

"Oh yes, please don't," Nell agreed. "We had no idea what we were getting ourselves into. We didn't even believe that the treasure was real until we saw it. And ..."

Dean's mother interrupted her. "Treasure? You found a treasure?" They could see her mood changing before their eyes.

"There are tons of old paintings and sculptures down there," Nell added.

"Any don't forget about the gold," Sam mentioned.

"Paintings, sculptures, and gold?" Dean's mother was stunned.

"Yeah, Mom, we think that all of the stuff may have been hidden during the Civil War, by Edward Gray," he added. "I can't wait to see it."

"There is a huge pile of gold bars down there," Sam informed them. "Clay, our kidnapper, seemed to think that it was the missing Confederate gold."

"So, the rumors about the Confederate gold are true," his mother said. Her eyes lit up with excitement. "Well if artifacts have been uncovered, they will need to be properly cataloged, inspected, and cared for, and we'll need the appropriate experts."

She rambled on. "You kids may have just discovered an incredible piece, or pieces, of history. If the gold is indeed the missing shipment of Confederate gold, it could be worth millions. I must get down there." There was a twinkle in her eyes.

Just then, Sam heard the sound that she had been dreading, the voices of her and Nell's parents. They were upset. Very upset. She turned and saw all four parents walking toward them at a brisk pace.

"That's it. We're dead," Sam said to Nell. Actually though, Sam's relief at having escaped with her friends made her feel almost giddy.

"You have some serious explaining to do young ladies," Nell's mother began. "I don't even know where to begin."

"If this is the way you two are going to repay us for trusting you to stay home alone, well then, I guess we will have to make sure we don't make that mistake again," Sam's mother declared.

"Your mother has been beside herself with worry," Sam's father informed her.

"You gave us quite a scare," Nell's dad informed them. He was the only one of the four looking at them with actual concern in his eyes.

"Yes, uh, you had us worried sick," Nell's mother hastily added.

"Are you okay?" asked Uncle Hank.

"We're fine," Nell replied, staying close to Sam.

Sam turned slightly to hide her bandaged arm. They would see it soon enough.

"We would like to hear an explanation," said Sam's dad.

Sam wanted to shrivel up and disappear. It was all too much. She was angry and embarrassed plus other emotions too many to count. It was torture having to endure the firing squad with Dean and his mother watching. Before she could respond, Dean's mother interjected.

"I'm sorry to have to meet under such circumstances," Dean's mother began, "but I'm Victoria Weston, Dean's mother. I wanted to congratulate you in person for your daughters' remarkable find."

Sam looked up in surprise. She wasn't sure why Dean's mom was coming to their aid, but she wasn't about to interrupt. Plus, Weston? Dean was a Weston?

"Remarkable find?" Sam's and Nell's parents sputtered.

"Yes, yes, the proper experts will need to get down there as soon as possible, but based on what I'm hearing, I believe that the kids here have discovered a long-lost Civil War treasure of sorts.

They had done a great service to this town and to our country for that matter.

"I know that this is a shock to all of us. However, with your permission, I would like to involve them in the recovery operations. I am a historical society director, and I think it would be a wonderful learning experience for them."

Sam could see that both sets of parents were stunned speechless. They clearly were at a loss for words. As much as they probably wanted to throttle their kids, this approach from the historical society director had thrown them off guard and prevented them from acting on that impulse. Nell's mother, in particular was big on public image.

Uncle Hank was the first to speak. "Our kids, discovering a treasure. That's incredible." Being an avid history buff, he, too, was clearly intrigued by what he was hearing.

Nell's mother was not ready to throw in the towel yet. "Well if it's true that they broke into the Gray house ...," she began.

Victoria gently cut her off. "Oh no, they did not break-in anywhere. Dean, like me, is authorized to access the house. He often assists with various functions and coordinates routine maintenance on the home. He tells me that he was showing the house to the girls. They had just discovered a hidden door and were about to contact me when they were viciously attacked by an intruder."

Sam suppressed a smile as she listened to Dean's mom give all four parents the short version of what happened.

"Your girls were so brave. You must be very proud of them."

"What? ... we ... well, I don't know ...," Nell's mother began to stutter. Uncle Hank was beaming. The parents obviously still didn't know what to say, and that was just fine with the girls.

Just then, they heard gunshots coming from the tunnel. The sound pierced the warm night air like a knife. Everyone turned to look in the direction of the tunnel entrance. Three more shots rang out. Sam held her breath, hoping that Mike was all right.

Then there were shouts. "We got him! All clear. Bring him out. Great job, Mike. This is one for the record books."

All eyes were trained on the bell. Sam saw Clay being dragged out of the opening by an officer. Following closely behind was Mike. He was grinning from ear to ear. After the officers took turns patting Mike on the back, Clay was loaded into a police car. Mike then turned his attention to the crowd of people. The sight of Clay's face made Sam shudder. The gravity of the events was really sinking in now. Sam tried to brush the goose bumps off her arms.

"Girls!" Mike yelled. "Where are you? Get over here so I can wring your necks, and then congratulate you!"

Sam and Nell turned to look at their parents. After receiving dumbfounded nods, they trotted off to talk to Mike. They reached him at the same time and gave him a combined hug.

"Mike, we can't thank you enough," Sam told him. "We are so thankful that you were here to save the day."

"You definitely are our hero," Nell agreed. "We heard gunshots. Are you okay? What happened down there?"

"I'm fine, not a scratch on me. When Clay realized that he was cornered, he panicked and started shooting. Luckily, his aim is terrible. I fired back, hit him in the leg, and he surrendered."

"Did he damage any of the artwork?" Nell asked.

Mike laughed. "Now you're art connoisseurs, huh? We'll have people who know what they are doing inspect the contents of the vault, but since he was shooting at the door, I think the art is probably safe."

"Now you two need to tell me everything that happened since we last spoke. Actually, you had better start from the beginning and tell me everything this time."

Sam looked at Nell and then back at Mike sheepishly.

"Here, take this," Nell said, reaching inside her pocket. "I recorded a lot of it on this recorder."

"You had a recorder in your pocket?" Sam and Mike exclaimed

together. They both stared at her with a mixture of shock, disbelieve, and admiration.

"Um, yes," Nell answered, now blushing. "I brought it along because it is really small, and it has a tiny but super bright light. I thought it might come in handy to have a backup light. My dad hasn't used it in ages, so I thought it would be okay to borrow for a day. After Clay kidnapped us, I remembered that I had it, and I pressed the play button. Supposedly, it is voice activated and records for something like five hours. I hope it helps."

"You are incredible!" Sam said. "I can't believe you didn't let on that you were taping the conversations."

"Well, Clay never left us alone, so I didn't have a chance to tell you. By that point, I had forgotten all about it."

"Mike, he confessed to killing Fred because Fred was going to go public with his search for the treasure we found," Sam said. "Clay didn't want to risk sharing the treasure with anyone.

"You two continue to amaze me," Mike said, clearly impressed. "Well, it will be quite interesting to watch Clay try to wriggle out of this one. In addition to the murder of Fred Gray, Clay and his family have been suspected of being behind other illegal acts including harassment, stalking, and breaking and entering."

"How did you know about his family?" Sam asked with surprise.

"When I called in asking for backup, I gave dispatch the name Nell had given me, Clay Davis. When I got out of the tunnel, one of the other officers informed me about the police file on the family."

"He also admitted to us that he and his family started a lot of the fires in town, including the fires here at the school, in an effort to find the treasure," Sam informed him.

"I don't think our Mr. Davis will be seeing the light of day anytime soon. We will, of course, need to take your official statements. Your *complete* statements of everything from the woods until today," he added. "However, it can wait until tomorrow, after you both have had time to rest."

"Officer?" Dean's mother said. "Would it be possible for me to take a brief look in the vault? I have called several experts in the area, and they are on their way. However, I would greatly appreciate the opportunity to have even a brief look at the items stored down there so that I can give the experts a better idea of what to expect."

"I think that can be arranged. However, it will need to wait until tomorrow. I think we've all had enough excitement for today."

"Can we go too?" Sam begged.

Sam heard Nell's mom start to object. She and Nell turned to look at their parents. They must have looked pitiful, because Nell's dad started to laugh.

"I have no objection," he said. "I think they have earned the right to see what they discovered. But I agree with Officer Mike. It will have to be tomorrow."

"I have no objection either," Sam's dad stated. "As long as there is proper supervision."

The girls were ecstatic. They were finally going to be able to look at the treasure that Edward Gray had hidden so long ago, without fearing for their lives.

Dean's mom gave her phone number to Sam's and Nell's parents, and they arranged to meet back at the school the next morning along with Officer Mike.

"I hate to break this up," Mike interjected after a moment of silence. "But it's getting late. You kids need to get home, and I need to secure the area. Oh, and don't forget to follow up with your doctor about that arm, just to be safe." He added. I'm going to write-up your statements based on what you told me, and I'll be by your houses tomorrow to have you read and sign them.

Although they hated to leave, they knew that Mike was right. Sam took one more look around and then led the way out the door and up the ladder.

The fresh air outside helped bring Sam of her private thoughts, out of Edward Gray's time, and back to the present. Sam and Nell's parents were waiting just a short distance from the bell. Sam, Nell, Dean, and Victoria walked over to join them. Knowing that her parents would have much to say once they were alone, Sam braced herself for the fallout.

19

◇

Punishment and Glory

Miraculously, Sam and Nell's parents actually let them return to the scene the following day. Sam knew that Dean's mom when a long way toward convincing their mothers to let them go. If nothing else, her mother had to save face in front of such a respected member of the community. Plus, it didn't hurt that Uncle Hank was a history buff.

After greeting Mike, Dean and his mother, Sam's and Nell's parents agreed to wait on benches on the property. Sam couldn't wait to see the treasure again.

"I think you should lead the way," Victoria said, motioning to Sam.

"Okay, no objection on my part," she replied, grinning from ear to ear. She led the way back to the bell and into the opening, with Nell, Dean, Victoria, and Officer Mike following close behind. When her feet hit the ground below, she felt as if she had entered a different world. Gone was the exhaustion, the pounding heart, the throbbing head, and the feeling of doom. Now she felt only sheer excitement. She entered the vault and waited for the others to join her. As she looked around, she was filled with renewed awe for the objects which now lay before them.

Sam heard Victoria let out a gasp of surprise. For several moments, they all stood there, trying to take it all in. The scene was surreal. Slowly, as if in some sort of a trance, Victoria began to walk toward the paintings. "I ... this looks like a da Vinci. I mean, of course, they would need to be examined by the experts, but ..." Her voice trailed off.

"Da Vinci? As in the famous painter Leonardo da Vinci?" Mike asked her with disbelief.

"Mom was an art history major in college," Dean whispered. "She's a bit of a junky on this stuff, really."

"Yes, you know, of course, that I usually only see most of these sorts of things in the art history books collected by the library, and in museums, of course. However, I recall seeing this paining of Medusa in one of the books. And this looks like the painting *Leda and the Swan* by Michelangelo."

"Like the Sistine Chapel Michelangelo?" Mike asked, his jaw hanging open. "Are you messing with me?"

"Honestly, their authenticity will need to be confirmed, but no, I'm not pulling your leg. You know I think this just might be *Autumn and Winter* by the artist Watteau."

She continued walking, mumbling, and throwing out names of artists and painting titles as she worked her way around the far side of the room. Raphael, Rembrandt, and many others Sam had never heard of. She also mentioned several names that she said were American artists whose work was thought lost during the Civil War. She reached the far end of the room and came to a stop at the pink wall Sam has noticed earlier.

"Brilliant," Dean's mom uttered with admiration.

"What's brilliant?" Sam asked. "Are you talking about the weird pink wall?"

Victoria laughed. "The weird pink wall to which you refer is actually a solid wall of salt."

"Salt?" Sam, Nell, and Mike all exclaimed in confusion.

"Yes, salt. I suspect that it was placed here to help preserve the paintings. You see, salt has long been used as a preservative. The salt captures moisture in the air. That, along with the cool temperature down here, would have helped to preserve the art. Simply inspired."

Dean's mom crossed the room and began walking along rows of tables and bookshelves. "This silver bowl, *Wedding of Neptune and Amphitrite*, by Cellini," she said in a voice that had an almost girlish pitch to it. "Did you see this bronze statute? *David resting his foot on severed head of Goliath*, Michelangelo. She hovered her hand over a stack of books. I don't believe it. No, it can't be—Quintus Tullius Cicero's Greek tragedies; Homer's *Margites*; Socrates verse versions of Aesop's Fables! Oh my word, I think this might be the Gospel of the Twelve." Her voice drifted away, and Sam could only make out the words "lost New Testament apocrypha."

"What's apocrypha mean?" Sam asked Nell.

"It means books of the Bible that the church found to be un-helpful or not divinely inspired; it's not part of the official Bible."

Victoria stopped and looked up at Sam, Nell, Dean, and Mike. "If a fraction of these works is authentic, this find, it's worth ... well, it's priceless."

"Hey, uh, Mom, you forgot to mention the massive pile of gold in the center of the room," Dean said with a chuckle.

They all watched with amusement while Victoria looked first at Dean, then over to the gold. She put one hand on her forehead and the other over her heart. "My stars!"

"Clay really seemed convinced that it was a lost shipment of Confederate gold that the North had intercepted during the war," Sam said. "What do you think?"

"What? Oh my, as I said, I have read about such speculation, but there was never any real evidence that the gold existed in the first place." She swiftly made her way over to the pile. "Based on these markings, it's certainly possible. Officer, we will definitely need round the clock guard on the contents here until they have been properly inspected, cataloged and moved to an appropriate location."

Watching Dean's mom react to the findings somehow made everything seem more real and even more exciting. Sam left her spot by the door and made a loop around the room, trying take in the enormity of it all. Her adrenaline was starting to subside now, and exhaustion was setting in again. She sat down on the floor to rest her feet.

"Oh!" she exclaimed, "I almost forgot I had this," she said, waving an envelope.

"What's that?" Mike asked.

Sam explained how she had noticed it laying on the desk near the entrance and had taken it before they made their escape. "It looks like Edward Gray's handwriting. Can we open it?"

"What makes you think that it's Edward Gray's handwriting?" Mike questioned.

"It's a long story," Sam replied, "but let's just say we have had the opportunity to see samples of his handwriting, and it looks just like this."

Nell and Dean came to her side and looked over her shoulder.

"We have to open it," Sam pleaded. "I think it will shed some light on all this."

Mike looked at Victoria, who nodded. She was clearly so excited at this point, she wanted it opened a much as Sam. "Okay, since you've already touched it, go ahead and open it, but go slowly and be *very* careful."

Sam now felt immense pressure. She tried not to think of her history of clumsiness. Her hands trembled as she carefully inserted her finger under one corner of the envelope and gently opened it. Once the flap was up, she lifted the letter out and eased it open. She took a deep breath to calm her nerves and began to read aloud.

I write this letter to whom
ever shall have followed the
path I have laid.

First, I thank you for undertaking the journey which
has led you to this place.

Second, I write to ex-
plain, in part, my reasons for
such clandestine activities,
and the method to my apparent madness. While serving my
country in its quest to remain resolute and unified, I
was an unwilling witness to
many tragedies. I had but little opportunity to stop many
of them. However, the split in
this great nation's fabric man-
ifested itself in diverse ways.
The divide tore at the very soul
of our country and caused its
citizens to turn upon each

other. Fear, anger, and des peration were decimating our history.

Sam stopped reading out loud, but she continued to scan the letter. "He talks about running into people who were looting Southern homes, that he couldn't stand for the country's history to be destroyed. He wanted to help."

She started reading out loud again.

I felt a pain deep in my soul, and I resolved to do my part to preserve history. Efforts to stop the looting failed. Using my name and rank, I per suaded several of the looters to turn the goods over to my care. I compensated them for aiding me in preserving items of historical value from dam age and destruction.

My beloved town would be the safe haven for the coun try's history. I knew that I could not share my burden with any of my family, friends, or business associates. Therefore, I told no one. The bunker in which you now stand was constructed in secret, the entire project known only to me.

Although the path commences at my brother Adam's residence. (He was aware of only of the tunnel connecting his house to our sister's, for it had served many purposes over the years. The middle door, constructed near the tunnel leading to my sister's residence, was my private monument to those who fought and suffered from the war. And so it does stand. My sister never set foot inside the tunnel and so knew nothing of its particulars.

Throughout the war, the collection grew. Attempts to

identify true owners were difficult under the circumstances.

Sam stopped reading again. "He goes on to write about the wounds left by the war and that he knew he couldn't reveal the items preserved without resurrecting more fighting between the North and South. He thought he had to wait until after his death so he left the clues in his Will, the windows, et cetera."

She picked up reading from the letter again.

The bronze star, given to me after the war, is meant to give you strength and guidance and to appreciate and preserve our great union. Ours is a great and noble country. It is the duty of all Americans to preserve, protect, and defend this great nation and with it its history.

It is my final wish that my family know of my actions and that I acted out of love and loyalty and of pure heart. I pray that I did the right thing and that my actions

have not tarnished the noble
Gray name.

Humbly yours,

Edward Gray

The room was silent. Sam looked up and looked around the room. Victoria had tears in her eyes. Nell was visibly moved. Dean had his hands behind his head and was shifting uncomfortably from side to side. Mike looked dumbfounded.

"Well, Sam said, that was ... informative."

"What an amazing man," Victoria remarked.

"He really did love his country," Nell reflected.

"The man certainly had a way with words," Mike said with envy.

"He sure went through a lot of trouble to protect some art," Dean added.

All the girls in the room looked at him and shook their heads.

"If we learned anything from all this," Sam said, addressing Dean, "it's that he believed it was his duty to preserve, protect, and defend this country and its history along with it. Perhaps his method was a little unorthodox, but I don't think you can question his motives. They were pure."

"That is most definitely true," Dean's mom agreed. She wiped a tear from her eye. "Good gracious, we've been down here for some time. Your parents will be wondering what's keeping us. I think it's above time for us to head up."

"Oh man," Sam groaned.

"It is a breathtaking discovery," Victoria began telling the other parents when they were topside again. "I'm not an expert in this area, but I believe the art and other artifacts down there are priceless. I am quite anxious to hear the experts' opinions on the find. In any event, we will be able to learn quite a bit from the pieces I observed."

She must have realized that she was rambling and that only Uncle Hank was matching her enthusiasm because she then directed the focus of her comments back to the kids.

"It's extraordinary that the kids were able to follow clues left so long ago," Victoria concluded. "You must be very proud of them."

Sam doubted very much that her mother was proud of her at this moment. She certainly had broken more than a few rules over the last few days.

"Of course, the kids will receive credit for the find," Victoria said. "And I was thinking, well, hoping, that they could work with me and the team that will be processing the find. It truly is a once in a lifetime opportunity. Plus, I suspect that it would look nicely on their college applications," she said with a smile.

Sam's and Nell's parents just stared at Victoria and muttered something to the effect that they would think about it.

"Pleasure meeting you," Victoria said, shaking their hands. Before excusing herself to speak with Officer Mike, she turned to Sam and Nell. "It was nice to meet you, Sam, and you too, Nell," she said smiling, "and I hope to see more of both of you." She instructed Dean to say his goodbyes and join her on the sidewalk.

It was awkward trying to talk with Dean in front of the parents. There was so much to say. The three just sort of stood there for a moment.

"Sam?" her mother repeated.

Sam looked up and saw that her parents were staring at her in utter confusion.

"Anna, why did she call you Sam?"

"Um, oh, because that's sorta what I go by," she responded matter-of-factly.

"But your name's *not* Sam," her mother stated, obviously offended.

Dean seemed equally surprised, but he had a huge grin on his face.

Nell stepped in at that point. "It started years ago. We were playing around, and we started calling her Sam, and, well, it stuck."

"Yeah, Anna Marie Sullivan, the initials rearranged spell Sam," Sam added.

Sam's mother's face contorted with obvious disgust. "We raised you to have more couth than that," her mother sputtered. "Well that's something else for us to address at a later time."

Uncle Hank came to the rescue again. "Hey, you know what? Why don't you guys say a quick goodbye while we adults pull the cars around? Meet us over on the side street," he said, motioning, "in about five minutes."

Nell's mother looked irritated, but she, along with Sam's parents followed his suggestion and ambled away.

"So Anna, huh?" Dean said. He was looking at her closely now as if trying to decide whether she looked more like a Sam or an Anna.

"Yeah, never really liked the name, it never seemed to fit," Sam admitted, shrugging her shoulders. "Hey, what about you?" She demanded. "Weston? As in the Weston family who were the original founders of this town?" Her eyes were narrowed in accusation.

Dean's cheeks turned a little pink. "Um, yeah. Look, though, you guys never asked. Besides, it's bad enough that my mom does what she does and ropes me into all her stuff. Sometimes our name and my dad's family come with more baggage than I can carry. I thought that you had figured it out during the home tours when you were interested in the Weston homes. I guess I should have told you then. I was just a little self-conscious."

Sam and Nell looked at each other and then back at Dean. "Well, I guess we're even," Sam said.

"Even," agreed Dean.

"Hey, so, do you really think that your mom can get us involved in working with all the things we found?" Nell asked with enthusiasm.

"Look, you guys found the treasure," Dean reminded her. "I'm sure my mom can swing it. Are you in?"

"Definitely," they responded.

"But we *all* found the treasure. We couldn't have done it without you. Thank you." She gave him an awkward hug. "I'm so glad that we all made it out alive."

Nell flung herself at him next and gave him a big hug. She was always much more at ease showing her affection for her friends and family. "She's right, you know, you were a huge help. I'm so glad we met you, and I'm glad that you're all right."

A car horn beeped. Sam looked over and saw their parents' cars. "We'd better get going. I don't think we can push their patience any more tonight. Thanks again. Tell your mom that we would love to work with her. Plus, it will help get us out of the dog house with our parents. Or at least get us out of the house she added with a wink."

"Will do."

The girls turned and headed for the waiting cars.

"This is going to be ugly," Sam groaned.

"I know," Nell commiserated. "I can tell my mom's just itching to have a go at me. She's eyeing me like I'm a convicted felon. Thank goodness for Dean's mom. I think she really feels sorry for us."

"Yeah, she does seem to be going out of her way to support us," Sam noted. "Dean is so lucky to have her. Good luck tonight, call me as soon as you can to let me know what your parents say."

"Okay. Cross your fingers that my dad can restrain my mother," Nell responded.

Sam gave Nell one last hug and walked off to her car.

Nell got off the easier of the two. In light of her father's intense love of history, her father was inclined to praise her. However, thanks to her mother, she was grounded from using her phone or computer for two weeks.

Punishment came swiftly for Sam. Her parents were outraged at the entire ordeal, including that she had not informed them of her conversation with Fred. She was forced to insure a lengthy lecture about how her decision to look for the treasure was immature, irrational, and reckless. They were especially unhappy that she had dragged Nell along. They repeatedly reminded her that she could have gotten herself and Nell seriously hurt or killed.

They could have saved her breath. The nightmare was still all too real in Sam's brain. Images of Clay's menacing glare still plagued her dreams and even slipped into her head when she closed her eyes. She would never forget what happened and just how lucky she was to escape Fred's fate.

Wow, Sam thought, I caught a murderer and assisted in locating a major historical find. Only my mother could find 'inappropriate behavior' in that. In the end, she, too, was grounded for two weeks. No phone, no television, no visitors, and extra chores around the house.

As it turned out, however, it was almost impossible for Sam's parents to enforce the punishment. The phone was ringing off the hook with congratulatory calls and requests for the girls to give interviews. Sam's parents were not big on giving lavish compliments, and so every call made them increasingly uncomfortable.

Officer Mike came over the day after the find to fill Sam in on Clay's arrest and to take her official statement. Sam was thrilled when Mike convinced her parents to let them speak in private. He told them it was often easier for younger victims to tell their story outside the presence of their parents. Since Sam's parents had known Mike since he was a baby, they agreed. After taking her statement, and asking countless questions, Mike admitted that he no longer wanted to throttle her.

"You know, Sam," Mike said, smiling at the nickname, "I wish that you guys would have come to me sooner and not put yourselves in danger, but I have to admire your bravery. The police department, and the whole town for that matter, owes you its gratitude. Thanks to you and your cousin, Clay will be going to prison for a very long time.

"We have also provided information on Clay's family to the FBI so that they can determine whether any action should be taken against any other members of Clay's family. Nicely done. We will need to talk to you, and your parents," he emphasized, "about your involvement in Clay's trial.

For now, though, just relax and enjoy the rest of your summer. And try not to observe any more murders, or other crimes, if you can restrain yourself."

Sam rolled her eyes at him. "Duh."

As luck would have it, Sam and Nell did enjoy the summer, but it wasn't exactly relaxing. They had become local, if not national, celebrities. They gave several interviews to various press interested in their story. Also, true to her word, Victoria contacted both Nell's and Sam's parents a few days after the discovery and persuaded them to allow the girls to be involved in the process.

Experts from around the country poured into town to inspect, authenticate, and preserve the objects in the vault. Dean was officially inside the girls' inner sanctum, and the three of them enjoyed hanging out. In fact, Sam finally admitted to Nell how handsome Dean was, and how much she enjoyed being with him. The feeling was obviously mutual, Nell had informed.

Now that the drama was over, and Clay was behind bars, a huge weight had been lifted. They felt like kids again, but they knew that the experience had changed them forever.

"You know," Sam informed Nell and Dean as they were carrying some boxes, "I could really get used to this whole mystery-solving business. Apart from the murder and kidnapping, it's really a rush."

"Me too," Nell responded enthusiastically. "This is much more fun than us pretending to solve mysteries in your backyard."

Sam blushed a little at Nell's hint about their years of make-believe.

"I'm in too," Dean said, smiling. "Except next time, I would like to avoid being knocked unconscious. But what do you mean about Sam being true to her word?"

"The day I moved back here, Sam promised me that this was going to be the most exciting summer ever," Nell informed Dean. "She definitely delivered on her promise."

"I would say so," Dean said.

"If only I would have known then, what I do now," Sam replied with a wide smile.

"Would you have done anything differently?" Dean asked.

The girls looked at each other and giggled. "Probably not," they replied in unison.

"Hey, did your parents tell you about the reward?" Dean asked.

"What? No. But it would be nice to have some spending money," Sam remarked. "That is, if my parents let me accept it. They once made me turn in a five-dollar bill I found at a football game."

"The reward money is more like college money," Dean informed them. "According to my mom, the monetary awards are sizeable. Like, you won't need to worry about how you will pay for college, at the very least."

Sam was dumbfounded. A reward had never occurred to her. She felt excitement and guilt.

The greatest surprise came when the Lillian Gray, Fred's mother, invited Sam, Nell, Dean, and their families over for dinner to thank them in person for their bravery and hard work. Of course, Sam's mother was flustered and dismayed by the invitation. Despite her protests, Lillian would not take no for an answer.

The moment they arrived at the home of Lillian Gray, she greeted them warmly. Lillian was easily the most elegant and graceful person that Sam had ever met. She was dressed in a white silk blouse, pearls and tan slacks. Her thick, chestnut-brown hair stopped short of her shoulders. She had perfect porcelain skin, and she looked like she had just stepped out of a magazine.

Lillian and several other Gray family members who were present thanked Sam, Nell, and Dean profusely for their efforts. They told them that they were "forever in their debt" for finding Fred's killer and for solving Edward's clues.

"I just can hardly believe that there really was a treasure," Lillian said. "Only Fred had the courage and conviction to follow the clues."

She fought back tears. She had a far-off look in her eyes as if she were someplace else. She paused for a moment before continuing.

"He tried to convince us that the message was important, and to get our support," her voice trailed off. "I just wish that we would have taken him, it, seriously. Maybe things would have turned out differently. Maybe he would still be alive today. The family has learned a lot from this and from him." Her eyes were misty with obvious regret.

"And you three," she continued, now looking at Sam, Nell, and Dean. "There are no words to fully express to you how truly thankful we are for your efforts. Thanks to you, Fred's killer was captured, and his quest was fulfilled. We can rest a little easier, knowing that he did not die in vain. In addition, as you may know, we had offered a $100,000 reward for anyone with information leading to the capture of Fred's killer. It is but a small token of our gratitude. You have clearly earned it."

"Oh no!" Sam and Nell objected together. "We couldn't take any money from you. We just wouldn't feel right."

Sam saw from the corner of her eye that she had just beaten her mother to the punch with her objection. She should have known that her mother would object to any reward.

Lillian was obviously touched by the girls' genuine protests.

She looked at them with the kindest eyes Sam had ever seen. She put her hand over her heart and smiled. "You have done this family, this town and this nation, a great service. Such service must be rewarded. It is what Edward and Fred would have wanted."

"We are so happy that we were able to finish Fred's work," Sam said. "Also, we wanted to return this to you." She held out her hand to Lillian. "This is the star we found with Edward's. We figured that it belongs to the Gray family."

Lillian's eyes welled up with tears again. "No, we could not accept it," she replied softly. "As you know, this was given to Edward after the war. He left it for the one, or ones, brave enough to follow his path. It most certainly belongs to you. I think it would be what Edward would have wanted. Please keep it as a reminder of the good that you have done."

Sam looked at Nell and Dean. It was a touching and awkward moment. After a long pause, the most they could muster was a hushed thank you.

"You are quite welcome," Lillian responded softly. She then turned to the parents and said: "My family and I strongly belief that courage and conviction such as your children possess is a true treasure. You must be so very proud of them."

The parents simply nodded in return.

"Well, you probably know by now that the Gray family will be commissioning a historical monument recognizing the location of the treasure and giving the three of you credit for the find," she said addressing Sam, Nell, and Dean again.

"Also," she said, now with a sparkle in her eyes, "the historical society has asked me to speak with you about the three of you conducting a tour of sorts for the visitors who will no doubt flock to this town to take a 'treasure tour.' I suspect that you will be quite busy for the rest of the summer, what with the treasure supervision and all." She leaned toward them and smiled. "But if you have any interest, please let me know. Now, that business is taken care of, let's move on to the dining room and enjoy our dinner."

Dinner, indeed, was an incredible affair. The food was unlike anything Sam had ever seen or tasted in her life, and the table glittered with china dishes engraved with the Gray family crest, ornate silverware, and crystal goblets.

Sam noticed that even the parents were having a good time. Sam knew her mother was still uncomfortable with the entire situation, but she refused to let that dampen the night. For once, she was being showered with accolades, and she was going to enjoy it.

CPSIA information can be obtained
at www.ICGtesting.com
Printed in the USA
LVHW092130070219
606840LV00005B/30/P